THE VISIONARY

THE VISIONARY

PAMELA S. THIBODEAUX

FIVE STAR
A part of Gale, Cengage Learning

GALE
CENGAGE Learning™

Detroit • New York • San Francisco • New Haven, Conn • Waterville, Maine • London

GALE
CENGAGE Learning·

LIBRARY OF CONGRESS CATALOGING-IN-PUBLICATION DATA

Thibodeaux, Pamela S.
    The visionary / Pamela S. Thibodeaux. — 1st ed.
        p. cm.
    ISBN-13: 978-1-4328-2549-2 (hardcover)
    ISBN-10: 1-4328-2549-6 (hardcover) 1. Women architects—
Fiction. 2. Twins—Fiction. 3. Self-realization in women—Fiction.
I. Title.
PS3620.H526V57 2011
813'.6—dc23   2011031288

First Edition. First Printing: November 2011.
Published in 2011 in conjunction with Tekno Books.

On high I dwell, and in holiness; to revive the spirits of the dejected, to revive the hearts of the crushed; I will heal them and lead them, I will give full comfort to those who mourn for them.

Isaiah 57:15–19

DEDICATION

All honor and glory belong to God for His wisdom, direction, and strength to get through such a painful—yet beautiful— story. This is dedicated to abused children everywhere; may you find the peace and joy offered through salvation, forgiveness, and the healing power of God's grace and mercy. To the people who counsel them and the doctors who treat them: may God bless you in your endeavors. To the perpetrators of violence against children and the people everywhere who are also their victims: may God reach your hearts and change your lives.

To Mirella, author, editor, friend—Thank *you* for your tireless efforts to help me improve this book and for your wisdom, direction, and understanding of these characters—May God Bless and keep you and yours in the palm of His mighty hand and may He bless your writing with infinite sales.

To the residents of Southwest Louisiana, I pray the descriptions in this book are a reflection of how much I love this area—my home.

To my beloved, Terry: of all the heroes in my stories, Alex Broussard is the one who most reminds me of you ∼ *oodles & oodles of charm and charisma by the case.* I'll love you forever and miss you always.

Last but certainly not least, for my grandson Karson: you are a blessing to my life.

CHAPTER ONE

Taylor Forrestier awoke with a muffled scream. Her feet tangled in the bedcovers when she tried to bolt, and she landed on the floor with a thud and a whimper. She kicked free of the sheets and blankets then crawled into a corner. Eyes wide with horror, she tried to make sense of the shadows that danced around her, to separate the ones in the room from those in her mind. Her heart thundered. Breath escaped in short pants. She drew her knees to her chest, took several deep breaths to keep from hyperventilating, then closed her eyes and rested her head. Shivers overtook her slender frame. A sob escaped. *Oh, God, would the nightmares ever cease, the ghosts ever rest in peace?*

Resolve straightened her spine. Eyes still closed, she inched her way to the bedside table. Her hand trembled when she turned on the lamp. The light forced darkness from the room, but only one thing would push it from her mind. Agility born of fear drove her to her feet. She fumbled into a sweat suit, socks and tennis shoes, scraped her hair up into a ponytail, then fled.

Alex Broussard turned right off Lakeshore onto Bor du Lac Drive. Though the name of the street meant "around the lake," the stretch of road encircled only the eastern shore along the body of water once known as Charlie's Lake. He parked his SUV in one of the far corners of the Civic Center's lot, slipped the keys into his pocket, and headed out for a brisk walk along the seawall. Though the early March morning air nipped at the skin, he noticed others out and about.

Walkers chatted up ahead, joggers passed with a smile, a nod, or a murmured "morning," and someone on roller blades whizzed by. A flash of color caught the corner of his eye. Alex watched a young woman jog down the steps, run along the water's edge and back up and around. Then she flew on down to the boardwalk.

His thoughts wandered back over the years and the changes to his hometown of Lake Charles, Louisiana. The legalization of gambling brought riverboat casinos to dock on the once peaceful lake. Hotels decorated the shores; the mayor built a small alligator park and molded the lakefront into a tourists' haven, all on a one-mile stretch of beach. Hurricane Rita destroyed one boat and now, instead of a thriving business, a deserted hotel and parking garage blighted the landscape. His heart pricked at the sight, and he wished once more someone would restore the buildings or tear them down.

He settled on a bench at the south end of the Civic Center grounds and turned his gaze toward the east while the sun ascended into the heavens. Fingers of orange and yellow stretched gloriously across the sky and tinted the clouds into fluffs of pink and peach as the gray of dawn gave way to the brilliance of morning. Colors expanded heavenward then reached down to caress the water and added hints of orange and gold to the silvery waves.

No matter how much things change, this would always remain true: sunrise or sunset on the lake was one of the most breathtaking sights he would ever see.

There's another breathtaking sight, his mind added when the woman jogger bounded into view again and headed toward him. The material of her peach sweat suit stretched across firm thighs. His heart jumped to the rhythm of her ponytail and bounced with each step she took.

10

Their eyes met. It was only a brief moment of contact, but he felt the touch clear to his soul. He smiled. She flushed, averted her gaze, and swept by without so much as a nod. Alex shook his head and chuckled under his breath. *Been too long without the company of a woman, old boy, and no time to become involved with one now. Been there, done that, and once was enough.*

"More than enough," he muttered as he rose from his seat. He would not let those memories spoil the beauty of his morning or put a damper on the rest of his day, especially this day. If the meeting he planned went as hoped, it would be the best birthday gift he'd ever given himself.

He glanced at his watch . . . time for another quick cup of coffee before he moved on to business. Fifteen minutes later he pulled into the parking lot of T&T Enterprises. The sign said they opened at eight, but cars were parked alongside the building. He hoped he could be seen early, especially since he didn't have an appointment.

The door swung open at the slightest tug. The aroma of fresh-brewed coffee filled the air. A bell on the door announced his arrival, so he waited in the small foyer until the receptionist appeared at her desk.

"May I help you?" she asked.

He glanced at the nameplate on her desk and smiled. "Yes, ma'am, Miss Pam LeBlanc, I'd like to see one of the T's of T&T Enterprises."

She laughed—a soft tinkling sound. Her eyes sparkled. *Pretty little thing,* Alex thought, *with her jet-black hair and emerald eyes.*

"Miss Taylor isn't in yet, but Mr. Trevor is," Pam said.

"Husband and wife team?"

Pam shook her head with another laugh. "No, brother and sister. Don't worry, you're not the first person to make that mistake and probably won't be the last. Let me get him for you. Your name, please?"

"Broussard, Alex."

Again the sound of pure joy bubbled up from her throat.

"Broussard first name or last?"

He couldn't help but chuckle. "Are you always so bright and cheerful this early in the morning?"

She nodded. "Yes, sir, it's my gift. Drives some people crazy, though."

Alex noticed the dreamy expression that clouded her eyes, and he cleared his throat. She looked up. A blush rushed to her cheeks. The corners of his mouth tugged into a smile. "Lost you there for a moment."

"Sorry," she breathed.

"No problem," he assured. "He's a lucky guy." He grinned when her blush deepened. Her buoyant personality returned in the twinkle of an eye.

"Yeah, he is, even though he doesn't know it yet."

A chortle rose from deep in his chest. "Uh, oh."

Laughter bubbled up in response to his humor and escaped her throat in a giggle. "You can wait in the lobby, and I'll let Mr. Trevor know you're here."

Alex leaned toward her with a conspiratorial wink. "I take it we're talking about the same guy?"

Pam groaned. Another rush of heat filled her cheeks. "How did you know?"

"Figuring things out is my job."

"What are you, a cop?"

Alex laughed, rich and quick. "No, a financial analyst." He handed her a business card. "And if you ever need a job . . ." his voice trailed off at the adamant shake of her head.

"I won't, but thank you. Now, if you'll wait just a moment, I'll inform Mr. Trevor you're here. Would you like a cup of coffee?" she asked, before he could turn away.

He shook his head.

"Okay, I'll be right back."

He watched her traverse down the hallway and slip into another room. She exited with a coffee pot in hand and continued down the hall and around the corner. He heard a door open, and beyond that, muted voices.

Pam refreshed Trevor's cup while she informed him of his visitor.

"Thanks, Pam."

The huskiness in his voice and softness in his eyes belied the strict sense of business propriety Trevor demanded of his staff. His voice slid over her like a caress. Pam's heart did a slow swirl into her stomach. She kept her smile professional and eyes lowered, afraid he would see what the mere sound of his voice did to her composure.

"Give me five, will you?" Trevor added, when she headed out the door.

Pam nodded and closed the door behind her, careful to be quiet when she did so. She returned to her desk and found Alex waiting right where she'd left him. "He'll be out in a moment. Are you sure you wouldn't like a cup of coffee or something?"

"No, thanks."

"Okay. Make yourself comfortable," she said and pointed to the room across the way.

Alex took the hint that they'd share no more pleasantries and walked into the waiting area, stunned at the world of difference between the clean professionalism of the foyer and the exorbitant luxury of the lobby.

Adorned in the Southwestern style that had swept the nation with its charm, the décor took his breath away. Luminous shades of cream, rust, and burnt orange enveloped him with their warmth. Thick, plush furniture in a rustic design beckoned, offering comfort to the body and soul. The coffee and end tables were crafted from rich, vibrant wood with wrought-iron handles. The carvings suited the atmosphere of the room.

Copies of architectural publications as well as several home decorating magazines lay strategically scattered and tempted Alex to pick one up and browse. Large, handmade pottery vases held shoots of cattail. Lamps made out of the same rich earth as the vases were covered with paper-like shades, silhouetted with an intricate geometric pattern.

Paintings of red-gold landscapes hung on the walls. A curio cabinet made from the same wood as the tables displayed artifacts, Kachina dolls, and replicas of tools and eating utensils used by the early settlers of the region.

Alex heard a movement behind him and turned to greet the young man who entered the room.

"Mr. Broussard?" the young man said.

"Name's Alex," he replied and reached to shake the proffered hand.

"Trevor Forrestier. What can I do for you?"

Alex felt an odd sense of recognition, but he knew he had never met the young man before and shrugged the feeling off. "I'm looking for someone to restore an old house and a friend suggested I give you a call. I expected someone a little older though. Is your father in?"

A wary look crossed Trevor's face and he swallowed hard.

"No, sir, my father is deceased. My sister and I own the firm."

Stumped, all Alex could mutter was, "Oh, I'm sorry to hear that." He glanced away to gather his thoughts then back at the young man with a smile. "Nice décor."

Trevor smiled. "Thank you. My sister is the interior designer."

"She's good," Alex remarked, surprised when Trevor emitted a quick snort of laughter.

"I take it you haven't heard the hype surrounding her," he

commented with a grin.

Alex shook his head.

"Follow me," Trevor offered. "We'll take a tour of the offices while I give you the lowdown. Then, if you're still interested, we'll talk about a bid."

At Alex's nod, he turned to lead the way through the building.

Alex listened with interest while Trevor filled him in on the details of his, and his sister's, careers. Both had attended upscale Ivy League schools and obtained degrees in Architecture and Landscape Architecture as well as Urban Planning and Design. Both had also interned in their uncle's architectural firm in St. Paul, Minnesota. After their uncle's death, the two had decided to move to their mother's birthplace and make their mark on the world.

Trevor paused for a moment outside a door. "Any questions so far?"

Alex shook his head.

"Okay, this is my sister's office," he remarked with a smile and opened the door with a flourish.

Alex stepped through the entrance and felt right at home in the tranquil atmosphere. Shades of pale green and peach coated the walls, accented by a hand-painted magnolia border. Thick, plush carpet the color of *café au lait* covered the floor. A huge leather chair sat behind a solid oak desk. A drafting table carved out of cypress, another leather chair, and matched loveseat were the only other pieces of furniture in the room.

A hanging lamp with magnolias and Spanish moss silhouetted in its paper-like shade provided extra light over the drafting table. Limited-edition prints by Louisiana wildlife and landscape artists, framed and matted to match the room's décor, adorned the walls, and a masterpiece of light and color filled the space behind her desk.

Trevor grinned. "My office is just through there," he said and nodded at the door which joined the two rooms.

"I can't wait to see it." Alex wondered what design Trevor's sister had chosen for his office. He wasn't disappointed in the least when Trevor opened that door.

Artwork depicting the heart and soul of Native Americans hung on beige walls tinted with rich, vibrant colors that looked as though they were applied with sponges and feather dusters. Headdresses, drums, tomahawks, and dream catchers filled every nook and cranny of the room.

Carved out of a redwood tree with pieces of the bark still attached, his drafting table sat in the corner. Wolves silhouetted the paper-like shade on his hanging lamp. A huge oak desk, two leather chairs, and a set of shelves that overflowed with books and Native American artifacts rested on thick, plush carpet a shade darker than that in his sister's office.

Overwhelmed, Alex sighed in gratitude when Trevor sat behind the desk and motioned for him to take one of the other chairs.

"Now that you're duly impressed, at least by my sister's talent, are there any questions you'd like answered?"

His topaz gaze glittered with amusement, and Alex could tell Trevor tried hard not to gloat.

"A couple," he admitted with a nod. "How did she get to be so good?"

The grin escaped, followed by a laugh. "You mean at the tender age of twenty-seven?"

Alex nodded.

"Blood, sweat, and too many tears to count," Trevor said solemnly then smiled. "Added to that, she's an ambitious little twit. She's exceptionally gifted, and she's worked extremely hard to obtain the success she's acquired."

Trevor rose from his chair, took a couple of framed clippings from architectural and design publications off the bookshelf, and handed them to Alex.

"The gift has brought her national recognition and . . ." his voice trailed off. Trevor raked a hand over his face, took a deep breath, and continued. "Anyway, she doesn't like to brag about it and you won't find copies of these in her office, but for the life of me, I can't help it."

A shiver of apprehension skipped down Alex's spine at the sudden pallor in Trevor's face and the way his hand had trembled when he had scraped it over his face. He sensed a wealth of emotion behind that unfinished sentence. His brow quirked with curiosity before he skimmed the articles. If he had harbored any ideas to shop around, they were demolished while he read.

Seasoned with adjectives such as "brilliant," "gifted," and "extremely talented," the reviews hailed Taylor Forrestier as a visionary with an instinct for beauty and an eye for the unique.

"Well, guess that answers any questions I might have had," Alex admitted with a wry smile. He handed the clippings back to Trevor. "I'd brag too. So what exactly is your part in the whole scheme of things?"

"I do all the work. You might say she's the brains and I'm the backbone of the company. We usually work together on sketches and blueprints, though she's much better at both than I am. Taylor does all of the interior and landscape design, I work with the crew to build what she creates."

"Trevor, Taylor . . . Are you twins?"

Trevor nodded.

"Do you suppose I'll meet her before we sign contracts?"

Trevor grinned with a shrug. "Knowing my sister, there's no telling." He emitted a tiny laugh then pushed the intercom button on his speakerphone. "Pam, has Taylor made it in yet?"

"Yes, she just walked in. I think she's in the kitchen."

Another female voice came over the intercom and curled through Alex like a soft caress.

"I'm here, Trev. Sorry to keep you waiting. Can I bring you or your guest something to drink?"

Trevor eyed Alex, his eyebrow arched in question. "No, thanks," he replied when Alex shook his head. "Where've you been, Tay? It's eight thirty."

"It's such a beautiful morning Trev, I couldn't stand to come in early and stay cooped up all day. I went to church for meditation then out for some air. I'll be right there," she promised and the intercom light went off.

Within minutes a soft knock sounded on the door and she entered. The two men stood up.

"Hi. Mr. Broussard, is it?" she queried, when he turned to greet her. "I'm Taylor Forrestier." She pronounced the name as Louisiana natives would, "Foresjay" instead of "Forester."

One thought crossed Alex's mind before it went stunningly blank: *Oh, boy, the pretty little jogger.*

CHAPTER TWO

He reached out and enveloped her proffered hand in both of his, then murmured, "So, we meet."

The gleam in his eyes and the low vibration of his voice made shivers dance along every nerve in Taylor's body. A flush rushed to her cheeks when her brother cleared his throat, and she disengaged her hand. A frown creased her brow. "I'm sorry, I don't mean to be rude, but there's something vaguely familiar about you."

He smiled and slipped his hands in his pockets. "I was at the Civic Center earlier and you whizzed by the bench where I sat." He glanced back at her brother. "I thought you looked familiar," he told Trevor. "Now I know why."

Taylor cringed at her brother's sharp intake of breath. *I wish you hadn't said that,* she thought. Trevor's words barreled over any she might have uttered. "You went jogging alone, again?"

Taylor rolled her eyes with a sigh then glanced over at Trevor. "Do you really think we need to discuss this right now?"

Much to Taylor's relief, Trevor bit back his familiar arguments. She turned back to Mr. Broussard, whose gaze glittered with amusement. A smile tugged at the corners of his mouth, and she could tell he struggled not to laugh.

"Uh, oh, seems I've committed a *faux pas,*" he said.

Taylor shook her head. "It's no problem. Trevor can be a bit protective."

"And Taylor thinks she's invincible," her brother snorted in response. "But you're right, now is not the time to indulge in this discussion. We will talk about it later."

The chuckle escaped. Mr. Broussard settled comfortably back in the huge leather chair he'd vacated when she arrived.

"By all means, don't let me stop you. I've often wondered how people who've shared their lives as far back as the womb settle their differences."

Taylor's throaty laugh cut through the tension in the air. "My apologies to you, Mr. Broussard."

"Alex," he insisted.

She nodded. "Alex. Sometimes we forget we're all grown up with a business to run, huh, Trev?" She perched herself on the arm of her brother's chair. Trevor's reply was a noncommittal grunt.

Alex sat, momentarily stunned at seeing the two side-by-side. He'd always heard fraternal twins weren't identical. If so, medical scientists hadn't had the chance to study these two.

Though Taylor presented a softer version of her brother, there was no mistake they were twins. Thick, honey-colored hair shot with equal proportions of red and gold highlights covered identically shaped heads. Flecks of green and gold danced in wide-set, topaz eyes that were fringed by thick, golden lashes. A hint of cheekbone, a curve of cheek, and full sensuous lips gave Taylor a delicate, fragile look while her brother appeared ruggedly handsome.

They even dressed alike, he noted, and wondered if it were intentional. Trevor's embroidered denim shirt had been tucked into his designer jeans. Her matching shirt, tied at the waist, lay open to reveal a white undershirt. A slim, gold belt matched the band in her hair. Gold hoop earrings dangled from perfectly shaped lobes.

Once again Alex felt a spark of intensity and shook his head, his smile self-deprecating. "Sorry, I'm not used to seeing double unless I've overindulged," he admitted with a laugh.

Taylor giggled.

Trevor grinned. "You mentioned you were restoring an old house. Want to tell us about it?"

Alex tried to focus on Trevor, to concentrate on the conversation at hand, but his gaze strayed often to Taylor. No makeup marred her peachy-cream complexion. She had a natural beauty—trim, firm frame and dewy soft skin that glowed with health and vitality. He could almost see the gears turn in her mind and a glazed, distant look clouded her eyes while he talked about the project he had in store for them.

He'd purchased approximately forty acres of land about seven miles outside of Lake Charles. Situated on the English Bayou, the LeBleu Estate dated back to the original settlers of the area and was rumored to have housed Louisiana's favorite son on his excursions in and out of the area.

The house was run-down and ragged and the land in sad disarray from years of neglect, despite the fact there were too many heirs to count. Alex dreamed of turning it into a showplace. He wanted to restore the house and construct additional rooms as well as a garage. He also wanted to landscape and improve the grounds while building stables, a large swimming pool surrounded by a patio, a bath house, and full-scale tennis courts.

"Is it true Jean Lafitte slept in the barn during his excursions in and out of the state?" Taylor asked when Alex finished outlining his plans for the property.

Alex shrugged. "That's the rumor. I've heard he carved his initials into a board in the barn. Haven't seen it, though. Of course, the barn's pretty ragged and I haven't really had the time to traipse around out there, until now."

He took a deep breath, paused, and then asked, "So, are you

interested?"

Hope thundered in his chest at the dreamy expression on Taylor's face until he noticed a quick frown crease Trevor's brow when he glanced up at her.

"I think we should go take a look at it," he interjected before his sister could utter a word.

Alex could tell by the myriad of emotions which played across her lovely features Taylor was interested but that she bit back her enthusiastic response at the tone of her brother's voice. He knew by their interaction which twin was more practical and which more creative.

Taylor smiled down into Trevor's adamant gaze. "I think you're right," she said and he visibly relaxed. "I'll just grab a few things, and we'll be outta here."

Alex rose when she vacated her perch and headed toward her office. "Uh, miss?" He interrupted her departure. She turned. He swept his eyes over her jean-clad figure, her tiny feet encased in strappy sandals.

"Do you have a pair of boots or sturdy shoes?" he asked, unable to quell the shock of awareness that shivered through him at the sight his eyes beheld. He heard Trevor's sharp intake of breath and glanced over with a prayer that her brother couldn't read his mind.

No such luck.

Alex could tell by the glint of emotion in Trevor's expressive topaz gaze that he knew, though didn't appreciate, the effect his sister had on men. "It's rough out there, she needs to protect her feet," Alex said in the most respectful tone he could summon, despite the heart hammering in his throat and the blood thrumming through his veins.

Trevor acknowledged his words with a curt nod and rose from his chair. "She has a whole wardrobe in there," he remarked and walked around his desk to open the door. "If you'll wait in the lobby, we'll be out in a moment."

The strained politeness of Trevor's voice amused him, his eyebrow quirked and a smile tugged at his lips, but he refrained from comment and exited the room as requested.

It took every ounce of self-control Trevor possessed to not slam the door on Alex's departing figure, but restraint vanished when he stormed into his sister's office. "We're not taking the job."

"Why on earth not?"

"Because I don't like the way that guy looks at you!"

Taylor's dainty laugh grated on his already raw nerves.

"Oh, please, Trev, a little healthy desire never hurt anyone."

Trevor snorted. "Healthy desire my foot, that's pure animal lust!"

Taylor's smile didn't quite reach her eyes.

"Trying to protect my honor, little brother?" she asked, a hint of annoyance in her voice. "You above all people know there's nothing left to protect."

"Don't say that! Your honor is still very much intact."

"Even though my body isn't?"

"Taylor, we agreed," he began. She shook her head and held up a hand to ward off the familiar arguments.

Trevor watched in frustrated fury while she tugged on socks and boots. Then he grabbed her by the arm when she crossed his path on the way to her drafting table. "I can't believe you went jogging alone again."

Taylor drew herself to her full five foot four inches and glared at him. "Is that what this is all about?"

"Don't you watch the news or read the paper?"

"No, I don't."

"Well, you should!" Fear obliterated any ounce of anger he felt. Every time he opened the newspaper or turned on the television to hear about another rape, murder, or abduction, of a woman molested, mangled or dead, he dealt with the gut-wrenching terror that one day he'd lose her. That he couldn't bear. Especially after what they'd survived so far.

Flesh of his flesh, blood of his blood, heart of his heart, she was more than a sister to him. She was his life. From the moment of conception they'd shared everything—dreams, hopes, fears, and the horrors of a childhood wracked with lies and deceit. A childhood filled with anger, pain, and the kind of repulsive abuse disgustingly prevalent in society.

Throughout the years of shame and fear, of therapy and counseling, and down the long, seemingly endless, road to recovery, he and Taylor had stuck together, grew closer, and vowed they'd never leave one another. They had shared home and hearth until the move to Louisiana. Both had decided the time had come to loosen the ties and rent separate places. Trevor still hadn't adjusted to her not being there in the morning when he awoke or late in the evening when he couldn't sleep. Many were the nights he called in the midnight hour just to check and make sure she was okay.

He knew Taylor recognized the raw emotions in his heart when she touched his cheek in a gentle caress. He saw the sorrow in her eyes and knew she, too, regretted how the past sucked them back with such ease. Would it ever stop haunting them?

"The past is over and done with, Trevor, and I'm sorry for bringing it up. But I'm not a helpless little girl anymore. I'm a grown woman and perfectly capable of taking care of myself. Besides," her voice trailed off and she bit back the remainder of her comment.

Trevor knew what she hadn't said. *Nothing could happen to her that hadn't already been done.* He cupped her cheeks in his hands. "I'm sorry too, Tay. I just worry when you go jogging alone. All we have, all we've ever had, is each other. I couldn't bear to lose you."

Taylor gave him a quick hug and brushed her lips over his cheek. "I promise to be extra careful when I go jogging if you promise to stop being so overprotective. Now, we shouldn't keep Mr. Broussard waiting any longer," she insisted. She grinned at his quick snort of disdain. She grabbed a sketch pad and pencils from her drafting table and left the office with him close on her heels.

Laughter sounded from the lobby and elicited another quick snort of disapproval from Trevor, along with a muttered oath. Taylor laughed and turned to face him, while she walked backward.

"Maybe you shouldn't be so adamant about what's proper, Trev. Wait too long and someone will stake claim to what you don't." She turned on her heel and practically skipped into the lobby.

"Pammy," she all but sang. "We're heading out to look at a job with Mr. Broussard. Hold down the fort, will you?"

Pam grinned. "Sure thing. Anything you need for me to take care of while you're gone?"

"Ask Trevor," Taylor suggested with a wink, then turned to Alex. "Tell me more about this property, Mr. Broussard," she urged, and led the way to the parking lot, which gave Trevor the opportunity to spend a couple of minutes alone with Pam.

Trevor knew his sister approved wholeheartedly of Pam's feelings for him, and, though he tried hard not to show them in the office, his growing feelings for her.

Pam's chuckle died in her throat when she turned to look at Trevor's flushed face and fierce eyes. "Is something wrong?" she asked, surprised when he stepped through the door to her office and boxed her in against the desk.

"Want to tell me what's so funny?"

Little shivers of delight danced through her system when she considered he might feel threatened or jealous. Her smile sweet, she fought the urge to run her fingers through his hair. "He was telling Boudreau/Thibodeau jokes."

Trevor's eyes narrowed. Pam resisted the temptation to drag him into her arms when he edged a notch closer.

"Quite the charmer isn't he?"

Pam inclined her head in subtle agreement. "I'm sure some would think so."

"And you?" he asked an elaborate arch to his brow. "What do you think?"

She smiled. "He seems nice enough."

Her heart skipped a beat when he cupped her cheek in his hand.

"Just don't forget where you belong," he ordered in a husky voice.

"Which is?" She could hardly force the words past the heart in her throat when he lowered his gaze to her mouth and lingered then returned to capture her in a heated embrace. Her heart stumbled in her chest when he threw propriety to the wind and lowered his lips to hers.

"Right here," he murmured, and pulled her against him.

The kiss was brief, devastating.

"Got it?" he queried, his voice soft.

Pamela rested against the desk, her knees threatened to buckle beneath her. "Yes, sir, and may I say it's about time you got it?" He laughed, brushed his lips over hers again and nodded.

"Now let me hurry before he charms my sister into agreeing to this project sight unseen."

Pam giggled. "If she's anything like her brother, she won't be so easily charmed."

"Oh, but that's where you're wrong, *mon cheré.*" He nailed the words if not the accent. "She's as easily charmed as her brother, though not quite as stubborn about it."

He eyed her with a meaningful grin. A quick flush of pleasure heated her cheeks. He turned on his heel and headed out the door but paused and tapped his cell phone.

"Holler if you need."

She nodded. Trevor hesitated then stepped back through the doorway.

"And don't make any plans for dinner."

She nodded again then slid bonelessly into her chair when he walked out of the office into the bright, morning sunlight.

Trembling fingers touched lips that were still tender from his kiss. Pam's mind replayed every word, gesture, and nuance of their encounter until convinced by her heart what she experienced wasn't a dream at all.

CHAPTER THREE

Trevor stepped from the dimly lit foyer and squinted against the brilliant sunlight. He scanned the area, and then spotted his sister with Alex, standing next to a dark green SUV. Taylor turned and her eyes danced with humor when he crossed the parking lot to join them.

"Are things squared away with Pam?" she asked.

"For now," he replied.

"We ready?" Alex asked.

Trevor nodded. "Shall we follow you?"

Alex shrugged. "Up to you. We can all ride together. I've plenty of room."

"That's fine." Trevor opened the back passenger door to help his sister into the vehicle. He heard her suppressed chuckle when she climbed onto the seat directly behind him while he opened the front door and entered. He smothered the urge to punch Alex when he walked around to the driver's side, opened the door, slid in and, with a wink and grin, adjusted the rearview mirror to where every time he glanced in it, his gaze would catch hers.

"You know what we need to do, Trev?" Taylor asked, while Alex maneuvered the vehicle through downtown traffic to head out of the city.

Trevor turned in his seat as much as the seatbelt would allow. "What?"

"We need to round up the gang and have a huge ball game

and picnic tomorrow."

"And where do you propose we do that?"

She shrugged. "Haven't a clue. But I'm sure Steve wouldn't mind if we hosted it at his place. He has plenty of room. The gang hasn't worked in nearly two weeks, what with finishing up the Guilbeau home and then all the rain. I'm sure everyone would enjoy it."

"Be good for morale too," Trevor agreed. "I'll give Steve a call when we return to the office."

"Good," she sighed with a smile. "You're welcome to join us, Mr. Broussard." Her saccharine tone earned a dark look from Trevor.

Alex glanced in the rear-view mirror then averted his gaze back to the road. "Please, call me Alex. I'm sure we'll be working very closely for quite some time once you agree to do this job."

Her smile was a combination of mischief and allure. "I'll remember that *if* we decide to do the job."

Alex chuckled. "And until then?"

"Until then it'll be Mr. Broussard and you may call me Miss Forrestier."

Trevor shook his head, rolled his eyes, and wondered what on earth possessed his sister. Taylor never behaved flirtatiously. He'd like to put it off as spring fever but he knew it went much deeper than that. Her actions were an attempt to put the past in its place and open herself up to the future. A future filled with love and peace and, hopefully, romance and children. They both wanted a chance to start over, to do better, a chance to provide for their own children what they had missed out on. He sighed and then asked how much farther they had to drive.

"Not far," Alex answered then maneuvered around a curve, yielded, then turned right onto the highway.

A couple of minutes later they pulled into the drive of a rundown property. Alex parked the SUV, disembarked, and pocketed his keys, then reached under the seat to pull out a pistol. "Hang on guys." The twins gasped. Alex glanced up then made sure the gun was loaded. "Take it easy, you two. This is just a precaution in case we rustle up any snakes."

Taylor, who had one foot on the ground and the other still in the truck, halted her descent. "Snakes?" she asked with a visible shudder and pulled her foot firmly back inside the vehicle.

Alex chortled at the response and the expression on her face. "Or rats, which is why I suggested the boots."

Trevor climbed out and took his sister's arm. "From the looks of things there's sure to be one or the other, or both. Stay close."

Waist-high grass and weeds grew in abandon. Rust corroded the barbed-wire fence and rendered the gate nearly useless. Alex fumbled with the lock then pushed the barrier far enough out of the way so they could pass through. He led, Trevor brought up the rear, and the trio made their way steadily toward the house.

"Are we going to look at the barn?" Taylor asked.

Trevor knew she too remembered the rumor that Jean Lafitte carved his initials in there and was surprised, impressed even, when Alex shook his head before he answered. He listened to their exchange with conflicting emotions.

"Not today. Once things around here are cleaned up a bit, we'll check it out. I'm anxious to see if the rumors are true too."

"We?" she queried.

"We," he agreed. "I'm sure your crew won't mind the extra work it'll take to clean up, especially since they haven't worked in two weeks."

"The crew doesn't mind any type of work as long as the money's right," she said, a delicate arch to her brow. "Besides, *we* haven't agreed to anything."

Alex turned as they approached the old home. "Money's no object," he assured her, his voice firm. "And you will."

Trevor heard the conviction in Alex's voice. He saw the wealth of emotions in his eyes and knew the man desperately wanted to touch his sister without the risk of being murdered by him. In a protective move, he took Taylor's arm.

"Watch your step," he cautioned, and guided her across the dilapidated porch and into the house.

The house, a mere box of a building, seemed sturdy despite its state of disrepair and years of neglect. Taylor fished in her pocket for a piece of charcoal and began to sketch the structure. When Alex spoke of changes and additions, she forced her mind off the way his voice feathered over her and added to the drawings. She flipped to a fresh page and drew the wallpaper pattern then found a spot where it had pulled away from the wall. She took a penknife out of her pocket, slid the blade under the paper and carefully cut a section and placed the piece in the book along with her sketch. A mental list of companies that specialized in the reproduction of old wallpaper and paneling patterns became notations alongside the sketch and sample.

She listened when Trevor noted aloud the quality of wood that could be restored or repaired to maintain the integrity of the original house. When he and Alex went outside she stayed in to examine walls and floors. She took notes of the hand-carved trim work, antique cook stove, and pot-bellied wood stove, but her mind continued to circle around the sound of Alex's voice and the light in his eyes when he looked at her.

She had no idea why he affected her so and welcomed the moments alone to focus on the job at hand. Her mind traveled back a few hours to her jog around the Civic Center, and she recalled with vivid clarity the moment she had passed by the bench where he sat. Their eyes had met for only a brief moment but she'd felt the warmth of his gaze clear to her toes. No one had ever touched her heart, much less jumbled her mind, with a simple gaze or smile.

She shook her head with a sigh and picked her way carefully up the ragged stairs, then stepped into what was once a loft or attic. The house reeked of history, from cypress-covered exterior walls and interior walls of bare wood, to the hardwood floors made of oak, the boxed staircase, and the wooden shutters with crosses carved out of the center.

Taylor knew the cuts were used to slip a gun barrel through in order to protect the property and family. Though a bit of a struggle, she managed to open one window and shutter. Sunlight filtered in to chase shadows from the room.

A glimpse of splendor, a glimmer of brilliance caught her eye, like fairy dust dancing on sunlight. She turned her head with caution when a pulse at the base of her skull began to throb and familiar vibrations stole over her. She lowered herself to the floor and let the sensations envelop her. Her eyesight blurred, fingers trembled and heartbeat quickened while her mind swam with images. Visions guided her hand until she filled the remainder of the sketchbook.

Trevor stepped back into the house and called for his sister. Excitement replaced the irritation he'd felt as Alex expressed his dream to turn this rundown piece of property into a showplace which rivaled that of the rich and famous. He paused just inside the door, looked, listened, and called for Taylor again.

Alex stepped up beside him. "Where is she?"

A muffled sound above drew their attention. Afraid she may be hurt or in trouble, both men scrambled for the staircase. Trevor reached the top first. She sat on the floor, head buried between her knees, sketchbook beside her. The full piece of charcoal she'd carried was merely a stub. He hesitated, then called her name, his tone soft.

"Is she alright?" Alex asked one step behind him.

Trevor walked over to his sister, ran a hand down her hair, and spoke her name again, careful to keep his tone soft. "Are you alright?"

She nodded. "Just a bit light-headed."

"It's no wonder, there's hardly any air up here," Alex insisted. He stepped over to another window and forced it open.

"How long have you been up here?" Trevor asked and squatted down beside her. She shrugged.

"What are you doing up here all by yourself?" Alex demanded, his voice tight with concern. "You shouldn't have negotiated those stairs alone."

Trevor knew exactly what had happened. He picked up the sketchpad and glanced through then handed it to Alex, not the least bit surprised by his reaction.

"Good grief, where on earth did these come from?" Alex exclaimed and flipped through page after page of sketches of the house and grounds. The last one showed a stately two-story home covered inside and out with plaster. There was a ballroom on the top floor.

"It's how the place used to look, how it should be again," Taylor answered, her voice shaky.

"Are you ready to get up yet?" he asked, then eyed Trevor. "Shall we help her to her feet?"

Years of experience hadn't made it any easier for Trevor to handle the weakness that overcame her after one of her visions. He eyed her a moment, then shrugged. "Tay?"

Taylor must have heard the concern in his voice for she lifted her head to smile at him.

"I'm okay, Trev," she said in quiet assurance and raised a

trembling hand to his cheek, "Really. Just give me another minute."

Trevor swallowed hard, nodded curtly. "Tell us when you're ready."

Alex bit back any further comments or questions and leaned against the window. He skimmed through the sketchbook again, and Trevor could tell by the awe on his face that what he saw amazed him. When Taylor cleared her throat and reached a shaky hand to Trevor, Alex scrambled over and assisted in helping her up. When she swayed, he shoved the sketchbook into Trevor's hands and lifted her in his arms.

"I can walk," she insisted.

Alex eyed her. "Bull. You're pale as milk and trembling. I won't have you fall head first down that poor excuse of a staircase. Lead the way," he ordered Trevor. "And stay close."

Once they reached the ground floor, Alex carried her outside. "Is she always like this afterward?" he asked, and sat her down on the porch.

Trevor nodded. "She's always a little weak, a bit dizzy, slightly disoriented, but it's usually not this bad."

"Probably a bit worse due to the lack of oxygen in the room."

"You're talking about me as though I'm not even here," Taylor complained.

Indignation brightened her eyes. Color bloomed in her face. Trevor crossed his arms over his chest and frowned down at his sister. "Probably worse because she skipped breakfast to go jogging, alone, and it's about near time for lunch."

"We'll have to see about getting some food in her then," Alex remarked, and placed a firm hand on her shoulder when she moved to stand up.

"Sit down, and stay down." He grinned when she glared up at him.

"Don't speak to me like I'm your pet dog, Mr. Broussard."

He squatted eye level with her and pointed a finger in her face. "I don't want to see you hurt, so stay put." His gaze locked with Trevor's. "Make sure she does."

Trevor stood in front of her, arms still crossed over his chest. "Don't worry, she's not about to get up or go anywhere."

"Back off, little brother," Taylor grumbled.

She knew he hated it when she called him that. Though born only minutes apart, Trevor had the misfortune to enter the world second. This fact irritated him royally while they grew up and still had the power to put him in his place when necessary. He tapped the toe of her boot with his and grinned. "Not gonna work this time, Big Sister," he chided. "You're gonna stay put until Mr. Broussard is ready to leave."

"It's Alex." Exasperation clouded his tone. "Don't you think we're past the point of formalities?" When neither answered him, Alex sighed. "I'll just run up and close those windows, and then we'll go."

Trevor nodded. "Okay."

Alex hurried indoors and up the stairs, his mind awhirl at what happened. Words from the articles he'd read in Trevor's office swam through his mind . . . *A gifted designer, a visionary with an instinct for beauty and an eye for the unique* . . . Suddenly he understood how accurate the statements were. He rested against the first windowsill, surprised at the quick shiver which shook him, not only from the shock she'd given him but from the memory of how she'd felt in his arms.

Chapter Four

Trevor surrendered the guard-like position in front of his sister and sat beside her on the porch. He slipped his arm around her waist, pulled her against him and brushed his lips across her temple. "Are you sure you're okay?"

Taylor rested her head on his shoulder and nodded. "I'm fine. Just ticked off at you for acting the way you are. I can understand Mr. Broussard's concern. I mean, it's his property. If I get hurt . . ." her words trailed off at his quick snort of disdain.

"I doubt very much he had a single thought of lawsuits when he picked you up. The man has itched to get his hands on you from the moment you walked in the office," he muttered. Her flush burned clear through his shirt, warmed his skin.

"Well, inform him that's against the rules will you?"

"What rules?"

"Can't mix business with pleasure."

Trevor chuckled. "I broke that rule this morning, so I can't very well be the one to tell him. Guess we'll have to renegotiate it."

She giggled. "It's about time."

"So I've been told." He sighed. "You about ready?" he asked when he heard Alex's footsteps.

"Yeah." She nodded as Alex walked through the door. He circled around, stepped off the porch, and turned to face them.

"Feeling better?" he asked Taylor.

"Yes, thank you."

He stooped down and cupped her chin in his hand. "You're still a bit pale."

"If you even think you're about to carry me, think again. I'll bloody your nose if you try," she warned, her eyes narrowed into dangerous slits of shimmering topaz.

He grinned. "Pretty feisty for someone who couldn't stand on her own feet less than five minutes ago."

Trevor laughed at the exchange, rose to his feet, and offered her a hand-up. Alex stepped out of the way and followed them back out to where he'd parked his vehicle.

"I believe you're right about why I'm so weak, Trev," Taylor admitted once they were buckled up. "I think my stomach gnawed a hole in my backbone."

Trevor reached for his cell phone. Before he could punch in the first number, it rang. The office number flashed on the display screen. "Yes?"

"Do y'all want me to have lunch here when you get back?"

"You must have read our minds," he admitted. "Call someplace that delivers and order us a plate lunch. You have enough petty cash?"

"If not, I have the credit card."

"Good, order one for Mr. Broussard also." He eyed Alex. "Okay by you?"

Alex shrugged. "I was about to suggest I take you two to lunch, but that's fine."

"We'll be back in fifteen or twenty minutes," Trevor told Pam, then hung up.

They rode back to the office in almost complete silence. Trevor hummed little sounds of surprise and admiration while he flipped through the sketchbook. Alex's gaze strayed often to the rearview mirror to check on Taylor, who rested against the seat, her eyes closed. When he pulled into the office lot and parked the SUV, Trevor handed him the sketchbook and disembarked from the vehicle to help his sister.

Pam waited for them in the kitchen, the table set with take-out plates which overflowed with rice, gravy, and beef tips. Whole-kernel corn and baby carrots soaked in a cinnamon & sugar glaze were the vegetables of the day. Homemade rolls, side salad, and thick slices of chocolate cake with vanilla icing were included in the meal. Three tall, frosted glasses filled to the brim with milk sat beside napkins, silverware, and bottles of salad dressing.

"What would you like to drink, Mr. Broussard?" she asked. "We have tea, cola, milk, or water."

"Milk's fine," he answered, and held a chair out for Taylor who slid into it with a sigh.

Pam took one look at Taylor's pale face and gave her a pre-moistened disinfectant wipe for her hands, and then filled another glass with milk.

"Thanks Pammy," she said, as the two men washed their hands in the kitchen sink. Once they finished, she rose to do the same, then returned to her chair.

Trevor held a chair out for Pam. Then he and Alex sat. Pam watched through lowered lids as Alex reached for a napkin and placed it over his lap, then hesitated when Taylor bowed her head and said grace. He grinned when Taylor reached for the salad dressing and Trevor pushed it and the salad out of her grasp.

"Eat," Trevor ordered and tapped Taylor's plate with his fork.

"I always eat my salad first."

"Not today. The salad will only curb your appetite and you need some food in you."

"You know I don't like rice and gravy," she whined. "Besides there's enough here to feed three people."

"Eat the meat then," Trevor insisted and passed her a roll. "And the vegetables. Then, if you're still hungry, you can have the salad and if you're a good girl, the cake."

Taylor picked up her fork and Pam could tell by the glint in her eyes she resisted the urge to stab Trevor with it. She had witnessed this scenario countless times since hired by the twins and waited in expectation for Taylor's response.

"Last time I checked, Trevor, I am twenty-seven not seven, and you're my brother not my nurse."

"Don't like rice?" Alex interrupted. "I've never heard of anyone not liking rice."

"I love rice," Taylor corrected. "Plain or with a little butter and sugar, not swimming in greasy gravy. And I prefer brown rice whenever possible."

"Sacrilegious." Alex turned to Pam. "Are they always like this?"

She nodded, smiled. "What's worst is you can never tell who wins."

Alex chuckled. "I can just about imagine, but this time he's right, you know."

"He sure is," Pam quipped and arched a delicate brow at Taylor. She smiled when, outnumbered, Taylor rolled her eyes and pierced a beef tip with her fork. A satisfied little hum escaped when the morsel melted in her mouth. They ate the remainder of lunch in companionable silence. When Taylor finished all of the meat and vegetables on her plate, Trevor handed her the salad, dressing, and cake without a word.

"Here, you can have mine too," Alex said, and pushed his salad in front of her.

"You don't want it?"

He shook his head and grinned. "I prefer rice and gravy to lettuce and tomatoes."

Taylor shook her head. "I'm about stuffed. But thanks any-way."

"We'll save it for later." Pam rose to throw her plate away, then began to clean off the table.

Taylor shoved her piece of cake toward Pam and stood to help. "Save this too. I can't eat another bite."

Pam accepted Taylor's help with a smile but watched closely to see if the meal had restored her energy or simply filled an empty hole in her belly. She'd learned long ago not to make a big fuss after Taylor had one of her visions, especially since Trevor fussed enough for an entire family. Gifted though they were, the episodes usually left Taylor spent. Much like an artist or writer, Pam supposed, who worked in a frenzy to finish that special painting, pivotal scene, or final chapter.

Trevor pushed back from the table, rose, and took the trash bag out of the can. He paused beside the ladies and touched his sister's shoulder in a tender gesture.

"Tired?"

She nodded.

"Want to rest a bit?"

Again she nodded, then turned to Alex. "If you'll excuse me, Mr. Broussard?"

Alex nodded, rose from his seat at the table, and reached for the trash bag in Trevor's hand. "Let me take that out for you."

"Thanks," Trevor replied and handed it over. He slid his arm around his sister's waist and escorted her to her office.

Once they left the kitchen Alex eyed Pam. "Is she alright? Does this happen very often?"

Loyalty bound Pam to choose her answers with care. "She'll be fine. She just needs to rest a bit. Shall I show you where the dumpster is?" She could tell by the way he hesitated and bit back any further questions that Alex understood loyalty very well, which pleased her.

"I think I can find it," he assured and stepped out the back door.

Alex returned to the kitchen to find Trevor sitting at the table with his face buried in his hands.

"Is she resting?"

Trevor nodded and lifted his head.

"Are you alright?"

Trevor swallowed hard and nodded again.

"My apologies to you Mr. Broussard, if we've come across as less than professional."

"Oh, please," Alex snorted, "Less than professional my foot. I'd be a fool to fault you for your concern over your twin, or her for what is obviously a rare and precious gift."

"Then I'll tell you this much," Trevor said and lifted a relieved gaze to his. "A venture of this magnitude will take an exorbitant amount of money and time. Taylor is a perfectionist when it comes to the restoration of an old home. She'll go above and beyond to preserve the integrity of the original style and structure no matter what you say. She'll take all you want into consideration, do her level best to accommodate you, but in the end, it's her way or no way, which is what makes her work so unique. And it always turns out beautifully.

"She'll probably have several more episodes like the one she had today, at various stages of development," Trevor continued. "They'll leave her moody, irritable and exhausted. You can't even speak to her when she's in the midst of one. It is almost like she isn't there, like she's outside herself.

"She's described the experiences as though a creative spirit, force, or energy consumes her every thought and guides her hand. She believes this is a gift from God. She takes that gift very seriously and uses it to glorify Him and His creation by creating the extraordinary and the unique. Let her have her way and you won't be disappointed," he assured Alex.

"Oh, and one other thing, we have the best crew of carpenters, concrete workers, and electricians this side of the Mississippi river. However, I do not believe in working them into the ground. They'll gladly give you forty, fifty, or even sixty hours a week when the weather permits. But weekends, holidays, and occasional three or four days off will be necessary to keep them at their peak. Many of them have wives and children, and Taylor and I are firm believers that families come first. Taking all of this into consideration, if you're still interested, we'll be happy to bid the job."

"I only have two questions," Alex said and sat in the chair across from him. "How long will it take and how soon can you get started?"

Trevor smiled. "You're looking at approximately a year to completion, give or take a month or two due to the weather or delays in the materials. Cleanup alone will take several days. Taylor probably won't even look at those sketches again until sometime tonight or tomorrow. It'll take us a couple of days to compile the figures and then another to draw up contracts. That is, if we can come to some kind of agreement."

Alex reached into his back pocket and pulled out the check book he'd retrieved from the glove compartment of his SUV. He tossed it on the table. "Name your price."

"You're looking at hundreds of thousands, possibly even into the low millions of dollars to develop this property to the specifications you outlined earlier, Mr. Broussard."

Alex acknowledged the fact with a tiny nod. "And as I mentioned earlier, Mr. Forrestier, money is no object. I have no qualms about letting your sister have her way. Or, should I say, exploiting her genius," he remarked with a chuckle.

"The last twenty years of my life I've worked, scrimped, saved, invested, and hoped this property would be available when I was ready for it. Believe me when I say the work will get done. I want you and your sister to do it.

"Now," Alex continued. "I'll save you a couple steps and give you the go ahead to start your crew on cleanup tomorrow. As soon as we get enough done, I'll furnish all the food and drink necessary for the ball game and picnic you and your sister discussed earlier." He took the pen from his pocket, filled out a check, tore it from the book and pushed it toward Trevor. "This should serve well as a deposit. We can deal with contracts next week."

Proficient in the art of negotiation, he sat back and waited while Trevor considered his proposal, no doubt in his mind Taylor would want to do this job. He also had a feeling that once she made up her mind, no one would be able to talk her out of it, not even her brother. Silence stretched between them until he began to wonder if he'd been adamant enough to show how serious he was about the project and the fact he wanted them to complete it. The breath he hadn't realized he held escaped in a relieved sigh when Trevor pushed the intercom button on the phone and called for Pam.

"Yes?"

"Round up the crew. We have a job to begin tomorrow," he said.

"Sure thing."

Trevor let go of the intercom button and extended a hand to him.

"Thank you, Mr. Broussard. You can rest assured everyone will do their best to accommodate you in every way."

Alex shook the proffered hand. "There's one stipulation I'd ask you to put in our contract."

Trevor's eyebrow arched in question. "Which is?"

"That you, your sister, and your employees call me Alex," he insisted with a smile.

"I don't see a problem with that one," Trevor replied with a grin.

CHAPTER FIVE

Taylor awoke groggy and disoriented. The room was dark and it took a few moments before she recognized her office. She rose from the loveseat and went to the closet. The tiny room contained a couple changes of clothes and shoes, but overall it was much more than it first appeared. She crossed to the altar, knelt, lit a candle, and began to pray. A short while later, she knocked on Trevor's office door, and entered upon his command.

He sat at the desk with her sketches, a legal pad, and calculator spread out before him. "You're working late," she commented.

"How are you?"

"Fine. Hungry, but fine."

Trevor put down his pencil and rose from the chair. "There's Chinese food in the kitchen. Pam and I ate earlier." He slipped his arm around her waist and led her there.

"You should have taken her out to dinner."

"I had planned on it. Didn't want to leave you though and neither did she."

"You two worry too much," she insisted, then turned to put her arms around him and rest her head on his shoulder. "But I'm glad you're here to take care of me. And I'm sorry for being so grouchy earlier."

Trevor hugged her. "I'll always be here to take care of you," he promised and rubbed her back and shoulders to soothe away the tension that lingered.

He smiled. "Besides, I'm used to it." He brushed his lips over her forehead, moved out of her arms and pulled a chair out from the table for her to sit.

He placed the salads and dressing left over from lunch in front of her. "Start with this while I heat up your dinner. After you're through eating, I'll drive you home."

Taylor smiled over at him. "I can drive home, thanks, but you can follow me if you wish." She knew he would accompany her whether she wanted him to or not.

Trevor nodded, put her dinner in the microwave to heat and then sat across from her while she demolished one of the salads. "I've agreed to do the job for Mr. Broussard. We start cleanup tomorrow."

Taylor smiled and reached for the other salad. "Good."

"You like him, don't you?"

"Yes, I like him. Don't you?"

Trevor studied her a moment then answered her question with a tilt of his head. "I don't like the way he looks at you but other than that, yeah, I like him."

"He looks at me no different than the way you look at Pam."

He flushed, stuttered. "I don't look at her like that."

"Like what?"

"Like I'd love nothing more than to gobble her up in one bite."

She laughed at the hint of insult in his voice. "Yes you do, especially when you think no one is paying attention."

Trevor had the grace to grin. "He doesn't bother or intimidate you?"

She shook her head and stacked the empty salad container on top of the other. "I haven't been bothered or intimidated by a man in a long time, Trev. But, no, in fact I feel rather . . ." Her voice trailed off as she searched for the right word to describe the warmth that consumed her in Alex's presence.

"Comfortable, I guess is the word I'd use to describe how I feel around him." *And alive.* She kept that thought private.

"Well one thing's certain: what he wants to accomplish with this property will be one magnificent project."

Taylor nodded in agreement. "What about contracts?"

"We'll get to them next week. He insists we include a clause to mandate everyone call him Alex," he said with a chuckle. "I've already started to work up the bid, but Taylor . . ." His words trailed off when she placed a finger over his lips.

"You don't have to say it; I've already been shown what to do to prepare, Trevor, and how to stay sane and healthy throughout the project."

"You have to take it easy," he implored. When the microwave beeped, he rose from his chair to retrieve the plate for her.

"Promise you'll take care of yourself," he insisted and set a serving of shrimp fried rice in front of her.

"I can do all things through Christ who strengthens me," she remarked, her smile tender. "But I promise. So, how far along are you in the bids?"

He shook his head, sighed. "Not far enough. I've looked over your sketches and tried to compile a few figures, but I've barely scratched the surface."

"Well, if you feel like working a little longer, we can look at it together."

Trevor shook his head. "You need to go home and rest."

Taylor rolled her eyes. "I've slept the whole afternoon away, Trev. I'm raring to go now."

"Well I'm not," he admitted. "I'm exhausted."

"Okay. I'll take what you've started home with me and work a little while this evening. We'll look at the sketches and figures together over the weekend or on Monday. Will you help with cleanup?"

He nodded. "Yeah. Pam will be there too."

"I'll be there sometime tomorrow then." She rose from the table to throw away her trash. When she finished, they gathered the things she needed from Trevor's office and left.

Trevor's car stayed on her tail as he followed her home. Taylor could tell weariness dragged at him, but she also knew he wouldn't rest until and unless he knew she was okay. She knew it would be useless to argue with him, so she opened the door to her cottage and allowed him to enter first. He kicked off his shoes, then headed for the shower and prepared to bunk down in her spare bedroom. When he exited the bathroom she handed him a cup of warm milk, said goodnight with a smile, and closed the door to her bedroom, which also served as an office and gym. She spread the sketches out on her drafting table and stared down at them, amazed and humbled they'd come through her.

She took a fresh pad from the endless supply in her nightstand and began to sketch out the plans Mr. Broussard, *Alex*, she reminded herself, had defined throughout their conversation. Though she and Trevor had computers loaded with programs to execute every aspect of a job from cost estimates to landscape design, they always started a bid the old-fashioned way, with basic sketches, measurements, and figures.

Step two for her was research, especially when it came to the renovation of an old home. She wanted to know everything she could about the original structure, the people who built it, and the time period in which it was built. Her first source would be the genealogy department at the local library. The wealth of information she found there always amazed her: old newspaper articles; photos or sketches of homes, families, and events; a number of books on the early settlers of Calcasieu Parish, as well as scrapbooks donated by their heirs. All of this helped her visualize a complete picture of the home and property she would restore, remodel, or redecorate. What she couldn't find there she sometimes found in the archives of the local university's library, on the Internet, or whenever possible by interviewing heirs. Those discussions usually included old photographs as well as stories, tales, and legends passed down through the generations.

In step three she entered the information into the computer in order to get a total cost analysis as well as estimated time span and profit margin. She could also utilize her PC to develop a computerized presentation of various stages of the project as well as how it would look upon completion.

Lastly, the bid would be handed over to Pam to insert into their standard contract. Once contracts were signed, they began the job.

Or that was how they'd always done it in the past, she mused, and wondered what Alex said to convince Trevor to agree to start this one so soon. Her mind went off in a whole other direction when she thought about him . . . his sandy-colored hair, merry hazel eyes, and velvety-rough voice.

The next morning Trevor slid into clean clothes. He always had an extra outfit or two as well as pajamas at his sister's house. He tiptoed into her room to check on her. He knew she had probably worked late into the night or into the wee hours of the morning, and he was careful not to disturb her. He watched for a moment, comforted by the steady rise and fall of her shoulders while she slept. He thought about their conversation last night and her assessment of Alex compared to his feelings for Pam and smiled. Maybe they'd both find the kind of love they dreamed about. Love that would heal the scars they carried.

A shiver shook his soul at the thought. Ghoulish memories rose from within the deepest recess of his mind and brought with them shame and fear along with a host of other emotions he dared not put a name to. He tamped down the beast within, buried it in the farthest corner of his heart, and covered the grave with a thin layer of hope that the move here would one day prove to be the end-all of their childhood misery.

He closed his eyes and sent a quick prayer of thanks for the blessing of his sister in his life, followed by a plea to God to watch over her, that she would rest peacefully, and that He would sustain and uphold her in the months to come.

Unsure if God heard him, much less cared, he exited the room as quietly as he'd entered.

He put on his shoes and socks and left the cottage. He stopped at a local deli and picked up biscuits, milk, juice, coffee, and doughnuts for the crew, then headed out to the jobsite. He arrived to find Alex as well as half of his crew already there.

"Good morning, Mr. Broussard, Alex," he amended with a chuckle at Alex's raised brow and nodded a greeting to his foreman. "Hey, Steve, how's everyone today?"

Steven Kyle Bourgeois was one of the first and finest carpenters hired for the firm, which made him more friend than employee. His smile reflected those emotions back to Trevor.

"Looking good. You?"

Trevor nodded. "Good. We ready to get started?"

"Yep, thought we'd begin here with the tractor and bush hog our way to the house. Alex and some of the others will stand by for a bit. They're armed with pistols, pitchforks, and various objects ready to destroy any snakes or rats or whatever else might crawl out of this jungle."

Again Trevor nodded. "Good idea. Once we get the front cleaned up and safe, we'll move on to the rest of the property. Let's be careful not to knock over or destroy any buildings until we see what's in them or decide otherwise."

"Will do." Steve climbed up on the tractor.

"I brought food." Trevor chuckled when Steve glanced at his

watch then at the rapidly rising sun and, with a grin, decided the bush hogging could wait long enough for a doughnut or two. He climbed back down and joined the other crewmembers who'd gathered around the truck.

Fortified with doughnuts, coffee, and conversation, the crew set out to work. Steve hoisted himself back onto the tractor and waited while a couple of guys, who'd brought hip-boots, started out ahead of the others and made their way with care up to the house. They swung sickles through the grass to encourage rodents and other creatures to evacuate their homes and to check for any objects that might damage the tractor or blades. Once Steve bush hogged far enough, another crewmember followed on a lawn tractor and groomed the grass into a more manicured appearance.

The process, slow, tedious, wrought with death and destruction, took most of the morning. Snakes, rats, and other creatures ran for their lives, some only to be caught or stopped by blade or bullet. Trevor appreciated the diversion when his cell phone rang at about eleven o'clock. He noted Pam's name on the screen.

"Hey, Pam."

"Hey, how's it going?"

"Slow. Are you coming out?"

"Yeah. Is Taylor there yet?"

"No. I left her asleep."

"Want me to run by and check on her?"

"If you don't mind."

"Not a bit."

"Thanks. Would you and Taylor bring some lunch? I brought doughnuts, biscuits and coffee earlier, but I doubt it'll hold the guys for much longer."

"Okay. I'll pick up some chicken and sides."

"Good deal."

"See you in a little while, then," Pam said, and they rang off.

Ten minutes after she hung up with Trevor, Pam knocked on Taylor's door. Taylor opened it with a smile. She was dressed and looked ready to walk out the door.

"Hey, Pammy, what's up?"

"I'm heading out to the jobsite, how about you?"

Taylor nodded. "Me, too."

"Want to ride together?"

Taylor smiled. "Love to, let me get my things."

She gathered her purse, sketches, and fresh sketchpads, and they headed out. Pam stopped to pick up buckets of fried chicken and side orders of French fries, mashed potatoes, potato wedges, corn on the cob, and coleslaw, as well as drinks. They arrived to find the crew gathered around Trevor's truck for what appeared to be a well-deserved break.

"Wow." Taylor's tone reflected her awe. "Hard to believe this beautiful lawn lay hidden beneath all those weeds. I can't wait to get into that barn."

Pam shot her a curious look. "The barn? Why?"

"Mr. Broussard said Jean Lafitte carved his initials in there."

"Interesting." Pam gazed at the dilapidated structure that leaned precariously to one side. "I doubt anyone will let you near it today."

"Irritating isn't it?" Taylor asked with a grin. "To be surrounded by overprotective men. It's like we've got a dozen husbands or brothers."

Pam's tinkling laugh made the whole crew smile.

"What's so funny?" Trevor asked.

"Private joke," Pam answered with a wink at Taylor and handed Trevor an armload of food.

Everyone murmured in approval when she passed out disinfectant hand wipes while the twins unloaded bags and boxes of food and drinks. Over lunch they discussed what to do next and decided cleanup was the most important step. No one minded that they'd have to put in a full day on a Saturday, especially since Alex promised barbeque and baseball for their entire families on Sunday afternoon.

When lunch ended, Steve climbed back on the tractor and headed toward the house to resume bush hogging. His sharp whistle about half-way brought the crew running. He turned off the big machine, scrambled down, and knelt on the ground.

"Hold up," he cautioned as, one-by-one, the crew gathered around him.

He reached gently into a mound of bloody grass and retrieved a baby rabbit. The tiny creature couldn't have been more than a few days old. Its eyes weren't open yet and it had no fur. One ear and half its nose had been cut off, but it was alive. He heard Taylor gasp and handed it to her. "It's alive, barely."

Taylor reached for the tiny creature with hands that trembled and tears on her cheeks. "It's a miracle, he is."

Steve nodded. "Yeah. Maybe you can get him over to Dr. Anderson at the Animal Clinic. Let him check him out, see if he can be saved."

Taylor nodded and Pam took her arm and walked with her to the car. Less than an hour later they returned.

The first to see them arrive, Alex asked, "What's the verdict?"

Taylor lifted a relieved gaze to his and replied, "Dr. Anderson couldn't do anything about the nose or ear, but other than those injuries, he seems to be miraculously intact. He gave us some milk and an eyedropper designed for kittens. He said it's been used to feed orphaned squirrels, so maybe it'll work. We'll have to emulate what the mother would do and feed him every two hours or so and wipe him down with a warm, wet cloth to ensure his bodily functions."

Alex watched in silence while they cuddled and cooed over the baby rabbit. Two women shoulder-to-shoulder, heads together, one dark, the other light. Pam's thick sable hair was pulled back into a ponytail, Taylor's honey-colored locks into a French braid. From where he stood, he could see the sweep of lashes covering eyes of vivid green and brilliant topaz while casting shadows on flushed cheeks.

He admired the picture they made.

CHAPTER SIX

That Sunday, two huge tables were set up close to the house. Although Alex had offered to provide all the necessities, wives and girlfriends of the crew brought side dishes, desserts, paper plates, and plastic utensils. Children played chase, baseball, and kickball throughout the yard. Alex stood by the barbeque pit, a cold drink in one hand, spatula in the other. He flipped hamburgers and rolled hot dogs to grilled perfection and waited for Taylor.

The woman intrigued him.

Yesterday he watched her and Pam put on work gloves and lug wheelbarrow loads of debris to the trash pile to be burned. As relentless and unflinching as the men, the two women raked and hauled and piled, stopping when necessary and only long enough to feed and nurture the baby rabbit, which they had named Bugsby. Never in his life had he felt such strong emotions for a woman so soon after he'd met her.

An only child, Alex was orphaned as a young teen when his parents died in a collision with a train. Having no next of kin, he became a ward of the state. Knocked around from pillar to post in the foster care system, he had never devoted much time to girls. Ambition fueled his dreams much more than the opposite sex. He had focused his energies, turned desire into determination, and set his heart to rise above the stigma of being a geek who loved math more than sports. His father, an investment banker, had used wisdom when he set up a trust fund at Alex's birth. Sound legal advice kept the fund intact even under the direst circumstances and thereby protected his inheritance. Small though it was, Alex took that start and built upon it layer by layer until he'd amassed a small fortune in a little more than twenty years. This house, this property would be the culmination of all his dreams save one, to settle down and raise a family.

Up until now, he hadn't had the time or energy to effectively pursue that goal, much less the emotional fortitude needed to nurture and sustain it. Oh, he'd dated off and on, been heavily involved on occasion, and even suffered through one disastrous marriage with a woman who spent more money on frivolous things than she did time with the one who earned it. The divorce cost him a fortune and made him wary and distrustful of giving his heart again. Despite his past experiences, none of the women he'd ever known affected him the way Taylor Forrestier did from the moment he laid eyes on her. That's what intrigued him the most. He wondered if she was what his heart had searched for all along, the one woman who would complete his life and give him the children he so desperately wanted. A ball whizzed by his head and forced his attention back to the moment at hand. He wondered for the umpteenth time if she'd ever get here.

He could tell the moment she drove up by the subtle shift of attention in the crewmembers and their families. Children raced toward her with cries of excitement, anxious to know what the shoebox she carried contained. Wives and girlfriends uttered little murmurs of joy and delight. This is love, Alex thought while everyone gathered around and reached out to welcome her with hugs, handshakes, or a simple brush of a hand over her arm.

He watched her make her way toward him and greeted her with a smile and nod. "Mornin' Miss Forrestier. How's your baby?" he said. Flecks of green and gold danced in her topaz gaze when she smiled back.

"It's Taylor, and my baby's just fine. How are you?"

Alex grinned. "Busy, as you can see." He waved at the food on the grill.

"Looks delicious. It's very kind of you to do this."

He shrugged. "A deal's a deal."

"Well, we appreciate it," she replied with another smile, then returned her attention to the children who clamored around, filled with curiosity.

"Let's all sit down and I'll show you," she responded to their consistent plea to tell them what was in the box.

Whatever Alex's initial feelings toward her, they grew by leaps and bounds when she gathered the children together and seated them in a tight-knit circle around her. She sat on the ground with them, placed the shoebox in front of her, moved aside the nest of cotton with a flourish and picked up Bugsby. He listened with interest and admiration while she answered their questions and explained to the children why they couldn't hold, feed, or play with the baby rabbit. Once he was fed and bathed, and the children's curiosity satisfied, she tucked Bugsby snugly back into his nest. After she made sure he was warm and comfortable, she proceeded to entertain the children with stories of war heroes and Indians, pirates, and buried treasures.

"I don't know, you'll have to ask Mr. Broussard," she replied to their fevered cries to hunt for those treasures.

It was a test. Somehow Alex knew it. He passed with flying colors when he agreed to take them on a treasure hunt after lunch. He laughed with her when they all ran off and urged their parents to prepare their plates.

He settled on the porch beside her and nudged Taylor with his shoulder. "I'll have you know you've just been recruited to come with me."

She laughed, a throaty, husky sound that made him long to take her in his arms.

"How do you know so much about Louisiana history?" he asked her. He fought the urge to wrap his arm around her with every ounce of self-control he possessed.

"My mother was born and raised here. She always told us wonderful stories about how Louisiana and its people came to be."

"So that's why you and Trevor decided to settle and establish your business here, instead of some major hub?"

"Among other reasons," she admitted. "Mother would get so aggravated when someone insulted the state and its people. Even romance novelists, not so much the historical as contemporary ones, tend to portray Louisiana as nothing more than swampland and its people little better than backwater hicks who don't know or appreciate progress. Dirt roads and pirogues, alligators and swamps, as though they're a world unto their own with no purpose or vision, abandoned by God to perish in the wilderness."

Alex chuckled at the obvious scorn in her tone. "So you've decided to prove otherwise?"

She shrugged. "Don't know if I can change the world's opinion, but I'll do my best to show and enhance the beauty and richness of culture that can be found here."

Alex smiled, no doubt in his mind she could do just as she suggested and would succeed. "What about your father? He must have been a genius at something to send you two to such a prestigious college," he remarked, curious and surprised at the instant change in Taylor. Her body stiffened, eyes frosted.

She sneered. "My father was a petty, selfish man, as cruel as he was rich, who lusted after things he had no business lusting after, things he couldn't, or shouldn't, have or control. It wasn't his genius that sent us to an Ivy League college, it was the family pride.

"Both he and my uncle had graduated from the same place, so it was a given Trevor and I would also. But my mother," the smile returned, "my mother was a saint. Huh, Trev?" She turned her attention to him as her brother walked toward them with Pam in tow.

Trevor's eyes searched hers for a moment before he nodded. "That she was. How's Bugsby?"

Taylor reached into the box, picked up the rabbit, and held him toward her brother. "He's fine. We're both fine," she assured, her voice soft. "Despite the fact I got up every two hours last night," she added as though to ward off any speculation as to why she would be otherwise.

But Alex saw the quick way Trevor's frame tensed, noted the guarded expression which crossed his face, and the flare of anger in his eyes followed by a flicker of emotion that could only be explained as protectiveness, and wondered.

Taylor pulled into the office parking lot at ten-fifteen the next day, excited and hopeful despite the fact that she arose every two hours to feed and nurture Bugsby. Yesterday had turned out to be a wonderful day. She and Alex had taken the children on a scavenger hunt. Though they had uncovered no treasures, she and Alex had laughed, talked, told stories, and managed to keep the kids' interest and enthusiasm at a continual high well into the afternoon. The conversation about her parents had not spoiled the atmosphere. Not even Trevor had brought it up again, and as a result, she had a very peaceful night. Now she was primed and ready to start her research.

She picked up the shoebox and carried Bugsby into the office so Pam could look after him.

"How's he doing?" Pam asked the minute Taylor walked

through the door.

Taylor smiled and handed her the box. "He's fine. I think he's going to make it." Each day he lived, every night he made it through, filled them with joy and confidence that he would survive and flourish under their care.

"Me too," Pam agreed.

"Trevor made it in yet?"

Pam nodded. "Here and gone, out to the jobsite."

"And how are things between you two?" Taylor asked. Pam flushed sweetly and her eyes sparkled like rare, precious gems.

"Fine, he stayed a while last night and we talked, really talked. The whole day and evening were wonderful."

Taylor smiled and lowered her voice a notch. "Has he kissed you yet?" Pam's flush deepened. She shook her head.

"No, not again, but I look forward to the next time."

"Again?" Taylor asked.

Pam nodded. "The other day when Alex first came in."

Taylor laughed. "Amazing what a little jealousy can do."

Pam giggled. "And how are things with you and Alex?" she asked her eyebrow arched with interest.

Taylor chuckled. "He's very sweet and very good with kids."

"And sexy?"

Taylor flushed. "Not exactly the tall, dark, and handsome type is he? When you consider he's not more than five foot eight or nine inches tall and a little generous around the middle."

"Maybe not," Pam remarked. "But there's a lot to be said for short and sexy."

Taylor smiled at the analogy. Her mind returned to the man in question. He wasn't really overweight or sloppy, but neither did he sport washboard abs. Probably due to his profession and the fact that he preferred rice and gravy to lettuce and tomatoes, she thought with another smile.

"There is something about him," she ventured. "Those bright

hazel eyes that laugh and mock and never miss a thing. Have you noticed they alternate between golden brown or light green?"

Pam shook her head. "Not really. What else have you noticed about him?"

Taylor flushed with a tiny laugh. "Everything. The trim, neat mustache; the curve of lips that smiles easily and often; that meticulously groomed, sandy-colored hair makes my fingers itch to run through it. He possesses oodles and oodles of charm and charisma by the case. And his voice, soft and husky and . . ." She shivered at the thought of the throaty lilt. "He always sounds as though he's just rolled out of bed."

Pam laughed. "Yeah, but he always seems so together. Even yesterday, when everyone else dressed in baggy sweats, ragged jeans, and tattered T's, his casual slacks were well pressed and his shoes polished to a spit shine."

Taylor sighed, her lips curved. "I know. I'm not sure exactly what it is about him that's so attractive, but when I figure it out, I'll let you know. Has he called or come by this morning?"

Pam shook her head.

"Okay, well if anyone should ask, I'm on my way to the library. I'll come by later to pick up Bugsby." She reached into the box to pet the rabbit.

"Don't worry, we'll be fine." Pam reached to pet the rabbit also but kept her eyes on Taylor. "Can I ask you something?"

"Sure."

"I overheard your conversation with Alex yesterday and, well, is there something I should know?" she ventured.

Familiar sensations stole over Taylor at the question, and she felt her guard go up, protective instincts kick in. "Did you ask Trevor that?"

Pam nodded. "Yes, last night. And he reacted the same way you just did. A flash of anger followed by cold, quiet, and aloof.

That quick flare of panic then total blank, as though you've forced the lid closed on Pandora's box. I don't want to pry or anything, but my gut tells me there's an issue I should know about."

Taylor saw the concern in Pam's face but hesitated with her answer. She and Trevor moved here to forget the past, to start over. Deep down she knew they'd both have to deal with it again, in order to be completely healed, but loyalty bound her to choose her answer with care.

"Sometimes, Pam, people think that just because you grew up with money or went to an Ivy League school, your life was perfect. But that isn't so. Our childhood was far from perfect. Trevor will have to be the one to tell you more than that."

"I love him so much." Pam sighed. "And you. I'd never want to hurt either of you."

Taylor smiled, tenderness poured through her at the light in Pam's eyes, and she hugged the other woman. "I know that. He needs someone like you, Pammy, we both do. Just continue to be patient. He's very shy and gentle. Unless pushed too far. He's unbearably overprotective. But he's generous and loyal to a fault. Now, I've got to get out of here or I'll never get started." She gave Pam another quick hug and left.

Taylor didn't have much time to think of the conversation with Pam in the short distance between the office and library. She entered the genealogy department and greeted the librarian with a smile.

"Hello, Ms. Henry, ready for another forage into the past?"

"Anytime. How are you, dear?"

"I'm wonderful, and you?"

"Just fine. Tell me about your new project."

"What can you tell me about the LeBleu Estate about five or six miles east of town?"

"That property was once in my family."

Taylor's eyebrow quirked with curiosity. "Really?"

"Yes, way down the line of course and on my husband's side, but family nonetheless. What do you want to know?"

"Everything and then some," Taylor admitted with a laugh. "Did you know the property has been sold to a local businessman? He wants to restore and remodel the home and build the entire estate into a showplace."

Ms. Henry nodded and handed Taylor a pair of gloves. "I'd heard something, but like I said, the family connection is way down the line." She led the way to a microfiche station and began to scroll through newspaper articles until she found the one she sought. "We'll start with this one, an interview with Mrs. Laonise LeBleu on her 100th birthday."

"Wow, a hundred years old, amazing," Taylor remarked.

"I know. Can you imagine living to be that old? In fact, she died at 103."

"No kidding? I'll read this in a moment but first, tell me what *you* know," Taylor invited, her interest piqued more by the woman's animated features.

Ms. Henry smiled again and pulled a chair up beside her. Taylor could tell that the more she talked, the more she warmed to the subject of her family lineage.

"There is so much history, and numerous legends surround this family and that piece of property. The ancestors of Arsene LeBleu, the original homeowner, were some of the earliest inhabitants of Calcasieu Parish. They settled here in the mid-1700's along with the family of Julian Charles Sallier, whom Lake Charles is named after. At the time of this interview, Mrs. LeBleu, or 'Grandma Jo' as her grandchildren and great grandchildren called her, was reported to be in good health and in possession of an incredible memory. She recounted visits by Indian natives to the area as well as Frank and Jesse James. It's said that she could outride, outshoot, and out-spit any man."

Ms. Henry chuckled then continued.

"Her family was from down around Eunice. Her father raised horses and sold them to the army. In fact, there is a story that she fought with a Captain over his desire to confiscate her favorite horse. Though Laonise was reported victor in the battle, the Captain took the horse anyway but left her with one just as beautiful and twice as valuable."

They laughed at the thought. "How wonderful it must be to come from a family with roots that deep. You must have a never-ending arsenal of stories."

Ms. Henry nodded. "Oh there are plenty more. I could sit here all day and regale you with story upon story, but I really must get back to work. I'll pull a few books for you to peruse, though."

Taylor thanked her and turned back to the microfiche. Within moments she found herself absorbed in the life of Joseph C., the son of Arsene, and his wife, Laonise LeBleu. Newspaper articles, legends, and scrapbooks revealed actual accounts of visits from the "gentleman pirate" Jean Lafitte, which confirmed what Alex indicated to be rumor. She couldn't wait to tell someone and check out that barn.

Another tale she enjoyed was that of the wedding between Laonise and Joseph. Of the pomp and grandeur that accompanied the event followed by the pain and joy of birthing ten children only to lose five of them at very young ages. She couldn't help but laugh when Laonise told of her husband's knack for collecting orphans and how at one time, they raised twenty-three foster children along with the ten of their own.

The more Taylor contemplated the trials, tribulations, and triumphs of the LeBleu family, the more convinced she was that God wanted her to approach this job with the intention to not only maintain the integrity of the home but also preserve the history of its inhabitants and their culture. To honor not just their memories but also the memory of an entire people who fought the odds to tame a wild and undomesticated land.

Three hours later, she left the library. Her mind swam with ideas as she tried to visualize how to preserve the old while they incorporated the new. Alex would have his home, she determined. The grounds would offer all the amenities of a modern, luxury estate. Except for contemporary facilities such as lighting, plumbing, central air and heat, the home would resemble a walk back in time. The key would be to mix old and new in a unique combination to complement one another instead of creating a mad clash between two eras.

The main project would be to restore the current one-story bungalow to its original two-story grandeur. The LeBleus housed up to thirty-three children in that home, so it was by no means a small one. They would improvise of course and change some of the bedrooms into a bathroom or study or possibly even combine two rooms into one.

She spent the next several hours in her office, pad in hand, and sketched her mental pictures of the house and grounds. She envisioned what each room would look like, how the floors and walls would be covered, as well as where every bush and tree should be planted on the grounds.

Oak, cypress, and magnolia trees would line the drive to the house. Honeysuckle mixed with ivy would create a backdrop for climbing roses along the trellises that would enclose the porch. The pool, patio, and bath house would be surrounded by color and scent; weeping willows interspersed with wisteria: blue, lavender, pink, and white. The stables would be tucked into a pecan grove, the tennis courts ensconced in a fruit orchard where pear, peach, and apple trees would intermingle with lemon, satsuma, and cumquat. A gazebo would hide in a private corner encircled by bushes and vines that would overflow with grapes, surrounded by blueberry, blackberry, and strawberry patches. The entire estate would provide a virtual smorgasbord of delight for the senses.

Taylor couldn't wait to consult with her brother and Alex, narrow down the sketches into a plan of action, and get to work. The more she thought about the project, the more her mind began to circle and hone in on Alex Broussard and the way she felt in his presence. She recalled the fun they had yesterday and wondered if he had had as good a time as she. No sooner than the thought crossed her mind when Pam rang in to let her know he'd arrived and wanted to see her.

"Give me five minutes then send him in." She rose to change her blouse, which was wrinkled and smudged with charcoal, and to brush out her hair. She answered his knock with a smile.

"Alex, hi, come on in."

He gazed down at her for a moment then shook his head with a grin. "I can't seem to catch my breath when I'm around you."

A flush warmed her cheeks, a tremble skittered down her spine. She turned and walked toward her desk, positive a little distance between them would prevent her from making a total fool of herself. "I'm not sure how, or if, I should respond to such a statement, but thank you. I think."

He chuckled, stepped through the doorway and strode to the chair, but he waited until she sat before he lowered himself into it.

"Would you like a cup of coffee or a cold drink?"

"Coffee would be nice."

She asked Pam to bring them each a cup then waited for him to initiate conversation.

Alex noted the flush on her cheeks didn't lessen and wondered if he made her as nervous and tongue-tied as she did him. Before he could comment, Pam arrived with the coffee. He thanked her and waited until she left, then smiled over his cup at Taylor. "I didn't see you at the Civic Center this morning."

"I don't go there often. Do you?"

He nodded. "Every chance I get. I love to watch the sun rise or set on the lake."

"Me, too, but as you've seen, Trevor doesn't like for me to go out like that alone."

"Can't say as I blame him," Alex replied, "Not that you're ever really alone with all the people about, but you can't be too careful these days."

She smiled, acknowledged his comment with a tiny nod. "What can I do for you, Alex? I'm sure you didn't come by just to talk about the weather or my jogging habits."

He grinned. "No, actually I came to ask you to have dinner with me."

Taylor flipped her calendar. "I'll have to check with Trevor and see if he's free but I'm sure dinner can be arranged. We haven't completed the figures yet on your project, but . . ." her words trailed off when he leaned forward and put the cup on her desk.

"I didn't ask Trevor to dinner, just you. And I don't care about the figures. Whatever the cost is to restore and remodel the property per my specifications, I'll pay."

He glanced down, caught a glimpse of her sketches, and picked them up. He flipped through the stack, whistled. "Can you really make the house and grounds look like this?"

"That all depends on what you agree to, but yes, we can."

"Can we spread them out, take a look?"

"Sure." Taylor rose from her seat to walk around the desk. She took the sketches from him and laid them out on her drafting table in correlated batches, then turned on the lamp.

Alex joined her, stood as close as he dared, and listened while she expounded on her ideas for not only the house but also the landscape design. Her animated features delighted and intrigued him.

"Wow," he breathed when she finished. "Are you sure your title is architectural designer and not magician?"

Pleasure sparkled in her eyes and covered her cheeks in a charming flush. His breath lodged in his throat. He traced a finger over her hand. "Have dinner with me."

She gathered up the sketches, held them against her like a protective shield, and lowered her gaze. "Trevor and I make it a point not to mix business with pleasure."

"Points, like rules, are made to be broken."

Something about the way she avoided eye contact made him uncomfortable, but before either could say more, Pam knocked and stepped through the door. "Tay, it's five o'clock. Do you need me to hang around?"

Taylor shook her head. "No, has Trevor called?"

Pam nodded. "He and the crew will work until dark, said he'll see us in the morning."

"Okay, lock up the front will you? We'll go out through the kitchen."

"Sure thing," Pam said then hesitated on her way out. "Hey, since we don't have Trevor here demanding meat, let's pick up a salad somewhere and chat a while."

Alex sensed more than professional protocol in her resistance to his dinner invitation when relief flickered over Taylor's face at Pam's offer. He stepped back without another word and let her off the hook. For now.

CHAPTER SEVEN

Trevor slammed the phone down, tugged on his boots, and stormed out of his apartment. Plagued by bad dreams, last night had left him feeling raw and running late. On top of that, he couldn't reach Taylor. A thought occurred to him, and he swung out of his driveway, proceeded to the Civic Center, and circled Bor du Lac Drive. Fear sliced through him when he didn't see her. Where could she be? Another idea flashed through his mind, and he turned his truck around to check it out.

Pastor Dan Hebert stayed in prayer for long moments after the meditation service concluded, as was his habit since he arrived at Way, Truth & Light Christian Church almost six months ago. He wasn't a man prone to question God. He'd always accepted His will with a calm sense of direction and purpose. Until now.

Fresh out of high school in upstate New York more than ten years ago, he'd enrolled in college and attended seminary in Canada where he had earned a master's degree in theology and a bachelor's in psychology with a minor in sociology. Upon graduation he had served both God and his country as a marine chaplain during Operation Desert Storm and the Gulf War.

And here we are, engaged in a war against the same irrational human beings. Dan shook his head to stop the tangent of thoughts. Suffice it to say, his stint as a chaplain was enough to convince him military life was not the kind of life he wanted.

In the ten years that followed that revelation, he'd worked as an evangelist, youth minister, and associate pastor in churches, as well as a youth counselor at college campuses all over the United States. His work fulfilled him until one beautiful morning in September when tragedy struck America in an act of terrorism so horrible it rocked the world. Violence that resulted not only in heroism but a wave of humanitarianism, as well as revitalization of God's Spirit that turned the hearts of the people back to Him.

Dan had rushed back to New York to aid and minister to the masses of souls left shocked and grieved in the wake of September 11, despite the fact that it shook his own faith to the core. He stayed three years and helped whenever and wherever possible. He awoke one day to find that the strain of ministering to others without taking the necessary time to refresh his bedraggled spirits had left him as dry and dusty as the pile of ashes that were once the World Trade Center towers. A year-long sabbatical in a monastery, as well as a year and a half on mission trips around the world, put his life and current events into perspective.

Hours of job searching on the Internet proved to be as fruitless as a grapevine in winter and yielded little but headaches and eyestrain until one fateful fall evening.

Way, Truth & Light Christian Church in Lake Charles, Louisiana, seeks Pastor.

The words leaped from the computer screen and straight into his spirit. But for the life of him, Dan couldn't figure out exactly what it was about the advertisement that had caused his spirit to quicken. He'd never wanted to live in Louisiana and still wasn't sure he wanted to now, even after nearly six months here.

Especially after almost six months here, he corrected himself with a mental shrug. He got up to wander through the sanctuary, careful to maintain the quiet, tranquil atmosphere.

Though non-denominational, the church proved to be a unique combination of ancient tradition and modern conviction, much like the congregants who gathered for service on Sundays and Wednesdays and on weekday mornings for meditation.

Stained-glass windows depicted the Stations of the Cross, adding grace and character to wood and stone. The arrangement of seats was a mixture of pews complete with kneelers and chairs. A podium stood on the raised platform instead of an altar. To the left of that, a wrought iron table with a kneeler housed various religious candles for those who wished to light one and pray. Rays of sun streamed in through the skylight and danced in beams on hardwood floors that gleamed with a high-gloss finish.

An old wooden cross made out of railroad ties leaned against the back wall. A hand-carved sign bore the words *Jesus, King of the Jews* and dangled from a nail in the top of the main beam. From the center of the cross hung a crown of thorns with splotches of red paint applied to its sharp edges. What appeared to be bloodstained spikes were driven deep into the crossbeam as well as the foot of the main one. Painted on the wall above and behind the cross was a portrait of the risen Lord in a glorious profusion of light and color. He walked amidst rainbows on a sea of clouds.

Dan knelt at the foot of the cross and prayed for a word from God as to why he was here.

All of his life, Dan had believed what he heard about Louisiana being a backwater state.

True, the people he'd met so far were different than any he'd come across in all of his years of travel and ministry. He wouldn't say they were better or worse, just different.

Louisianans were a people rich in tradition, steeped in

culture, who celebrated life to its fullest and the bounties of life in festivals throughout the year. Rice Festival, Frog Festival, Crawfish Festival, and Marshland Festival: events that honored the blessings provided by God to the inhabitants of this land.

Regardless of his slowly growing appreciation of Louisiana and its people, Dan still had no idea why God had sent him here. Here, where they called him Pastor "A-bear" instead of "He-bert," as he'd been called all of his life.

Why was he here, in this city, in this state, with these people who celebrated Mardi Gras as religiously as they did Christmas and Easter? People who put aside two weeks every year to remember the days of pirates and privateers in a festival known as Contraband Days?

People who ate things which crawled out of mounds of mud.

Why was he here, in this tiny church, lovely and peaceful though it was, instead of some huge city in a large house of worship where he could do great things for God?

When you continuously ask God "why," you become a "whiner," words from his own past Sunday's sermon rose in Dan's mind to prick his conscious and convict his heart.

He heaved a sigh and pressed the heel of his hands to his eyes. "I hear You, Lord," he murmured, and rose to his feet. Guilt and remorse stabbed at his heart. His fingers trembled when he reached out to touch the crown of thorns.

"I'm sorry," he continued and lifted his gaze to that of the Lord. The instant his eyes met those in the painting, he felt as though the image came to life. The eyes sparkled, brimmed with compassion, and overflowed with love. The arms were open wide in acceptance.

Okay, Lord, You win. I'll wait until You're ready to show me.

Dan stood transfixed, gained strength and peace from the embrace of God's Spirit with his, and knew he'd been forgiven. Again.

"Makes quite a statement, doesn't it? Quite a concept too."

The voice startled Dan out of his reverie. His breath escaped in a hiss, and he flinched when a thorn pierced his finger. He raised it to his mouth in automatic reflex.

"Sorry, didn't mean to startle you," the young man continued and stepped out of the shadowed entrance and walked toward him. "It's hard to imagine though, isn't it? That He would sacrifice Himself for people when most people could care less about anything but themselves."

"I imagine it's hard to believe, for some," Dan admitted, his tone quiet. He moved forward to help close the distance between them. "I'm Pastor Hebert. I don't believe we've met. Are you new to the congregation?"

The man shook his head. "No, sir. My sister sometimes comes to morning meditation. I thought she might be here."

Dan glanced down at his watch. "Meditation concluded more than an hour ago."

"Well, thanks anyway. Sorry if I bothered you," he said and turned to go.

"Wait," Dan insisted. He understood the flash of urgency which overcame him. "I never caught your name," he said and reached a hand to the stranger.

"Oh, sorry, it's Trevor. Trevor Forrestier," the man replied, shaking Dan's hand.

"Nice to meet you, Trevor. Does your sister come here often?"

Trevor shrugged. "I'm not sure. I just know she sometimes attends the meditation service."

A woman's image flashed in his mind. Dan scrutinized Trevor a little closer. "What's her name? What does she look like? Shall I keep an eye out for her and tell her you came by?"

Trevor answered the questions in the same manner they were asked, all at once.

"Name's Taylor, looks like me only prettier, and I guess so.

Thanks," he added, then turned to leave once more.

"I'll be sure and keep a lookout for her," Dan promised. He still felt a sense of urgency as well as a hint of unease. "I hope to see you in service sometime," he remarked, hesitant to end the meeting. "Take a bulletin."

He picked one up and held it toward Trevor in an attempt to delay his departure until directed by God otherwise. Trevor's eyes narrowed, and his lips quirked into an uneasy smile. It was obvious to Dan he bit back words when he reached for the bulletin.

"Thanks," he said again, then hurried out.

Dan took a deep breath and clenched his trembling hand into a fist, then forced it open and shoved it into his pocket. Alive with electricity, the air crackled with tension. Never in his life had he felt so much in one short meeting, heard so much in so few words, or seen such emotion in so brief a glance. It was a sign, of that he was sure, a mere glimpse of God's reason for why he was here. And though a piece of the puzzle had fallen into place, the big picture was still far from clear.

Trevor tossed the bulletin onto the seat of his truck and wondered for the umpteenth time where his sister might be. For the past three weeks they'd worked side-by-side with Alex to perfect the sketches and blueprints of the house and grounds. Today she'd disappeared. Contracts had been signed weeks ago. The crew had worked to prepare the house and grounds for major restoration and here it was, nine-thirty in the morning, and he hadn't heard a peep out of her. She wasn't at home, she wasn't jogging at the Civic Center, and she wasn't at church. Where on earth could she be? He picked up his cell phone and dialed the office number. "Pam?"

"She's not in yet, Trevor," Pam answered before he could ask, and his concern doubled.

"Do you have any idea where she might be?" Pam's sigh reverberated with frustration. He'd called and questioned every five minutes for the past hour and a half about whether or not Pam had heard from Taylor, and he could feel Pam's tension over the line. Her words sounded as though she forced them through clenched teeth. Her tone placated when she answered and tried to reason with him.

"Who knows, Trevor? Maybe she went to a park to jog, maybe she took a drive, or maybe she's at the jobsite. She's a grown woman and perfectly able to take care of herself. I don't understand why you're so worried."

"That's right," he growled. "You don't."

"Then why don't you explain it to me?"

Trevor felt a cold stab of fear in the pit of his stomach at the thought of baring his soul to her. What would she think if she knew the real reasons behind his worry over Taylor? He shook his head, bit back the words. "I haven't got time, Pamela. I've got to find my sister."

He ended the call before she could argue, then tore out of the church parking lot and headed to the jobsite.

He arrived to find Steve and Alex engaged in an avid discussion over blueprints and sketches. Various crewmembers traipsed about. They hauled lumber, set up scaffolds, and measured for framework. Steve was the first to spot him as Trevor walked toward them.

"Hey, Boss. Thought you'd be here earlier. When you didn't show, we figured you weren't coming at all."

"Has Taylor been around?" Trevor raked his fingers through his hair in an agitated gesture.

A gesture neither of the other men missed.

"No. Why?" Steve asked.

Concern turned to panic. Trevor's hands clenched into fists by his side. "I haven't heard from her yet this morning, and I thought she might have come out here."

"Haven't seen her. But I'm sure she's fine," Steve said, his tone soft and gentle.

Trevor knew Steve's tone was an attempt to ease the panic and fear he radiated, but the only reply he could summon was a curt nod. He took a deep breath, scrubbed his hands over his face, and tried to gather his scrambled thoughts. He forced a measure of calm into his voice when he asked, "How are things going around here?"

"Got it all under control," Steve assured. "Want us to help you look for her?"

Trevor shook his head. "No, but if she shows up, have her call me, will you?"

"Why all the panic?" Alex asked. Before Steve could answer or Trevor could turn away, he added, "The woman has worked her tail off for the past three weeks. Surely she's just slipped away for a few hours of downtime. She's entitled if you ask me."

Trevor's calm vanished. "Well no one's asked you, now have they? And no, she's not entitled! Not without at least a phone call," he burst out, then turned on his heel and stomped off before Alex could utter another word.

The two men watched in puzzled silence as Trevor slammed into his truck and roared away.

"Where on earth did that come from?" Alex pondered aloud.

Steve could tell by Alex's tone he was more than a little confused and put out by Trevor's reaction. "It's not like Taylor to not show or at least call if she's not coming in," he replied.

"Yeah, but gee, the guy's all bent out of shape because his sister, a twenty-seven-year-old-woman mind you, hasn't gotten permission to take a few hours off."

Steve wondered at that too. He'd known the twins for a little over two years and had always felt there was something different in the way they behaved toward each other. They were close, as twins usually were, but it was more than that. It was as though every gesture and every word between them was laced with undercurrents of something other than the mutual affection of one sibling for another. As though something sinister lurked just below the surface of their obvious love, something evil that, if unleashed, would destroy the sacred bond that held them together.

And it looked as though that something was tugging at the restraints.

Steve shook his head to banish the thoughts. Though he considered himself a very close and trusted employee, practically a friend, their personal lives were none of his business.

"Guess it's a twin thing," he said with a shrug. "They're very close."

"Extremely close," Alex observed. "Makes you wonder what's happened to or between them to make them cling so tight to one another."

"I'd watch the insinuations if I were you," Steve warned. "They've got some pretty loyal employees around here, people who'd fight you tooth and nail for talking like that. And you're standing mighty close to one of them."

"My point exactly," Alex said, his tone mild, unruffled. "How long have you known them?"

"More than two years."

"And the others?"

"About the same."

Alex nodded. "And you still don't know what makes them that way. Strange, isn't it, that they seem to be surrounded by loyal people, people who care about them, love them even, but none who'd call themselves friends? Like they're in a world of their own, a world people can get close to but can't really enter.

Something's wrong with that picture. Now, don't misunderstand me," he held up a hand in defense against the sharp breath Steve took and the intense look that hardened his eyes and set his jaw.

"I didn't say I think anything out of line is going on. I'm just saying I find it odd that two obviously talented, generous people have such a small circle of associates, none of whom they'd call close friends."

"Their personal lives are none of my business," Steve insisted in a firm but polite tone. "It's none of your business either. And like I said, I'd be careful. Talking off the cuff like that could get you in a boatload of trouble."

"Point taken," Alex assured in a quiet voice. "I know we've only known each other a few weeks, but believe me when I say I'm not out to hurt anyone. I liked those two from the moment we met. I'd love to get to know them better. Especially her." He smiled.

"You and every unmarried man out here. I'd be careful not to say that too loud also," Steve warned with a chuckle when Alex glared at him.

"Why? Has every man around here appointed himself her personal guardian?"

Steve shrugged. "Pretty much."

"I'm sure you've all tried to get close to her at one point or another."

The comment was more statement than question. Steve nodded. "Some harder than others. She's always real sweet about it, all sugar and smiles, loving and kind, never standoffish or rude, and incredibly generous to everyone. But there's a part of her that's quiet, reserved, vulnerable even."

"Especially when she has those visions," Alex interjected.

Steve nodded. "You know about that?"

Alex nodded in reply. "The first day we came out here she

had one. She scared the daylights out of me. It pulls at you in an odd sort of way to see her so weak."

Again, Steve nodded. "Makes you want to protect her. And, even if you can't have her, you certainly won't stand around and watch while someone else hurts her. So mind yourself. And as far as I'm concerned, that's about enough of this conversation. I've got work to do."

Alex glanced at his watch, then back at Steve. "So do I. I'll see you all tomorrow. Thanks for the insight. And the admonition," he said with a grin, then turned to leave.

CHAPTER EIGHT

Trevor slammed the door of his truck, thundered into the building, and cornered Pam in the lobby. "Has she called?"

Pam shook her head and sighed. "No, Trevor. She hasn't called. My goodness, she's not even three hours late. Calm down, will you?"

"Don't tell me to calm down," he growled, then pointed his finger at her. "You don't know anything about it."

Pam drew herself to her full five feet and three inches and went on her tip-toes to go nose to nose with him. "Don't you dare point your finger in my face, Trevor Forrestier." She slapped his hand away. "I know you're concerned, but you have no reason, no right, to get in my face. And you're correct I don't know anything about it because you won't confide in me! I do know this much though, I love my brothers as much as you love her, but I don't get all paranoid if they don't report to me their every move."

Pam took a deep breath and forced herself to calm down. "I love you, Trevor. Why won't you talk to me? Tell me what's wrong."

"You have no idea what love is." He hissed through teeth clenched as tightly as the fists by his side. "Most people have no inkling as to what true love is. True love is sticking together when your whole world is falling apart, trusting each other when you can't depend on another living soul, and being willing to die or kill for each other."

Fury lit his eyes into golden flames. Tension coiled the entire length of him, poured from every pore. Dark. Dangerous. Animalistic. Fear pumped through her. Pam gasped and took a step back. "My God, Trevor, what are you saying?"

Trevor must have seen the fear on her face because he also took a step back and swallowed the remainder of his wrath. A low moan escaped him, and Pam could tell he was shocked at his own behavior when he raked a hand over his face and muttered, "I have no idea what I'm saying."

Pam felt the denial like a knife in her heart. She went to him anyway, and wrapped her arms around him. Her heart swelled in her throat, tears filled her eyes. "What's happened to you?" Trevor remained stiff in her embrace.

"You don't even want to know what's happened to me. I've done things, and had things done to me, that would make you sick. I'm not fit to love you or anyone else for that matter. Nor do I deserve to."

"These things happened when you were a child?"

He nodded.

"They happened to Taylor too, didn't they?"

Again he nodded and squeezed his eyes shut to hold back the flood of tears that rushed to fill them.

"I couldn't stop it," he mumbled, his voice hoarse with emotion. "I couldn't protect her."

"And now you worry incessantly that something else will happen to her," she concluded. Her hands ran over his back and shoulders in a soothing caress.

"Whatever it was, it must have been horrible," Pam said. "Maybe someday you'll be able to tell me, but right now it doesn't matter. I do love you, Trevor. I've loved you since the first day we met. I'll always love you. No matter what," she promised and cupped his face in her hands.

★ ★ ★ ★ ★

Emerald eyes sparkled like sunlight dancing off the surface of smooth, flawless gemstones. Love shone brightly in them, a beacon calling to the depths of his soul. Trevor wondered if the power of it would be enough to erase the darkness of his past so he could finally walk in the light. He hoped so. Like a prayer, so was her name on his lips. He pulled Pam firmly in his arms with a groan of surrender. His mouth covered hers in a heated embrace.

Her knees buckled beneath the power and desperation of the kiss. Trevor lowered her gently onto the couch. His lips clung, molded, and shaped hers until each ragged breath he took robbed her of badly needed oxygen. She jerked her mouth from his.

"Trevor, stop." She twisted her face away and placed a firm hand on his chest. "This can't happen, not now, not here, not like this."

His heart thundered against her palm. Breath came in harsh, uneven gasps. His face felt taut, his jaw muscle twitched. Trevor shuddered, surprised he'd scaled the walls of control so quickly. He took her hand in his, lifted it to his mouth, and kissed the palm.

"You're right. I didn't mean for things to get out of hand. It won't happen again," he promised, and then pulled her gently to her feet. "Just one more kiss," he whispered against her mouth.

His arms remained gentle, his lips tender. Pam trembled against him, then slid her arms around his neck and surrendered to the sweetness of the embrace.

Taylor walked into the office to find Pam wrapped in Trevor's arms, his mouth glued to hers. She watched a moment, surprised, a bit envious even, and then grinned. "Gee Trevor, let the woman breathe."

He practically flung Pam away and turned on her in an angry whirl. "Where in the world have you been?" Taylor's eyebrow arched in annoyance, fury leaped to life in her eyes.

"I couldn't sleep, so Bugsby and I drove down to Cameron and watched the sun rise on the Gulf of Mexico." She turned on her heel. "Sorry, Pam, for my untimely arrival."

"Don't you have your cell phone?" Trevor demanded.

"Yes," she answered, but continued on the way to her office.

Trevor started after her. "Well, why on earth didn't you answer it?"

Pam grabbed him by the arm. "Trevor, wait. Don't do this."

He shook her off. "Stay out of this, Pam," he ordered and followed in his sister's wake.

His coldness affected her like a slap in the face after the intimacy they'd shared. Pam hesitated before she followed, not long, but long enough for the argument to be in full swing when she reached Taylor's office. She paused just outside the door. Their angry words stunned her into immobility.

"This has got to stop, Trevor! I can't take it anymore! You're driving me crazy!"

"You know how I worry about you, yet you run off anyway without as much as a phone call! All I ask is for you to keep me posted!"

"All you ask is to know my every move!"

"That's not true!"

"It is true," Taylor countered. "You worry over every little detail of my life. I want it to stop, and the only way I can figure out to make it stop is for me to do what I want when I want and let you learn to deal with it!"

Her voice softened. "He's not the monster in the dark anymore, Trevor. You saw to that. You've got to let it go and let

God heal you. Let Him heal us. I can't make any progress in my own life until you let go, and I can't be the one to help you. I've tried for so long but I can't bear the burden anymore. You shouldn't either," she added and laid her hand against his cheek.

Trevor shoved her hand away with a snort. "God? Where was God when we needed Him, Taylor? Answer me that! Where was He when Daddy beat Mama or molested you? Where was He when he beat me, tied me up, and made me watch or worse, when he held a gun to my head and forced me to have sex with my own sister? If God's so almighty and powerful, why didn't He stop it? Why did I have to be the one to kill him?"

Pam felt the bile rise up in her throat. Her eyes blurred and ears buzzed so loudly that Taylor's reply was muted. She backed away from the door, shaking her head in denial. "Oh, God," she moaned. Her heart refused to believe what her ears had heard. She began to sob.

"Oh, my God," she mumbled over and over. It couldn't be true! How could anyone do that to his children? His own flesh and blood!

But it was true. She knew deep down it was, and it explained why Trevor was so overprotective, paranoid even, when it came to his sister.

Pam made her way blindly back to her office and turned on the answering machine. Before she could reach the front door to lock it, Alex walked through.

"What's going on?" he asked.

Pam had no doubt he could hear the twins' raised voices. Barely holding it together, she locked the door behind him and collapsed into a sobbing heap.

Alex caught her as she slumped toward the floor. They glanced up in time to see Taylor, her face a mask of pained fury, run through the hall. She disappeared into the kitchen and slammed out the back door. Unable to follow Taylor because of his hold on Pam, he carried her into the lobby and set her on the couch.

"I'm going to be sick," she moaned and rocked back and forth with her head buried between her knees.

Alex grabbed the trashcan. "Hang on," he soothed, and rubbed her back in a gentle caress. "Can I get you something?" She shook her head.

"Can you tell me what's going on?"

Again she shook her head. Before he could rise to find out for himself, a loud crash sounded from Trevor's office. They rushed down the hall and stood in the doorway, paralyzed at the sight before them.

The drafting table was turned over and the chair upended. The desk had been swept clean and the bookcase had crashed to the floor. Trevor stood in the middle of the room. A gun trembled in his grasp. He looked at them, his face ravished with horror. One moment of madness was all they glimpsed before he turned the gun on himself.

Pamela screamed his name. Alex lunged for him. He managed to wrestle Trevor to the floor and deflect the shot, but the bullet ricocheted off the windowsill, tore through Trevor's back and lodged somewhere in his chest.

"Call an ambulance!" Alex shouted while he tried his best to staunch the flow of blood that poured from Trevor's wound.

Pam stumbled through the door, picked the phone up off the floor, and dialed 9-1-1.

Within minutes the place swarmed with police and paramedics. Police took statements from Pam and Alex while paramedics stabilized Trevor. When they wheeled him out and into the ambulance, Pam followed right behind them.

"Wait," Alex called. "How do I find Taylor?"

"I don't know!" she cried and ran a shaky hand through her hair. "Try the church," she suggested, then climbed in the ambulance with Trevor. "Way, Truth & Light!" she added a moment before the doors were closed and the ambulance sped off.

Alex was back inside, in the kitchen, when shock set in. He collapsed in a chair and buried his face in hands that trembled. "Jesus," he rasped, and took deep, calming breaths.

Every time he closed his eyes he saw Trevor's face etched with horror, an exact duplicate of Taylor's when she'd stormed out of the office. He knew he had to find Taylor. He rose and went into the bathroom and washed off as much of Trevor's blood as possible. He left the bathroom, crossed the hall, and stepped back into the kitchen, but before he could exit the back door, an investigator walked in. His eyes widened in recognition.

"Alex?"

Alex nodded. "Hey, Russ."

"What in the world happened here?"

His heart thundered, and his voice shook, but Alex relayed the incident in detail and answered each question Russ asked to the best of his ability while Russ examined Trevor's office.

"I'll have to speak to the sister."

Alex sighed. "I know. But can it wait until she finds out whether or not he'll live?"

Russ stared at him for a long, tense moment. Curiosity lit his gaze along with a hint of concern. A frown creased his brow. "How involved with this woman are you?"

Alex scrubbed the heels of his hands over his face. "She's come to mean a great deal to me in a very short period of time. They both have, as well as the entire crew and office staff. I've never felt so comfortable around complete strangers in my life. You know how difficult it can be to get close to people, Russ. We grew up in the same boys' home. But these people are different. They're honest and loyal and genuine to a fault.

Something about them inspires dedication from those they meet, those they work with. I'm not talking on the surface either, but true devotion."

"Are you in love with her?"

Alex felt the blood drain from his face at the question. "Yeah, I think I am, or at least I seem to be headed that way. You know how it is, how I am. Other than business, I'm not real good with relationships so I'm not sure where this will lead."

"But there are definite feelings here?"

Alex nodded.

"Great," Russ grumbled. "And I thought I'd get an objective view of what happened."

"You got a first-hand account, Russ, and the truth. The man turned a gun on himself. I tried to stop him. The gun went off, and the shot ricocheted off the window sill and hit him in the back. As well as we know each other I can't believe you'd doubt even a word of what I've said. Let me find her and take her over to the hospital. Once we know Trevor is okay, I'll give you a call. You have my word on it."

Russ hesitated, and Alex knew he weighed friendship and trust against protocol. At length he nodded, then handed him a business card. Alex thanked him and they left the office together.

Pastor Hebert hadn't been able to get past the encounter with Trevor Forrestier or concentrate on anything else. As usual when faced with a dilemma, he found the most peace in the sanctuary. He was in a pew, on his knees when a woman burst through the doors, stumbled upon the platform and collapsed at the foot of the cross. Sobs tore through her in painful torrents and her whole body shook. She pulled herself to her knees and began to pray, broken words uttered amidst passionate tears.

What had once been just another face in the small crowd of

worshippers became an individual, and Dan recognized her at once: Taylor, who looked like Trevor, only prettier. Everything about her cried out to him and suddenly he knew without a doubt why he was in Louisiana.

CHAPTER NINE

Alex pulled into the parking lot of Way, Truth & Light Christian Church alongside Taylor's car and realized he had prayed more in the last half hour than he had for most of his life. As a boy he had completed all the rites of passage connected to his family's religion. First Confession, First Communion, Confirmation. However, angry when his parents had died and left him orphaned at thirteen, he all but gave up on God and religion.

The anger led to rebellion which had jerked him out of the foster care system and landed him in the local boys' home. There he found a modicum of stability and the encouragement he'd needed to pursue his chosen career. Though he attended Sunday Mass as expected, that was the limit of his faith. Oh, he believed in God, but he never depended on Him to accomplish the goals he had set for his life. Up until today, the crux of his prayer life consisted of, *Lord help me,* and *Thank You, Jesus.*

He liked to think he and God had an agreement of sorts. He did his best to be a good man, and God did His part by not expecting more than that from him. He was honest and fair and did whatever he could to help widows, orphans, and those less fortunate, and so far, theirs had been a perfectly satisfactory arrangement. Now he had no idea what to do or say, much less how to pray. All he knew was he'd never survive the next half hour, not to mention the rest of the day, without some help.

His hand trembled. He raked it through his hair, then grasped the steering wheel in an attempt to stop the shudders racking his body. He took a deep breath and closed his eyes. He saw Trevor's face, the gun quivering in his grip, the crimson stain on his shirt. Tears filled Alex's eyes and burned the back of his throat. He swallowed hard the cold lump of dread that clogged his airways.

"God," he whispered. His voice sounded hoarse even to his ears. "There's no way I can do this by myself. You've got to help me."

An odd sense of calm, or maybe continued shock, cloaked him as he disembarked from the SUV. The first thing that struck him when he walked in the door of the little church was a strong sense of awareness, the second nostalgia. Though there was a large cross, there was no crucifix, no statues, and no tabernacle to host the Eucharist, but there was an achingly familiar feel about the place of worship. Maybe it was the stained glass windows or the pews in the center flanked by two rows of chairs. Maybe it was the table of candles that waited to be lit while one knelt in faith to pray. Whatever it was, he felt as though he'd returned home after a long and perilous journey. Much like the prodigal son had felt, he imagined.

He heard the murmur of voices and turned to see Taylor. She was with a man he assumed was the minister or pastor of the church, their words too quiet to be heard. He stepped forward and called her name. Her head jerked up, face paled, eyes widened then focused on his. Instinctively she knew and cried out her brother's name.

"What is it? What's wrong?" she asked and rushed to meet him.

Alex placed his hands on her arms as gently as possible, considering the degree they shook. "There's been an accident," he hesitated, then forced the words past his raw throat.

"He tried to shoot himself," he whispered, and tightened his grip when her knees buckled and she slumped toward the floor.

Sobs racked her slender frame.

"Oh, no, oh, dear God, no!" she cried. "How is he? Where is he? I've got to go to him!" She strained against the firm hold he had on her.

Alex nodded but made no move to release her. "He was alive when they picked him up and took him to the hospital. I'll take you there now."

Taylor turned and held a beseeching hand toward the other man. "You've got to help us. Please."

Without thought or hesitation, the man took her hand, squeezed it in a gesture of support and nodded in acquiescence. "I'll be right behind you."

Alex led her out the door and helped her into his SUV. Once she was safely buckled in the passenger seat, he hurried to the driver's side and climbed in.

"What happened?" she asked, deathly pale and just as quiet.

Alex shook his head. "I'd hoped you could tell me. That must've been some kind of argument y'all were engaged in. Pam nearly passed out at my feet. I was trying to calm her down when you bolted out the back door. We heard a ruckus from his office. By the time we got there, he'd wrecked it and was holding a gun. When he turned it on himself, I lunged for him and managed to deflect the shot, but it ricocheted off the windowsill and got him in the back."

Taylor buried her face in her hands and sobbed. Before Alex could question her about the argument, he pulled into the emergency entrance of the hospital where Trevor had been taken. He stopped the SUV, leaned over, and unbuckled her seat belt then cupped her cheek in his hand.

"I'll park and meet you inside."

She nodded.

"He's gonna be alright," he told her.

"God, I hope so," she murmured, then fumbled with the

door handle.

Alex placed his hand over hers, stopped her fevered movements, then opened it for her.

Taylor stumbled from the vehicle and rushed through the double doors which led into the emergency room, spotting Pam right away. Pam fell into her arms.

"Taylor! Thank God he found you!"

"How is he? Where is he?"

"He's in surgery. I didn't want to go up in case you got here. We can go up now."

"I'll go on up. Will you wait for Alex? He went to park."

Pam nodded. "Oh, Tay, I heard your argument. I'm so sorry."

Fear tightened her chest, humiliation heated her cheeks. "I'm sorry too, Pam. Keep it just between us, will you?" she asked, and then continued at Pam's nod. "Thanks, we'll talk later."

Satisfied that their secret shame would go no further, Taylor left Pam in the emergency lobby and went up to the surgery waiting room. Within moments Pam, Alex, and Pastor Hebert joined her.

Everyone waits in their own way, and it was no different with these four. Pastor Hebert waited with an attitude of prayer. Prayer not only for Trevor's surgery to go well and for him to be restored, but prayer for himself, that he'd be able to help these two people who'd lived more horror in their young lives than most could even imagine. His heart shuddered at the thought of what they'd endured.

Dan knew he'd have to rely on God to get him through the counseling sessions with the twins. That is, if Trevor agreed to them. Though he had a degree in psychology and though he'd helped many broken souls, not once in his entire life had he worked with someone who'd been abused the way these two were as children. He'd sometimes heard stories like theirs on the news and cried out to God over such cruelty. Now he cringed at the thought that he might not be experienced enough to do them any good.

Maybe I'm not, Lord, but You are. And that was the only truth, the only promise Dan could count on.

Alex waited impatiently. He paced the room and wondered what in the world took so long. His thoughts circled around one question: What could have driven Trevor to such drastic actions? His conversation with Steve earlier that day repeated itself over and over in his mind, and he knew without a doubt that something horrible had happened to the twins. Thoughts of them abused as children, of Taylor being mistreated at all, in any manner, filled him with an impotent fury. Though he had no idea as to the extent of the abuse, he wondered how God could allow such things to go on.

Taylor and Pam sat huddled together, their hands clasped. They talked softly. Silent tears slid down silken cheeks. Alex walked over to where they sat, squatted down in front of them and took one of each of their hands in his.

"Can I get either of you anything?" Both shook their heads.

"One of us needs to get back to the office," Pam muttered and stifled a sob. "But I don't want to leave him."

Taylor hugged her close. "We'll work that out as soon as we know how he's doing."

No sooner had the words left her mouth when the doctor walked into the waiting room and called for them. They all gathered around as Taylor introduced herself and waited for his news. The doctor ran a weary hand over his face before he addressed the questions in her eyes.

"He's in serious but stable condition. He's a lucky man. We got the bullet and patched him up but one inch either way, we wouldn't have been able to do anything to save him. He'll have a breathing tube for a while. We usually remove it in recovery or shortly after, but the bullet nicked one of his lungs. When we tried to take it out, he went into respiratory distress, so we're going to leave it in for several hours and give that lung a chance to start healing. However, he's young and healthy so, unless infection or unforeseen complications set in, he should recover nicely."

Taylor nodded. She understood completely what the doctor meant. Surgery on his physical body was the least of what her brother needed for his wounds to heal.

"Thank you," she whispered. Tears of relief and gratitude streamed down her cheeks, "When can we see him?"

"He'll be in Intensive Care for at least twenty-four, possibly forty-eight hours. Family can go in one at a time during visitation hours."

"Guess that leaves me out," Pam muttered once the doctor left.

"Nonsense, you're as close to family as we've got," Taylor assured her. "We'll take turns."

"Thank you," Pam whispered, "But what about the office, what about Bugsby?"

"As soon as he gets in ICU, I'll go to the office and take care of Bugsby. We'll figure out the rest later," Taylor assured her, then turned to Pastor Hebert. She took both of his hands in hers.

"I want to thank you for coming with us."

"You're very welcome. I'll check in on you tomorrow. If you need me during the night, here's my card," he said, and removed one hand from her grasp to retrieve a card from his pocket.

Taylor took the card, thanked him again, and walked with him out of the room. Within moments of her return, she, Pam and Alex went up into yet another waiting area while the staff moved Trevor into ICU.

Taylor was first to go in and see him. She stood beside Trevor's bed, held his hand, and stroked his cheek. "Trevor?" she queried, her voice tremulous. "Can you hear me?"

He moved his head slightly.

Encouraged, she tried again. "Don't try to talk, Trev, just nod or squeeze my hand."

His fingers closed around hers in a strong embrace. Taylor sobbed in relief. "Thank God," she whispered her lips against his forehead. "I love you, Trev, and I'm so sorry."

He jerked his head as though to say "no" and tried to lift his hand. Taylor brought it to her cheek.

"Just rest, Trev," she soothed and brushed the hair off his forehead. "Just rest, we'll talk later." When he drifted off once more, she tucked the covers around him and went into the waiting area.

Once there, she assured Pam and Alex that Trevor was waking and responsive, then touched Pam's arm. "It'll be a couple of hours before we can go back in. You go next. I'll go to the office and get things sorted out for the next couple of days. I'll be back later." She turned to Alex and asked him to take her to retrieve her car.

She managed to hold herself together while he brought his SUV around, but once seated, dignity gave way to the gamut of emotions that roiled in her soul. She buried her face in her hands and wept.

Alex left the hospital and headed toward the Civic Center. He parked, then pulled her into his arms as much as the bucket seats would allow and rocked her gently while she soaked his shirt with tears.

"Oh, God," she sobbed. "I can't believe this has happened. What am I going to do? How am I supposed to keep things together without him?"

Alex stroked her hair.

"It'll be okay. We'll get things lined up. You're not alone in this, Taylor."

"I have no idea what to do or even where to start. I'm so numb I can't even think straight," she muttered.

"Tell you what, let's go to the jobsite first and talk to Steve. He can keep things operational around there. Then we'll go back to the office, and you can check on Bugsby, listen to any messages you might have on the machine and whatever else you need to do and then we'll head on back to the hospital. How does that sound?"

"What about my car?"

"We'll get it later. You're in no condition to drive right now anyway."

"I'm so sorry you had to be involved in all this mess," she whispered.

Alex cupped her cheek in his hand. "I want to be involved," he said, his voice soft, husky with emotion.

"Very much involved." He brushed his lips across hers in a tender caress.

Taylor's head swam with the sweetness of his mouth on hers. A tiny hum of pleasure sounded in her throat when he pulled her tighter against his chest. His lips took a sensuous journey over her cheek to linger a moment at her temple then across her forehead.

Awareness sizzled between them.

She drew back, shocked at how quickly she'd been swept away by his kiss. "We'd better get going."

Alex nodded, and she could tell by the mixed emotions in his eyes that he was equally surprised to feel so much in such a brief encounter. He raised her hand to his mouth, brushed his lips over her knuckles, and squeezed it in a tender gesture before he released her. Once they buckled up, he turned the truck around and drove out to the jobsite. Steve was the first back from lunch and the only one there.

"Hey," Steve greeted when they disembarked from the Dodge. "I went by the office but no one was there."

Taylor knew she must look horrible with her red-rimmed, swollen eyes. Concern flickered across his face.

"What's wrong?" he asked.

"Trevor's been in an accident," she answered.

"What happened? Where is he?"

"He's in Intensive Care. Pam's with him now. Can you keep things under control around here for a couple of days?"

"Sure," he assured.

She could tell he was curious at the lack of information she gave him and was grateful when he bit back the questions. "Thanks, Steve. Come by the office in the morning, and we'll get y'all lined up for the next couple of weeks."

Steve nodded. He touched her arm before she could turn away. "Okay. Taylor? If you need anything at all please don't hesitate to ask."

A tiny smile tugged at the corners of her mouth. "Thanks, Steve. We'll talk more tomorrow. I need to get back to the office for a bit and then relieve Pam at the hospital."

"Is he going to be alright?" he asked when she turned to go.

Taylor hesitated. "God, I hope so," she whispered.

Alex slid his arm around her waist and helped Taylor back into the vehicle. He turned back to Steve after Taylor had buckled up, and closed the door. "It's pretty serious. We'll keep you posted on his recovery. I can't tell you more than that," he answered before Steve could question him further.

"I understand, man." Steve nodded in Taylor's direction. "Take care of her. She looks like she's about to break."

"I will." Alex shook Steve's hand then walked around to the driver's side. "If you or the guys need anything, give me a holler, and I'll see what I can do to get it to you."

"Good deal," Steve commented. "We'll be fine. I'll see you two in the morning. Assuming, that is, that you'll be there too?"

"Count on it," Alex answered with a nod, then opened the door and climbed into his seat. He backed out of the drive and headed to the office. He wondered how to tell her about Russ. He cleared his throat and reached for her hand. "An investigator came into the office. He needs to talk to you about all this. He's an old friend of mine, and I promised I'd give him a call after we found out if Trevor pulled through. If you want, I'll see if he can meet us at the office. Or, I can bring you to the police station."

She shuddered. "I'd rather meet him at the office."

Alex nodded and pulled off the road to call Russ who agreed to meet them. A startled sound escaped her when he pulled into the parking lot of T&T Enterprises a few minutes later. He touched her arm. "Are you alright?"

She nodded. "I, just . . ." She took a deep breath, shook her head. "I didn't realize the police would have everything taped off."

"The building has to be treated as a crime scene until they collect enough evidence to prove otherwise."

She turned another shade of pale. "Crime scene?"

"Strictly procedure, everything will be fine."

"We need to make sure Trevor's truck is locked." She bolted out of the SUV.

Alex hesitated before he followed her. Not until that moment did he consider the impact coming here might have on her. He hurried, catching up with her before she could enter the building, and touched her arm. "We need to wait until Russ arrives before we go in." They turned in unison when an unmarked police unit pulled into the parking lot. Russ climbed out and joined them. Alex introduced the two.

Taylor acknowledged Russ with a cordial nod then turned back and unlocked the door. They stepped into the kitchen, closing the door behind them. Taylor turned to Russ. "I need to see about Bugsby and check the answering machine. Can we talk afterward?"

Neither man missed the tremor in her voice or the fear in her dark eyes. Russ nodded. Relief flickered across her features and poured out of her in an audible sigh.

"Thank you. Bugsby is in my office. I'll check the messages first."

The three walked down the hall to Pam's office. When Taylor pushed the button on the answering machine, all they heard was static, the tumble and thud of items hit the floor, and then sheer pandemonium. Pamela's scream, "My God, Trevor, no!" was followed by a scuffle and a shot then came Alex's shout for her to call an ambulance.

Taylor's knees buckled. Her hand shook when she tried to turn it off. "Oh, God," she sobbed then covered her ears with her hands. "I can't make it stop! Please, make it stop!"

Alex pulled her in his arms and unplugged the machine. When she started to hyperventilate, he pushed her down in Pam's chair and shoved her head between her knees. "Breathe, Taylor. C'mon now, deep breaths," he urged and squatted down beside her. "Easy does it," he crooned while he rubbed her back. "It's okay now."

"But it's not okay," she whined. "Don't you see it'll never be okay again? He's scarred for life. Another scar from a war he couldn't control, couldn't stop. Jesus, why couldn't it just stop?"

Alex waited in silence until she pulled herself together. Once she calmed somewhat, he stood. "Where's Bugsby?" he asked.

"In my office."

"C'mon, I'll get him and bring him into the kitchen." He took her by the arm, led her to the kitchen, pulled out a chair, and settled her in it. "You stay put."

"No, Alex . . ."

He cut off her protests with a firm hand on her shoulder. "Yes, Taylor, you need to calm down. Take a few minutes and tend to the rabbit, it might help. I'll take you into Trevor's office after you've had a chance to get your emotions under control. Do you understand?"

His eyes searched her face for some sign that her mind registered his words. She stared at him for a long, blank moment, eyes wide, cheeks pale, then nodded.

"Okay, I'll be right back with Bugsby."

Once they'd realized the rabbit would survive, Steve had built Bugsby a wire cage large enough for him to have room to grow, yet small enough for Taylor to carry. At a little over three weeks old, the rabbit had thick, honey-colored fur nearly the same shade as Taylor's hair. His eyes were open and he was beginning to nibble on food pellets. A tiny board separated his sleeping area, which consisted of a thick cottony nest and one of Taylor's old T-shirts, from the rest of the cage so that it stayed clean. When the rabbit graduated from an eyedropper to a small baby-doll-sized bottle, Steve rigged up a holder and tied it to the cage upside-down where he could have milk anytime he desired. But whenever possible, Bugsby still preferred to be held and cuddled while he nursed. Alex hoped the chore would sooth Taylor and give her a moment or two of peace before she faced Trevor's office.

While she tended to the rabbit, he went back to Pam's office, took the tape out of the answering machine, and handed it to Russ. "Do you still need to talk to her?"

Russ shook his head. "No, this answers any questions I may have had. I'll take it with me. If anyone wants more info, I'll call you and set up another appointment. I'll remove the crime scene tape, and she can clean up the office."

"Thanks," Alex said.

"You okay, Alex? You look a bit rough."

Alex shrugged.

"If you need anything, call," Russ said.

Alex thanked him again, walked with Russ to the front door, and locked it behind him when he left. He reset the answering machine to record incoming calls using a pre-programmed message, then rejoined Taylor in the kitchen. When she indicated she was ready, he took her by the arm and led her down the hall to her brother's office.

She gasped. "Oh, my God." Her fingers trembled when she raised them to her mouth.

He left her in the doorway, walked into the office, and righted the chair then the drafting table. When he reached for the bookcase, he heard her moan and turned to watch her kneel on the floor next to where Trevor's blood had spilled onto the carpet. Her hand shook when she touched the spot. She clenched it into a fist, clasped it to her breast, and began to rock back and forth while sobs wracked her tiny frame.

Chapter Ten

Hers was a deep, wild sound of grieving that pierced his soul, ripped at his heart, and rooted him to the spot. Alex let her cry as long as he could stand it, the total of about thirty seconds. He left the bookcase, walked to where she knelt, and reached for her.

"Taylor, c'mon sweetheart," he urged, his voice thick with unshed tears as he remembered every detail, every aching moment of the incident.

"No," she cried, struggling against him. She crawled to where the box of tissue had tumbled to the floor when Trevor swept his desk clean, picked up the box, and hurried back.

"Let me help you," he offered and reached for the box.

"No! You don't understand! Now his blood is on my hands too, I've got to be the one to do it! I've got to make it right. No one can see this," she sobbed and attempted to sop up the blood with the tissues. "No one can know!"

"What are you talking about?" Alex demanded and stopped her fevered actions with a firm hand. The horror and devastation in her eyes tore his heart out.

"No one can know," she whispered. "That's why we came here. So no one would know."

"Know what?"

Taylor shook her head and covered her face with hands that trembled. She began to pray and mutter about inherent evil and generational curses, oblivious to the fact that she smeared blood all over herself.

Alex gathered her up in his arms and carried her into her office. He settled himself on the loveseat and cradled her against his chest, curious at what she rambled about and yet desperately afraid to find out. When the sobs subsided into soft, hiccupping sounds, he brushed the hair off her face. "It tears me to pieces to see you like this, but I don't know how to help you. I don't know what to say."

"There's not much you can say," she sniffled. "What's done is done. I just don't know how to make it right."

"Why is it just your responsibility to make it right?" he admonished in a gentle voice. "Trevor's a grown man. He has some responsibilities here too."

"You don't understand."

Alex cupped her cheek in his hand. "I want to. Tell me whatever it is I need to know in order to understand why your brother tried to take his own life." She trembled violently in his arms. Fear and panic darkened her brilliant topaz gaze to a murky brown.

"I can't," she whispered. "Not now. Not yet."

"You need to talk to someone, Taylor. And it's obvious Trevor does too. Hopefully someday soon you'll know me well enough to trust and confide in me. Does Pam know?"

She nodded.

"She overheard you arguing, didn't she?"

Again she nodded.

"Tough way to find out," he observed. "But she's in love with Trevor. She'll pull through and fight to pull him through. She'll be there for him, but who'll be there for you?"

"God is my refuge and my fortress. In Him only do I trust and rely," she whispered.

Alex nodded. He could tell by the tremor in her voice, the hope and the desperation with which she wanted, needed, to believe the words she spoke aloud.

"Maybe so," he agreed. "But I want you to know you can trust and rely on me too."

"Thank you."

"Are you okay now? Do you want to leave? I can bring you to the hospital then come back here and clean up."

Taylor took a deep breath, shook her head, and stood. "No, I want to do it. I want you to leave me alone, though," she said and hurried to continue before he could argue. "You can help me pick up the furniture, but I'd like to be alone to clean the rug."

Alex hesitated, wary and concerned that to leave her alone was not the wisest thing to do. He held her steady gaze a moment, then nodded and rose. "I'll leave you alone, but not for long, and I'll be close by."

A tiny smile tugged at her sensuous lips but didn't quite reach her eyes. "Thank you." She turned and led the way back to Trevor's office. When he reached for the bookcase, she helped him hoist it upright. One by one, they picked up the items that belonged there and on Trevor's desk and put them back, surprised at how few were actually broken.

Alex worked alongside her until the office was once more in some semblance of order. The broken hanging lamp, the dented windowsill and the blood on the rug were the only indications of what had taken place. He took a deep breath, sighed, and placed a gentle hand on her shoulder.

"I guess this is the part where I leave you alone," he said, though the tone of his voice indicated he'd rather not.

"I promise not to be long."

He nodded, unable to shake the uneasiness he felt. "Okay, I'm going to wash up a bit and be back in a few minutes to check on you. I don't feel comfortable leaving you totally alone in here, though."

His eyes swept the room and spotted the reason for his anxiety. The gun lay on the floor just under the corner of Trevor's desk. Alex picked it up.

Taylor held out her hand. "I'll put that away."

"I don't think so," Alex replied and slipped it in his pocket. "I'll take it home and clean it. Get it back to you tomorrow or the next day. But I'd suggest that you put it somewhere safer."

Taylor smiled slightly at the defensive gesture.

"Trevor insisted on having it here for protection. Pam and I both knew where it was. I had no idea he'd even consider something like this."

"Well, people in turmoil do strange and senseless things."

"He's been tormented by our past for so long . . . too long," she insisted. "Maybe now, he'll get some help. Maybe now we can both be healed and hopefully, someday, be made whole again."

While Alex went into the bathroom to wash up, Taylor went into the kitchen to retrieve what she'd need to clean the rug. She gathered a bucket of cold water, a sponge, and stain remover, then went back to Trevor's office and closed the door behind her.

She knelt beside the spot where his blood had seeped into the carpet, and reached a hand to touch it. The blood wasn't warm, but cold, and still damp enough to stain her fingers. She pressed a trembling fist to her lips, bit back a sob, and set her mind to the task and her heart to prayer. With a deep breath she squared her shoulders and began to scrub, oblivious of the tears that streamed down her cheeks. Scriptures of the cleansing and healing power of the Blood of Jesus repeated themselves in her mind . . . *As far as the east from the west, He removes our transgressions from us and remembers them not . . . Old things have passed away and all things become new . . . The blood of Jesus washes us as clean as snow . . . When we are born again, we become new creatures in Christ.*

As she worked, Taylor prayed these truths would become as real to her and her twin as the blood that now stained the carpet. Once satisfied the blemish would be removed when the rug dried, she wiped the tears from her face, stood up, and carried the bucket into the bathroom to empty and rinse, then washed herself.

Alex heaved a sigh of relief when Taylor emerged from Trevor's office and went into the bathroom. He waited by the door until she walked out again, then took her in his arms, brushed his lips over her forehead, and asked if she was okay.

Taylor nodded and stepped out of his embrace. "I'm going to change my shirt. I'll be out in a minute," she said and disappeared into her office.

He paced the lobby for fifteen minutes before worry set in. He went to her office and knocked on the door but got no answer. He let himself in only to find it empty. He looked around, confused then anxious. He walked over to the closet, knocked then opened the door, half-afraid of what he'd find, even more surprised at what he did. Taylor knelt at a tiny altar, obviously deep in prayer. "Taylor?"

She looked up, obviously unaware of how long she'd been there.

"Oh, I'm sorry. I didn't mean to worry you."

"I didn't know this was here, certainly didn't mean to disturb you."

She rose, blew out a candle, and joined him.

"It's okay. I need to get back to the hospital. Would you take me to get my car first?"

"If that's what you want. I'd rather take you to the hospital, stay with you, and maybe give Pam a break. She's been there by herself for a while and has probably gotten a chance to see him only once. We can get your car later or in the morning, after we see how he's doing and y'all decide how to handle the office and stay with him, take shifts or whatever."

Taylor nodded. "Okay." She hesitated a moment, touched his cheek. "Thank you, for everything."

Alex covered her hand with his, moved it around to his mouth, and kissed the palm. "You're more than welcome. Like I said earlier, I want to be here for you."

Tears rushed to Taylor's eyes, and he could see she was overwhelmed at the emotions he knew were reflected in his. A smile trembled on her lips. In silent acquiescence she let him take her hand, escort her out, and help her into the SUV.

Alex was right about Pam. She had only seen Trevor once all afternoon, and she needed a break. The visitation was all too brief. He'd opened pain-filled eyes and traced a T in her palm. Pam assured him that Taylor would be back soon. After that all she could do was cry, so much so that the nurse asked her to leave to avoid upsetting him more. She sighed with relief when Alex and Taylor walked into the room. Taylor sat down, slid an arm around Pam's shoulder, and hugged her close.

"How is he?"

"Okay, I guess," she mumbled and fought back the tears she hadn't been able to stem all day. "He asked for you, but I was crying so much that they ran me out."

"Alex's going to take you down to the cafeteria and maybe for a walk or a drive." She looked to Alex for confirmation and continued at his silent nod. "I'll check with the nurse, see if they'll let me visit with him a minute or two and let you know how he is when y'all get back. Okay?"

Pam nodded and let Alex help her to her feet. Her heart lifted a little when he caressed Taylor's cheek before he offered her his arm.

"Are you hungry?" he asked, once they left the waiting area.

She shook her head. "Not really. I don't think I could stomach anything right now even if I was."

"How about a walk then?" he suggested and punched the elevator button when she nodded.

"How is she?" Pam asked once they were on the elevator and he'd pushed the first floor button. He shook his head and sighed. His eyes showed concern.

"As well as can be expected, I guess. She lost it when she saw his office. I had to get her out of there before she could calm down."

"I can imagine," Pam remarked.

"The answering machine recorded the whole incident. She heard it right off the bat so that didn't help matters. I reset it."

Pam gasped. "Oh, Lord. I didn't think about that. It's a safety feature Trevor insisted on. If any phone is knocked off the hook, the recorder automatically records what's going on in that room. God, it must've been horrible for her to hear that."

"Pretty rough," Alex admitted. "But the real challenge was when she saw his office."

"I shouldn't have let her go there. I should've gone with you."

"Don't feel guilty. She needed to deal with it. We went out to the jobsite and talked to Steve. She only told him that Trevor was in an accident and that he was in Intensive Care. He's supposed to come by the office tomorrow so they can get things lined up for the next couple of weeks."

"Good," Pam remarked. "How's Bugsby?"

"Bugsby is fine. What about you? How are you, really?"

Pam shrugged. "I'll be better when I know he's out of ICU and when I get a chance to digest everything that's happened."

"Taylor told me you'd overheard them," he ventured.

"Considering the shape you were in and everything that happened, they must've had a pretty bad argument."

"Worse than you can probably imagine," she assured him, and choked back a sob when their words replayed in her mind. She turned to face him. "Please don't ask me to tell you what I heard. I can't do that. I know you're probably curious and by the way you treat Taylor, I assume it's more than curiosity. But I can't be the one to tell you anything. I can't. I won't violate their trust that way."

Alex hugged her. "I wouldn't ask you to." He moved away so she could see his eyes. "And you're right, it is more than curiosity. I've never felt so much for someone so soon."

Awe and wonder, mixed with confusion, colored his tone. Pam sensed his surprise at how true those words were and how real and deep his feelings went considering the short amount of time he'd known Taylor.

"Anyway," he continued, "from the things she said when she saw the blood on the carpet in his office I can only imagine the secrets they hold in their hearts."

Pam shuddered. "You can't even begin to imagine."

Tears streamed down her cheeks, sobs shook her shoulders. Alex pulled her close and stroked her hair. "As Taylor said earlier, maybe this will be the impetus for them to seek help. Hopefully it'll be the one defining moment in their lives that constitutes change. God knows they need deliverance from the demons of the past that continue to haunt them. Maybe now they'll get it."

"I sure hope so," Pam muttered. "I only hope that I can be of some help, y'know?"

"Me too." Alex sighed. "Me too."

Taylor watched for their return and noted again how swollen and red-rimmed Pam's eyes were. "Are you alright?"

Pam nodded. "Did you see him? How is he?"

"Recovering nicely, from what the nurses say. They think he'll be moved into a room tomorrow if he keeps on doing as well as he is now. He opened his eyes and squeezed my hand when I talked to him. Tell you what," she continued at their relieved sighs, "why don't you go home, try to get some rest and take over for me later tonight? I'll go to the office first thing in the morning and relieve you after I meet with Steve and get the guys lined up for the next few days."

"That's fine," Pam said. "I'll take Bugsby home with me and bring him to you later."

"Good idea."

"Can you take me to get my car?" she asked Alex.

"I'm at your service, ladies," he assured them with a tiny nod and an encouraging smile. "What can I do or get for you, Taylor?"

She opened her mouth to say "nothing" but reconsidered when she thought about the long hours between visits. "Maybe a sketch pad or two and some pencils. Perhaps I can relax a little or at least be somewhat productive between visits."

"Okay. May I make a suggestion?" he asked, and then continued when they nodded. "How about Pam and I get your car and drive it to the office. From there she can go home or whatever and I'll come back up to stay with you for a while tonight."

"But how will I get home?" Taylor asked.

"I'll drive you home and pick you up early tomorrow."

"But how will you get any rest if you're constantly carting one or the other of us around?" Pam wanted to know.

He shrugged, and they could see that his mind was made up. "I'll be fine. I've spent hours on the road before. This is a piece of cake for me," he admitted, and then pulled out his trump card. "Besides, it'll be one less thing for Trevor to worry about when he wakes up."

No doubt in either mind he spoke the truth, the women had no choice but to agree.

CHAPTER ELEVEN

Pam asked to see Trevor once more before she left and promised the nurse she wouldn't cry. She swallowed the lump in her throat, took his hand in hers, and brushed the hair off his forehead. "Trevor?" she whispered. "It's Pam."

He opened his eyes. She sighed, blinked back tears of relief, and offered a tiny smile.

"I'm gonna go home for a while. Taylor's here. She'll stay for now. I'll relieve her tonight, so I'll see you later. Okay?" He nodded a little and squeezed her hand.

"I love you," she whispered, then brushed her lips across his forehead. His eyes filled with tears. He jerked his hand from hers and shook his head as though to deny her words.

Pam laid her forehead against his to stop his movements. "Yes," she whispered, and fought hard not to cry. The last thing she wanted was to upset him or be thrown out.

"I'll always love you, no matter what," she promised and swallowed the pain of his rejection. "I'll see you later," she insisted.

She feathered her lips across his forehead once more and then left before he tried to further deny her declarations. With a quick swipe, she brushed the moisture off her cheeks before a nurse or Taylor could see. But once seated in Alex's SUV, she let loose the torrent. He stroked her arm then held her hand until the sobs subsided.

"I'm sorry," she mumbled.

"No need to be sorry," he assured. "It's been a rough day for everyone. Felt like crying myself a time or two," he admitted, and then pulled into the parking lot of Way, Truth & Light Christian Church.

"Do you mind if we go in for a minute?" she queried.

"Not a bit."

"It's such a lovely church," she whispered when they stepped inside. He nodded in agreement.

Pastor Hebert rose from the foot of the cross and turned when he heard the door open. He stepped off the platform and greeted them. "How's Trevor?"

"Holding his own," Pam replied. "We've come to get Taylor's car."

"So, she's alone up there?" Pastor Hebert asked.

Pam nodded. "For now, Alex's going to take me home after we drop her car off at the office, then pick me up to relieve her later."

"Think I'll run up and visit with her a while. She shouldn't be alone for long."

"She won't be," Alex interjected. "I'm going back up."

Pastor Hebert smiled at the possessive note in Alex's voice. "That's good. Like I said, she doesn't need to be alone too long."

He turned back to Pam and took her hand in his. "So, how are you doing?"

Tears rushed to her eyes. Pam blinked them back with determination, swallowed the lump in her throat, and then shook her head. The tears spilled over. "Not good," she admitted with a sob.

Dan pulled her close. "Why don't we sit down and talk a minute or two," he offered, his gaze moved to include Alex.

"Do you mind?" Pam asked Alex.

He shook his head. "No. You go ahead. I'm going to run over

to my apartment and clean up a bit. I'll be back in thirty or forty-five minutes. Is that okay?"

They turned to Pastor Hebert, and he nodded. Alex touched her arm.

"Don't go to the office without me. You don't need to be there alone just yet. There's time enough for that tomorrow," he added, glad when she nodded in agreement. Pastor Hebert's words halted his exit.

"Are you sure you wouldn't want to sit with us a minute? Strictly informal, you don't have to say anything unless you want," he assured Alex with a smile.

Alex hesitated, tempted to vent some of the emotions that had ruled his heart and mind all day. He shook his head. "I'd love to," he replied with a pointed look at Dan. "But not right now."

Dan nodded that he understood then offered his hand. Alex shook it, squeezed Pam's arm in a gesture of support, then left. He kept a tight rein on his emotions until he arrived safely in his apartment. Once there, he collapsed.

"Jesus," he moaned over and over and sank into a chair. He buried his face in hands that shook and wept until no tears remained. Purged of the vicious emotions for the moment, he headed straight for the shower. He stripped as he went and hoped the hot, pulsating spray would sear the incident from his mind, wash the blood from his hands. When it failed and the water ran tepid, he dried off and dressed. He stuffed a few things in an overnight bag, hung a change of clothes, and stowed his laptop in his SUV, then went to the church to meet Pam. Within moments, they bid farewell to the pastor. She climbed into Taylor's car, and he followed her to T&T Enterprises.

When they reached the office, Alex pulled into the parking lot beside Pam's car, emerged from his vehicle, and waited while she parked Taylor's car next to Trevor's truck. The sight of his vehicle made her gasp, reminding Alex of Taylor's sudden urge to make sure her brother's truck was locked up. She stopped beside it and ran a hand over the fender. Sobs shook her slender frame.

Alex stroked a hand down her back. "Give me the keys. I'll get Bugsby and bring him out to you." Pam handed them over without a word. Once inside, he grabbed a couple of sketchpads and pencils from Taylor's office and the rabbit from the kitchen. He loaded the items into the back of his SUV and helped Pam into the passenger seat.

He hesitated before starting the truck. "Are you sure you're going to be alright? Maybe you shouldn't be alone tonight, either." Pam shrugged and looked away. "Is there someone I can call for you, or somewhere you can go so you won't have to be alone?"

She nodded. "My parents' house," she replied and gave him the address.

When they arrived, Alex sent up a silent "thank you" to see a car parked in the driveway of Pam's parents' house. He followed Pam up to the back door. Together they entered the kitchen and Pam called for her mother. Within moments the room bustled with people. One look at her mom and Pam collapsed.

"Oh, Mama," she sobbed and was quickly enfolded in loving arms.

Alex waited and watched in complete silence. Between sobs Pam told them what happened. Though she didn't go into detail about the argument she'd heard between Trevor and Taylor, she did tell them enough to allude to the fact that the twins had suffered a horrendous childhood. He shook Pam's father's hand when the man extended one to him with words of thanks for bringing her to her family.

Once assured Pam would be safe in her parents' care, Alex

brought Bugsby in, then left for the hospital. His stomach growled, which reminded him he'd skipped lunch. A glance at his watch confirmed suppertime had long since passed also. He figured Taylor hadn't eaten either so he picked up a sandwich for himself and a salad for her. Looks like their first dinner date alone would be in an ICU waiting room. He frowned at the thought.

He'd wanted to ask her out again, but between his business and hers, the opportunity hadn't presented itself. Though he longed to know her on a more intimate level, he'd discovered a few very important things about Taylor Forrestier in the three weeks he'd known her. She had the sweet tooth of a child and a sense of humor that sometimes surprised him with its spontaneity and depth. She loved salads, especially ones filled with seafood, and she'd live off Chinese food if her brother would let her.

Alex smiled at the memory of Taylor's argument with Trevor that if the Chinese lived on Chinese food, she would do just fine emulating them. He wondered if she'd ever enjoy such light-hearted banter with her brother again. Emotion, thick and suffocating, clogged his throat and stung his eyes. He swallowed hard several times and blinked furiously to dislodge it.

On impulse, he decided to pick up a gift to show his support, then hesitated. What could he buy that wouldn't add to an already complicated situation? Candy? Roses? Both? One of his clients owned and operated several successful florist shops. He pulled off the road and dialed the man's cell number.

"Hey, Frank, you closed yet?"

"Yeah, but I'm still at the shop. What can I do for you?"

"I need a gift, but I'm not sure what to get."

"Come on by, and we'll fix you up."

Alex glanced at his watch and figured another few minutes wouldn't hurt. He arrived at the florist's, and Frank let him in the back door.

"So, tell me what's going on."

"A friend's brother's been in an accident, and I'd like to bring something to show that I care, but I'm at a loss. She loves chocolate, but I'm thinking flowers. What would you suggest?"

"Do you want roses? What color?"

Alex remembered the many conversations he and Frank shared about roses and the symbolism of each color. He figured Taylor loved history and tradition enough to know what the colors meant too, so he picked out peach, white, and yellow, then bought a vase in the shape of a teddy bear to put them in. Frank added a few other flowers, greenery and baby's breath to round out the arrangement. He then tied a tiny bag of assorted chocolates around the bear's neck with a bow, smiled and deemed the gift perfect. Alex thanked him with a generous tip, then left.

He arrived in the ICU waiting room to find Taylor curled up in the corner of the couch, head back, eyes closed. He watched a moment to gauge whether or not she might have dozed off. A single tear slipped from her eye to leave a moist trail down her cheek, and she wiped it away with a sniffle. Alex set his laptop on the floor and put the food and roses down on the table next to her. He brushed his knuckles over her cheek and whispered her name.

Taylor opened her eyes, and the worry rushed back into them after her brief respite. She smiled, a tiny movement of lips that did not reach her eyes or relieve the lines of tension in her face.

"I'm okay. It's just that every time I see him and then have to leave, I can hardly believe this is all real."

Alex sat next to her, pulled her to his side, and cuddled her head against his shoulder. "I know," he said, then brushed his lips over her forehead. "How was he when you last saw him?"

"Good."

"When can you see him again?"

She shrugged. "They haven't been too strict about the rules. The nurses said as long as things were quiet in there, and they didn't need to settle in a new patient or attend to an emergency, I could pretty much come and go as I please."

"Good," Alex remarked. "You need to try to rest a little too. I know it isn't easy, but you won't be any good to anyone if you collapse."

"I'll rest later. How's Pam?"

"She's all right. I took her to her parents' house. Her dad will bring her up here around ten or so. That way, you can go home and get some sleep."

"I'm glad you did that. She doesn't need to be alone."

"Neither do you, which is why I got back as soon as I could."

"Pastor Hebert just left," Taylor told him.

"Perfect timing," Alex said, trying to smile. "I picked up some food. I thought you might be hungry." She nodded. "You want to go down to the cafeteria or outside?"

"No, I'd rather eat in here."

"Okay," Alex said, and cuddled her a moment longer. When she moved out of his embrace, he handed her the roses.

"Oh, they're beautiful."

"Do you know what they mean?" he asked.

She smiled, a real smile this time, and nodded. "Yellow for friendship, white for purity, peach for sympathy, chocolate 'cause you're so sweet, and a teddy bear to make me think of you."

He chuckled and cupped her face with his hand, brushing his lips over her cheek. "I want you to know how much I care and that I'm here for you."

She flushed, buried her nose in the sweet fragrance of the flowers, and whispered, "Thank you."

He reached for the bag, opened it, and handed her the salad.

She put the roses down and sighed in appreciation. "Oh, I love these things."

"I know. But don't tell Trevor, he'll probably chew me out because I failed to buy you 'real' food," he teased. She smiled as he'd hoped she would.

"I won't," she promised, then dug in. Twenty minutes later she closed the empty salad container with a groan. "Now I'm stuffed."

Alex grinned. He enjoyed the way she demolished the generous salad, with crab meat and shrimp mixed with boiled eggs, pasta, cheese, olives and peppers. He watched her rise, stretch, and rub her lower back with a weary sigh.

"I feel like I've been here for days instead of hours." She did a few shoulder and neck rolls.

Alex stood. "Come here." When she obeyed, he turned her around and did his best to massage the tension out of her shoulders. "Want to go for a walk or a drive? We don't have to stay away long."

She rolled her head, sighed. "No, thanks, but I think I'll go sit with him for a while if you don't mind."

"Of course not. Taylor?" She hesitated when he called her name and turned to face him. Alex cupped her cheeks in his hands. "Tell him 'hi' for me."

She touched his cheek with gentle fingertips. "I will."

While she visited with her brother, he called his answering service to check for urgent messages from clients or prospects, glad to find there were none. He picked up his laptop and tried to work but found himself too wired up to concentrate so he played Solitaire until his brain stopped spinning.

Trevor passed a quiet evening. He stayed awake for longer periods, and though still heavily sedated, he appeared somewhat alert. The breathing tube, inserted in his mouth and down his throat before surgery, seemed to bother him the most. He tugged at it a time or two, then frowned when Taylor stopped him and took his hand in hers.

"They have to leave it in for a while, Trev. Let it be."

He shook his head, tried to speak around it. "Go home," he croaked, barely intelligible.

She stroked his cheek. "Not yet, Trev, you have to stay here a few days. They'll probably move you into a regular room tomorrow if you pass a peaceful night."

He shook his head, frowned again. "You, home."

"Not a chance, little brother," she insisted, and then touched her lips to his forehead. "I'm not about to leave you alone here. I'll go home later when Pam gets back."

Again he shook his head. "No Pam."

Taylor frowned. "You don't want Pam up here?"

He shook his head.

"Why?"

Tears filled his eyes, rolled slowly down his cheeks. Taylor saw the fear in them—and the shame. "Oh, Trev," she whispered. "It's okay. She loves you so very much. Let her show you, let her in."

His lips trembled around the tube. "Afraid," he mumbled.

"I know," she whispered. "Me too, but there is a time for every purpose under heaven, a time to heal and a time to love. It's time Trevor, time for both of us to let it all go and move on. Time for us to trust others and to let them in our hearts and our world, time to fall in love, get married, and have children. Pastor Hebert will help if you let him. But let's not worry about it now," she insisted, her voice gentle. "We'll talk about it later, when you're feeling better."

"Love you," he muttered, "so sorry."

"I know, and I'm sorry too. I love you little brother," she assured him, her voice tremulous. "I love you so very much. Rest now," she urged, grateful when he closed his eyes and dozed off once more.

Pam arrived at ten-thirty. Taylor hugged her. "How are you? Did you rest?"

She nodded. "Mama fixed me one of her famous hot toddies then stayed with me while I slept." A tiny smile trembled on her lips. "You'd think I was still five the way she coddled me."

Taylor smiled and hugged her again. "You deserve to be coddled. Where's Bugsby?"

"I left him with Mom and Dad. They've offered to take care of him for a few days."

Taylor nodded in approval.

"How's Trevor?" Pam wanted to know.

"Better," Taylor answered. "Awake more and more alert. He even tried to make me go home."

"Good."

"Yeah, I never thought I'd be grateful to hear him fuss at me," Taylor agreed.

Pam smiled. "Well, you need to go home and try to rest."

"I will," Taylor said, then went to see Trevor once more before she left for the night. As she walked out the door she heard Pam tell Alex to take good care of her and his answering promise.

When Taylor returned, Alex handed her the roses. He took her by the arm, escorted her out of the ICU waiting area and out of the hospital to where he'd parked his SUV in the covered, multi-level garage. Minutes later, they arrived at the cottage she leased.

"What time do you think you can be here in the morning?" she asked when he pulled into the driveway.

"I thought I'd stay with you," he said and turned to watch her reaction. "I can sleep on the couch or something."

Her eyes met his. "There's no need for you to go to so much trouble."

"It's no trouble, and you don't need to be left alone any more than Pam did. It's not going to do you any good to argue," he insisted when she opened her mouth to protest. "You're not staying alone."

Torn between gratitude and frustration, Taylor shut her mouth. Didn't anyone understand that sometimes she just wanted, needed to be alone? In light of all he'd done for her that day, she bit back on the irritation.

"Well, thank you," she said with a strained smile, and handed him the key to her house. "There's no need for you to sleep on the couch. I have an extra bedroom."

Alex chuckled, took the keys, climbed out of the SUV, and walked around to open her door. He took her by the arm, escorted her to the house, and unlocked the door. He waited until she entered before he followed her in, then dropped her keys on the coffee table. He turned her around and drew her into his arms.

"I don't mean to barge in where I'm not welcome, Taylor. I care about you and your brother. I want to help you through this, and I really don't think you should be alone tonight."

Taylor surrendered and rested her head against his chest. "I'm sorry. I didn't mean to be rude. You've been so much help to me, to all of us, today. I am grateful. Honestly."

"Shhh, it's okay." He stroked her back. "I know you'll need some time alone to deal with what's happened, but I think tonight is too soon for that."

"You're probably right," she admitted, feeling tired and gritty. "I think I'll take a hot bath then go to bed. Make yourself at home," she said and showed him the room where he would sleep.

Alex did as she suggested. He rummaged around in the refrigerator, surprised to find an unopened bottle of wine. He carried the bottle to the counter, found a corkscrew then searched out two glasses. He uncorked the wine, poured a glass for each of them, then carried one and the roses into her room and placed them on the nightstand by her bed.

He took the other glass with him, kicked off his shoes, stretched out on the bed and sipped the sweet, white liquid until he'd emptied it. He changed into pajamas, climbed beneath the covers, and dozed, unaware of the nightmare that would plague the woman in the next room.

Chapter Twelve

Taylor thrashed about and fought the fear clamoring in her throat. Panic stole her breath. The monster held her while Trevor grappled with a gun. She struggled and kicked, but the monster held her fast. She had to get away. She had to stop him! She begged and pleaded, but the monster just laughed. His gnarled, horrid sound sent shivers of terror through her soul. A blast of gunshot, a flash of lightning, and the scream tore free from her throat and echoed through the room.

The door burst open and strong arms encircled her. Gentle hands stroked and soothed, a soft voice caressed, tender words flowed over her. Taylor buried her face in Alex's shoulder while he cradled her against his chest and rocked.

"I'm sorry. I didn't mean to wake you," she murmured. A pulse hammered against her skin, a tremble shimmered down her spine. She pushed herself closer, found safety and comfort in his embrace. Alex tightened his arms around her, smoothed her hair.

"It's okay. That's why I'm here and exactly why I didn't want to leave you alone tonight. Is there anything I can do or get for you?" She shook her head.

He noticed the untouched glass of wine on the bedside table and picked it up. "Try this. It might help."

She turned her head away. "I don't like wine."

"Then why did you have a bottle in your refrigerator?"

"A Christmas gift from Steve. I didn't have the heart to throw it away."

He chuckled, cuddled her closer, and held her until the shudders stopped and her breathing leveled. He left her alone once more, careful to close the door behind him.

The scenario repeated itself more than once in the hours that followed. He offered the comfort she needed every time. Taylor knew she wouldn't have slept at all if not for his presence.

Alex awoke to the hum of a motor and the steady rhythm of Taylor's feet pounding on the treadmill. He glanced at the clock—not quite five-thirty in the morning. He groaned. He had no idea what time either of them had finally slept. How on earth she could be awake, much less running, at this ungodly hour?

He propped the pillows up behind him and examined the décor in the room. Adorned in an early American style, he could distinguish Taylor's distinctive flair in every nook and cranny. The bedroom ensemble included a four-poster made of unfinished wood, an armoire, and a nightstand. An antique butter churn, decorated with the same design as the hand-painted border on the walls, held large artificial flowers. The country pattern even embellished the ceiling-fan blades. Everything about the room, the almond walls, wainscoting, shadow boxes filled with knick-knacks, handpicked paintings, quilted bedspread and curtains, all spoke of Taylor's unique talent.

He closed his eyes and listened. His heart picked up the rhythm of her footsteps. He remembered the first time he saw her, how the peach sweat suit clung to her body and revealed curves of taut muscle and soft flesh. The memory of that morning drew him from under the covers. He changed into slacks, slipped on a shirt and buttoned it, but didn't bother to tuck it in. He padded barefoot past her closed bedroom door to the kitchen.

He heard the treadmill slow then come to a stop, poured them each a glass of juice, and placed the carton back in the refrigerator. He took a sip. The glass had yet to reach his mouth for a second time when she walked out of her room. No sweat suit clung to her figure today. Instead she wore shorts and a tank top. Though not long, her legs were firm and well toned. She patted her flushed face with a towel. Her chest heaved with exertion and skin glistened with a thin sheen of perspiration.

Swift and fierce, a wave of desire washed over him. The glass froze on its way to his mouth, which was suddenly as dry as dust. His breath backed up in his lungs; his body tightened with need.

Alex turned his back to her and all but slammed the glass down on the counter. He clenched his fists in an effort to keep himself from leaping across the tiny kitchen to drag her into his arms and devour her mouth with his. The last thing he needed at this point in their relationship was to frighten her off with the force of his physical reaction. He heard her pause in the doorway.

"Oh, hi, hope I didn't wake you," she said.

He shook his head.

"Good, did you sleep well?"

He nodded.

"This juice for me?" she asked. "Thanks," she added, when he nodded again.

"You're welcome," he rasped.

"Are you alright?" she asked. "You sound a little hoarse this morning."

Alex chuckled and scrubbed the heel of his hands over his face.

"I'll be fine," he muttered and then turned to gaze at her. His eyes swept over her in a look as potent as a caress. "As soon as I get my breath back."

He watched a multitude of emotions flicker across her face. Some sent shivers of awareness down his spine, quickly followed by shudders of trepidation. Only a few feet separated them.

It felt more like a chasm.

She gasped, clutched the towel against her, and stepped back. "I'm going to jump into the shower." She took another step back. "Make yourself at home," she murmured and turned on her heel.

Alex called her name and halted her escape. She turned to face him, her eyes a kaleidoscope of emotions: a hint of excitement, a glimmer of desire, and a sparkle of pleasure all shadowed by the sharp edge of fear. The fear stopped him from simply snatching her up in his arms and wallowing in the feel and taste of her. He hesitated, then took a step closer. When she didn't bolt, he took another. Still an arm's length away, he cupped her cheek in his hand.

"Relax, enjoy your juice, and cool down a minute. Though tempted, I'm not going to pounce on you," he promised with a tight smile. "I would like to kiss you though," he murmured and brushed his thumb across her lips.

He felt her tremble and responded with a shiver of his own as every nerve ending in their bodies reacted to that simple touch.

She swallowed hard and shook her head.

"Please," she whispered, but he wasn't sure if it was a plea for him to stop or an invitation to continue. The mixed signals emanating from her added confusion to his already haywire system. He took another step closer and felt her stiffen and tremble. Desperate for contact, he brushed his lips across her forehead.

"That'll suffice for now," he said and stepped back. Her heartfelt sigh of relief pierced his heart.

"What's on the agenda this morning?" he asked, when she sipped the juice with a hand that trembled. The towel, still clutched against her, shielded that luscious view from his sight.

Taylor brushed the towel over her face. Though he'd stepped back from her, she could still feel the tension oozing from him.

"Well," she began, then cleared her throat and walked around him to put her glass in the sink. Her breath came easier with a little more distance between them.

"I thought we'd run over to the hospital and one of us would take Pam to breakfast, give her a little break at least, then head over to the office. I figured I'd stay there until noon or so, and then relieve her for the afternoon and evening. She could go back to the office for a couple of hours then home to rest, and relieve me again later tonight. Once Trevor's in a private room, we'll work out another plan." She smiled over her shoulder then continued.

"I'm sure he'll fuss soon enough and say we've neglected the office to tend to him when that's what the doctors and nurses are paid to do."

The thought of him was so strong that she could actually hear his voice in reprimand.

Alex chuckled. "I'm sure you're right. It's still early though, so why don't you get ready, while I finish up, and we'll grab a bite of breakfast first. I'll make sure Pam gets something to eat before we leave for the office."

Though anxious to get to the hospital and see her brother, Taylor nodded. "On one condition," she remarked.

His eyebrow quirked with interest.

"Breakfast is on me."

Alex grinned. His eyes kindled, danced with wicked humor. Taylor flushed when she realized what she said and how it sounded.

"I mean, that you let me buy your breakfast," she amended.

"It's the least I can do after all you've done for me, for us."

The grin turned into a chuckle that rumbled deep within his chest. Alex cocked his head, and she could tell from the quick way he tensed then clenched his hands that he wanted to touch her.

"If you insist," he remarked, his voice tinged with laughter.

Taylor had the grace to grin. "I walked right into that one, didn't I?"

He nodded, continued to smile, but refrained from comment.

"Well, if you'll excuse me, I'll take my shower now," she said and walked past him. She hesitated, turned back, and found he watched her, as she knew he would. She clutched the towel against her then took a step closer and brushed her lips across his cheek.

"A kiss on the cheek," he groaned and reverentially touched the spot her lips caressed. "Enough to put me in my place, thank-you-very-much," he mumbled, the complaint uttered in a husky, teasing tone.

Her laughter rang out like music on the morning, and she made her escape into the bathroom.

Breakfast was sweet, lightly romantic, and not at all awkward. They arrived at the hospital to find Pam pale and tense, pacing the ICU corridor. She rushed up to them.

"Oh, Taylor, I was about to call you. He had a terrible night. He ran a fever, and it got pretty high, so high it made him delirious. He even pulled the breathing tube out of his mouth. Of course, that tore up his throat. They tried to put it back in, but he fought them so hard, they were forced to restrain him. Once the doctor found out what happened and that he spit up blood, he told them to leave it out and just watch him."

"When did all this happen, Pam?" Taylor asked.

"Two or three o'clock I guess. I've been in and out of his room so much I lost track of the time."

"Why didn't you call me earlier?"

Pam shrugged and buried her face in shaky hands.

"I didn't know what to do."

"You should have called," Taylor insisted.

"I'm sorry," Pam said. "You needed to rest, and there was really nothing you could do. You were so worn out when you left and I know that's what Trevor would have wanted. I did what I thought was best."

"I'm so tired of you and Trevor treating me like I'm some kind of porcelain doll. I'm not fragile. I won't break, and I can take care of myself!" Taylor declared. She clenched her teeth and all but stomped her foot in agitation.

"You had no right to keep me from my brother when he needed me," she added, her tone scathing.

Alex placed a hand on each of their shoulders, surprised at Taylor's anger, even more shocked at her outburst. "Easy. Let's all calm down. I'm sure no harm was intended here," he soothed. Pam bit her lip and turned another shade of pale, her eyes wide and dark with shock.

Taylor shook off his hand with an ill-tempered shrug. "I'm going to check on my brother," she muttered, and turned on her heel when Pam collapsed into the nearest chair.

"C'mon, Pam, let's go get some breakfast," Alex urged. She shook her head.

"Yes," he insisted. He took her firmly by the arm and pulled her to her feet. "You've got to get out of here for a while." When they returned forty minutes later, Taylor was still in ICU.

Pam sat down with a heavy sigh. "I can't believe she got so mad."

"She's not mad, just upset."

"What's the difference?" Pam muttered.

Alex smiled, stroked a hand down her arm. "Let me rephrase that. She's not mad at you, just the situation. This whole ordeal has been a terrible strain on everybody. There's bound to be harsh emotions, raw feelings. She'll be better once she finds out for sure how he is."

Pam's eyes searched his, concern and sympathy reflected in the brilliant green gaze.

"I love them both so much. Taylor is like the sister I never had. I'm closer to her than my own sisters-in-law."

Again he smiled. "She's probably just really tired of being fussed over and needs a little room to breathe."

"Trevor is very overprotective, almost to the point of domineering. I guess it's her turn to do the fussing," Pam admitted.

"And you're incredibly sensitive and generous to understand to that degree," Alex complimented.

"Love does not take offense," Pam murmured, as Taylor walked into the room.

"How is he?" Alex asked. Taylor sighed, her expression resolute, and swiped at the tear that slipped from the corner of her eye.

"He's better. The fever's down, almost normal, but the doctor said to keep him in here until they're sure infection hasn't set in. They have him on an IV with antibiotics to be safe. His throat is raw from when he pulled out the tube, another reason for the antibiotics, but he's breathing on his own. They removed the restraints."

"Was he awake? Did he talk to you?" Taylor nodded in answer to his questions then eyed Pam.

"He asked for you. But I don't want you in there if you're going to cry. He needs to stay calm. If you're upset, he'll just worry."

Pam flinched at the sharp edge to Taylor's voice and her chin jerked up a notch. She rose from her seat but paused beside Taylor.

"I'm sorry, Tay," she whispered.

Taylor accepted the apology with a curt nod but didn't speak.

Pam stiffened her shoulders, then went in to see Trevor. Alex's heart ached for her. He turned to Taylor. "A little rough on her, don't you think?"

Taylor glared at him.

"So now I'll have you telling me what to think and how to feel too?" she burst out.

He inhaled with a sharp hiss and bit back the angry retort that came to mind. He stopped her when she tried to storm past him.

"Now you hold on just one minute, Miss Forrestier," he told her. "You've a right to rant and rave all you want, but not at her. She's been nothing but your friend and his. You've certainly no right to rage at me," he asserted, teeth gritted and fists clenched as he fought the urge to shake some sense into her.

Taylor's hands curled in automatic defense against his anger. She fought back shudders of fear in the face of it, unaware until that moment how much resentment she still harbored in her heart, resentment against being dominated by overbearing, overprotective people.

Resentment or unforgiveness?

She felt the blood drain from her face at the thought and with a pang of guilt realized she'd never offered forgiveness to Trevor for his part in their past. She slumped into a chair and buried her face in her hands.

"Oh, God, help me," she mumbled.

First Corinthians 13 swam through her mind in bits and pieces, pricked at her heart and conscious. *Love is patient and kind, never jealous or rude, does not take offense, is never resentful and is always ready to excuse.*

She took a deep breath and swallowed the lump of emotion that clogged her throat. Shame washed over her. She raised tear-drenched eyes to Alex's.

"You're right," she admitted. "I'm sorry."

She rose when Pam walked into the room and enfolded her in a hug. "I'm sorry, Pam. Please forgive me." Pam hugged her back with all she was worth.

"What's there to forgive? I understand. But thanks anyway. Do you want me to go to the office so you can stay here a while?"

Taylor shook her head. "No. Steve is supposed to meet me there this morning." She glanced at her watch. "He's probably there already, pacing the parking lot. So we'd better go. Just call, Pam, if there's any change, good or bad," she insisted. Pam promised. Taylor hugged her again. "Thanks. Again, I'm sorry I behaved so ugly toward you."

"Don't worry about it," Pam said in a firm voice. "Go and do what you have to do. I'll keep you posted. See you later."

Taylor went to Trevor's room once more before she left. "Trev?" she queried, her voice soft. She brushed her fingers through his hair and sighed with relief when he opened his eyes and smiled.

"I'm going to the office for a while. Pam will stay. She'll call me if you need anything. Okay?"

He nodded.

"See you later," she promised and kissed his cheek, surprised and delighted when he wrapped his arm around her and hugged her.

"Go," he said, his voice barely more than a harsh whisper. "Pam, too," he muttered. "She fusses too much."

Taylor grinned. "It's about time you got a taste of your own medicine," she teased with a gentle laugh. He smiled, but his eyes were worried. She hurried to ease his fears before he could speak.

"Everything's alright, Trev," she assured. "Everything's going to be just fine. You rest now. Get better so you can get out of here and come home."

Trevor nodded, blinked away the moisture that filled his eyes, and swallowed hard. Taylor could tell by the way he winced his throat ached and was relieved when he slid once more into the peaceful void of sleep.

CHAPTER THIRTEEN

Alex and Taylor rode to the office in strained but polite silence. Taylor worried over her brother, her behavior, and what she'd say to Steve. She could tell by the way he held her hand and his conscientious glances, Alex worried over her. She turned to him when they pulled into the parking lot.

"I feel like I should apologize to you again, Alex, for what I said. Words can't express how grateful I am for all you've done."

He cupped her cheek in his hand. "You don't have to apologize again, Taylor. Once was enough. I know you're hurt right now and probably afraid and confused. I've said it before and I'll say it again, I care about you a great deal. I want to help you through this, but I can't do that if you don't talk to me."

"I don't know what to say," she said and blinked back the tears that rushed to her eyes, determined to be strong, to overcome. "I'm afraid to say too much or say the wrong thing."

"When I consider what's happened, I assume that you and Trevor had a rough childhood?"

She confirmed his observation with a quick grimace. He paused a moment then continued when she didn't elaborate.

"I'm sure you find it difficult to trust people. But you have to start sometime. You are surrounded by people who care about you, love you. Open up to them. Maybe not all at once, and certainly not everyone, but start somewhere. Start with me," he urged.

Taylor closed her eyes and fought shudders of apprehension

at the thought of sharing her and Trevor's secrets, with anyone. But she knew he was right, on one count at least. The time had come for her and Trevor to open up to people, to learn to trust someone besides each other. She smiled slightly and reached for the door handle. "I'll think about it."

Alex stopped her with a gentle hand, and brushed his lips across her cheek. As he opened the door for her, Steve drove up beside them and disembarked from his truck in time to meet her next to Alex's SUV. He took her hand in his.

"How are things this morning?"

Due to Steve's six-foot height, Taylor had to tilt her head in order to look into his eyes. "He had a rough night, but he's doing better," she answered. "They've got him on antibiotics to fight off infection. Hopefully he'll be moved out of ICU tonight or tomorrow."

Steve eyed Alex with a measured look when he walked up beside them, then pulled Taylor's hand through his arm, and escorted her to the back door of the office.

"Are you going to tell me what happened?" he asked, his voice laced with concern.

Taylor took a deep breath and disengaged her hand from his arm to unlock the door. She shook so much that Steve took the keys from her and opened it himself. The three of them were in the kitchen before he spoke again.

"I hope you know how much I love and respect the two of you, Taylor. Whatever's happened, whatever you say will remain in strictest confidence if that's what you want. And if there's anything you need or anything I can do, just ask."

Taylor nodded. "Thanks," she whispered. Her lips trembled in an attempt to smile.

"How about some coffee?" she asked. Her gaze caught Alex's, and she could almost read his mind: *If you're going to open up and learn to trust people, now's a good time.* His slight, imperceptible nod encouraged her to take the next step.

She turned back to Steve. "Then we'll talk."

The men sat at the table and conversed about the job while Taylor fidgeted at the counter. In the time it took to clean the coffee pot, measure out grounds, and wash cups for them to drink with, Taylor thought about what she'd say to Steve. Her mind wandered back to the day they'd met and how well they'd gotten along since. Though muscular and well-proportioned for his height, his lean frame and gentle personality were more of a comfort to her than a threat. She'd accepted dinner dates with him once or twice, and though she'd found him incredibly kind and sweet, there were no sparks between them. Not like what she'd felt the first time Alex had taken her hand in his.

She remembered how both men liked their coffee, prepared and handed them each a cup, then poured her own. She took a sip and slid into the chair one of them had pulled out for her. She put the cup down on the table, clasped her hands in her lap, and swallowed hard.

She knew she must look scared to death because both men reached for her hand under the table. Their hands collided over hers. A cool, calculated look passed between them. Taylor took each of their hands in hers, squeezed, and then released them. She propped her elbows on the table, clasped her hands and rested her forehead on them. *Father in heaven, help me,* she prayed silently. *Give me courage and wisdom. Most of all, Lord, give me the words.*

The truth will set you free, came the reply.

She took a deep breath, cleared her throat, and turned to Steve. "Trevor tried to shoot himself."

It was a good thing he'd put his coffee down before she spoke. "What?" he gasped.

Tears rushed to her eyes. Taylor blinked them back with determination. "We had a horrible argument, one that brought up all the pain and shame of our past. It pushed him over the edge."

Steve held up a hand to halt her words. "Whoa, wait a minute. Back up and say that again."

A single tear slid from the corner of her eye and rolled slowly down her cheek. Taylor knew she'd have to give him more details than that in order for him to understand and, hopefully, not judge Trevor too harshly. She took a deep, shuddering breath, brushed the moisture off her face, and swallowed the bitter emotion clogging her throat. She took a chance she never had before and trusted their most valued employee and friend.

"Trevor and I had a horrible childhood. Our father was a hard, domineering man who ruled his household with an iron fist." She tucked her hair behind her ear with a hand that trembled.

"He was abusive to our mother as well as us. Our uncle took us in after their deaths. When he died nearly three years ago we moved here in hopes to forget and start fresh. I've sought the help of the Lord to move forward, but Trevor hasn't." She fiddled with her coffee cup but didn't dare try to drink for fear she'd choke.

"We were counseled as children so he thought that by just being here, where no one knew us or anything about our past, it would all go away. But it's continued to haunt us. Yesterday, when I didn't call or touch base with anyone, he got really worried." Her voice broke on a sob. "We had a huge fight and I threatened to leave . . ."

Her words trailed off when both men gasped, "What?"

"I threatened to leave after the job is finished and strike out on my own. I could never really do that! We've vowed never to leave one another. I was just angry and frustrated because he's so overprotective. I didn't think he'd take my words to heart or that they'd have this kind of impact on him. It's all my fault."

She collapsed, unable to hold back the tears a moment longer.

Both men knew the situation had to go much deeper than that, be far worse than she described for Trevor to take such drastic action. Before Steve could vacate his chair, Alex rose and took her in his arms. When her sobs subsided and they sat down again, Steve reached over and took her hand. She lifted wide, pleading eyes to his.

"Please don't judge him too harshly," she said.

"I hope you know me better than that," Steve chided, his voice gentle. Taylor's smile mocked slightly and didn't quite reach her eyes.

"We know you as well as we've allowed ourselves to know anyone, which doesn't say a whole lot," she told Steve. "But you have been a trusted employee and as close to a friend as we've ever had," she admitted.

Alex gritted his teeth but refrained from comment when Steve smiled and tucked her hair behind her ear. "Thank you. Now what can I do to help you two through this?"

Taylor shrugged. "Keep progress on the job, I guess. And, maybe once he's in a room, go visit with him, offer your support, show him you care like any friend would."

"I don't think that's too much to ask," he remarked with a tender smile. "So it's business as usual?"

She nodded. "Pam and I will take turns here and at the hospital until he runs us off, which probably won't be too much longer. Trevor hates to be fussed over. He'd rather be the one fussing," she admitted with a smile.

"How long do you think he'll be laid up?"

Taylor sighed. "Not long, I hope. Right now the threat of infection is our biggest worry. At least that's what they said earlier. Once that's out of the way, when his age and overall health is taken into consideration, they believe he'll recover quickly. I'm sure he'll be anxious to get out there with you guys soon enough," she remarked. "I just hope he'll take it easy and not push too hard too soon."

"We won't let him," Steve promised and rose from his seat. "You tell him not to worry. The job is well under control."

Taylor stood too. "Thank you, Steve. And, I would appreciate it if this conversation remains confidential, for now at least. Trevor and I both need to learn to trust people more, but it's not going to be easy after so many years of having no one but each other."

Alex tensed but remained seated when Steve replied with actions not words and pulled her into his arms. He hugged her to his chest and stroked a hand down her hair. Steve's eyes narrowed in silent dare for him to protest, but Alex understood the man was her friend. He couldn't expect that to change just because his own feelings went a level deeper. They eyed each other for a long, tense moment. Once clear to each of them by unspoken communication where they stood, Steve released her. They talked a few minutes longer, then he headed out to the jobsite.

Alex pushed back from the table and rose from his seat when she closed the door. "That wasn't so hard now, was it?"

"You tell me," she replied and turned to face him. A tiny smile tugged at her lips. "I had the distinct impression you wanted to punch him a time or two."

He grinned and pulled her against his chest. "Only when he put his hands on you," he admitted with a chuckle.

She went into his arms, allowed him to wrap her in his embrace, and rested her head on his heart.

"Feel better?" he queried.

She nodded.

"If God didn't want us to trust other people, He wouldn't put them in our life," he remarked.

"That's true, I guess," she replied, then took a deep breath and stepped out of his embrace. "So, now you know why Trevor did what he did . . ." she hedged.

Alex could tell by the tremor in her voice and the way she avoided his gaze that she was anxious to know how he felt about them now, yet also afraid to find out.

"I don't know near enough, lady," he murmured and pulled her back in his arms, stroking her hair. "There's no doubt in my mind that you glossed over the harsh truth with mild words. Steve knows it too, but neither of us will pry. Not yet anyway," he added.

He eyed her, a meaningful lift to his brow, and brushed his knuckles over her cheek. "It's enough that you've opened up a little and want to trust us."

"I don't know if I'll ever be able to say more than I have already," she admitted. "But it does feel like a huge weight lifted off my shoulders."

"You will," he assured. "You'll have to, eventually, in order to be rid of it for good. I'll be here when you're ready." He cupped her face in his hands and lowered his lips to hers in a tender caress.

He felt her relax as she allowed herself to be caught up in the sweetness of the kiss. Her arms crept around his neck, lips parted, body swayed against his in subconscious surrender.

She may as well offer a feast to a starved man.

A primitive grunt escaped him. Alex pulled her tighter in his embrace and plundered the taste and texture of her mouth. His actions must have frightened her because she stiffened in his arms and whimpered. He ended the kiss by slow degrees and loosened his hold until his hands roamed over her back and shoulders in a restless caress.

"You are so beautiful," he whispered, his voice thick with emotion. He cuddled her to his chest and stroked her hair in a soothing manner. "I have never felt so much for anyone so soon."

Taylor rested her head against his chest and felt his heart thud against her cheek. His kiss elicited so many emotions—surprise that she could feel so much pleasure, embarrassment at how quickly the pleasure turned to fear, amazement at how easily he sensed both and relaxed his hold so she wouldn't feel intimidated or threatened. Still, she wondered what he would say if he knew how defiled she really was?

She stepped out of his embrace and laid her hand against his cheek. "I've never felt this way at all."

Alex covered her hand with his, brought it to his mouth, and kissed the palm. "We'll take it slow. What's on your agenda for the rest of the day?"

She smiled. "I'm going to stay here for a while, try to get some work done, and then relieve Pam a little later."

"You want me to hang around? I'm still not sure you should be alone, especially here."

Taylor shook her head with a sigh and tried not to smile. "You men are so hard-headed when it comes to me being alone. What's up with that? I mean, I know Trevor's reasons, but what's your excuse?"

Alex grinned. "Call me old-fashioned, call me un-feminist, but there's just something about a woman with such beauty and talent that cries out to be protected and brings out all my manly instincts," he admitted with a chuckle. "Besides, Trevor needs to rest, not worry about you here all by yourself."

She made a face at him. "Don't try to use that against me again. It won't work a second time. Besides, don't you have a business to run, tax returns to prepare?"

He shook his head. "Except for a few select clients, I no longer prepare taxes. I leave that to the CPAs. Speaking of which, who does your accounting?" he asked.

She told him the name.

"Great firm, but I'm better and more qualified to advise you on investments and long-term financial planning. Both personal and professional."

Taylor grinned. "I'm sure you are better in both aspects. I'm also fairly positive you're aware that loyalty is the first order of business."

"Loyalty is the first order of life," he replied.

She laughed. "True. They're the ones who told us about Pam," she continued. "One of the partners had talked with her and was impressed with her resume but had no position to offer. When I contracted them to do our accounting, I asked if they knew anyone who could do general office work. They suggested I give her a call."

"Well, you sure got a prize when you hired her. She's a real gem."

"You should have seen the look on Trevor's face the first time he laid eyes on her," Taylor reminisced. "She wore a pale green business suit and high heels. She'd plaited her hair into a French braid, which accentuated those high cheekbones and wide, emerald eyes. Trevor looked as though he'd been hit over the head with a baseball bat."

Alex chuckled. "I can imagine. She is a looker."

"She's more than a looker," she said. "She's a talented office manager. She's friendly and fun-loving, honest, and loyal. You can't ask for more in an employee or a friend."

Alex grinned at her quick defense of Pam's character. "This from a woman who has a problem getting close to people."

The phone rang before Taylor could respond. Pam's voice came over the line.

"Hey, Tay, the doctor's making his rounds. He should be in to see Trevor in about thirty minutes or so. You want to be here?"

143

"Of course, I'll be right there," Taylor answered then hung up the phone and relayed the information to Alex.

"C'mon, I'll take you. I'm self-employed. My business can wait," he said. "Besides, I'd much rather spend my day in the company of a pretty lady than in front of a computer."

He laughed when she rolled her eyes and called him a chauvinist before she allowed him to take her arm and lead her to his truck.

CHAPTER FOURTEEN

Pam met Taylor the minute she and Alex walked into the Intensive Care lobby.

"The doctor is with him now. They wouldn't let me in."

"They'll let me in," Taylor insisted, and walked through the closed doors of ICU. The nurse glanced up, saw the determined jut to her chin, and waved her on.

Taylor knocked softly on the closed door to her brother's room, entering before anyone could reply. Dr. Fontenot glanced over his shoulder then went back to his examination. She mustered up every ounce of patience she could and waited until he finished checking Trevor's eyes and throat and wound before she asked, "How's he doing?"

The doctor slid the penlight into his pocket. "As well as can be expected. His progress is good considering the fever he had. Blood tests show no sign of infection, but since he ran such a high temperature last night, we're going to keep him on antibiotics for at least twenty-four hours. From the way the bullet entered his body, there's been some damage to the muscles and tendons in his back and shoulder. He'll need physical therapy. I'd like to start him on a mild anti-depressant, but he doesn't want it."

"You want to put me on drugs when you don't know anything about me," Trevor muttered. "I'm not depressed."

"I know this much, people don't usually attempt suicide unless there's something wrong somewhere," Dr. Fontenot replied.

Trevor snorted.

"Hush up, Trevor," Taylor insisted before he could utter another word. "What kind of anti-depressant?" she asked the doctor.

"One that's mild and non-habitual to keep him calm and help him rest while he heals."

She took her brother's hand in hers. "Maybe it's not such a bad idea, Trev," she said. Her tone reflected her concern.

"I'm not depressed, Taylor," he reiterated. "I messed up, big time. I know that," he muttered. Tears rushed to fill his eyes. He blinked them back with determination. "I'm not depressed. Stupid, yes, I can't believe how stupid I've been, but I'm not depressed. I don't want to get on a bunch of drugs."

"He said they're mild and non-addictive . . ." her voice trailed off when he shook his head. She turned back to the doctor with a resigned sigh. "Can we wait a few days and see how he feels when he gets out of ICU, out of the hospital? Then if he has trouble with sleep or rest, we'll get a prescription."

The doctor nodded.

"How soon will he be moved into a private room?"

"If he continues to progress well today, we'll move him this evening or tomorrow morning."

"Good," she said. "I think he'll rest better when he's in a regular room and someone can stay with him. I know I will."

"I'll rest better when I can get out of here and get back to work," Trevor grunted.

Taylor lifted his hand to her cheek. "Well, you'd better get used to chilling for a bit because you're going to take care of that wound if I have to make Steve or Alex hog-tie you to the bed," she threatened. "And I'll tell you another thing, little brother, if I think you need those pills, you're going to take them even if I have to shove them down your throat. It's my turn to take care of you. Understand?"

Trevor glared up at her. He nodded, bit back a smile, and forced a frown. But Taylor saw the love and laughter in his eyes.

"Good," she sighed, turned back to the doctor, offered her hand, and thanked him.

Dr. Fontenot chuckled at their exchange. He took her hand in his, shook it then motioned with his head and eyes for her to follow him out of the room.

Taylor nodded that she understood and then turned to her brother. "I'll be back in a minute, Trev."

"Going to talk about me behind my back?" Trevor mumbled.

Dr. Fontenot paused at the door when he heard Trevor's comment, stuck his head back in. "Yep," he admitted.

This time Taylor did glare at her brother. "You sound like a surly six-year-old, Trevor, instead of a grown man," she chided, and turned on her heel to follow the doctor.

Dr. Fontenot's grip was gentle when he took her by the arm and led her into the hallway just outside of the ICU doors. He gazed at her for a long moment, and she could see the concern in his eyes.

"I'm sure you know the reasons for his actions?" he queried.

A flush of embarrassment rushed to her cheeks, emotions filled her soul—fear, pain, shame. Taylor nodded. Kindness filled his gaze. He offered a tentative smile.

"I've been in practice for a long time and seen a lot of crazy situations but never felt such a deep, emotional pull for a patient as I do with you two. Most attempted suicides I've witnessed are usually drug or alcohol induced or related to some mental illness. It makes me sad and curious as to what happened to drive Trevor, an obviously bright, intelligent young man, to such actions. In fact, under normal circumstances, he'd be moved from ICU straight to the psychiatric ward, but I don't feel that is necessary. However, you will both need to meet with the staff psychologist before I allow him to be put in a private room."

When she didn't comment, he continued. "I won't pry into your lives, but I will ask if there is anything I can do for you. Give you something to help you rest, recommend a private psychiatrist for you and your brother?"

Taylor shook her head. "No, thank you. Like I said, I'll be better when I know he's out of Intensive Care and someone can stay with him. As for the other, I'll counsel with my pastor. Hopefully Trevor will now as well."

"Well, it's obvious he needs something. If you change your mind, just give me a call. I'll leave an order in his file for that prescription if you need it."

Taylor sighed at the reprieve when he didn't question her further or delve too deeply into their personal life. Once again she shook his hand and thanked him, then went back in to see Trevor.

"Can I get you anything?" she asked, and brushed her fingers through his hair.

"My throat hurts," he mumbled.

"Don't try to talk then. Just nod. How about a cup of hot tea with lemon and honey to sooth it?"

He shook his head no.

"Water?"

Again he shook his head. "Coffee," he breathed.

"You got it," she promised and went to the nurse's lounge to get him a cup. "I talked to Steve this morning," she said after he'd taken a couple of sips. His eyes flew to hers, wide with worry and fear.

"What did you tell him?"

Taylor sat beside him on the bed and took his free hand in hers. "The truth," she said with a tender smile. "As Alex said, I glossed over the harshest parts with mild words, but he knows what happened and why. He said for you not to worry, that the job is well under control. And he'll be up to visit you once you're out of here and in a private room."

"I can't believe you told him everything," Trevor muttered and jerked his hand from her grasp. "We agreed to let it go and start over. That's why we came here."

Taylor sighed. "I know, Trev, but don't you see it's not working out the way we planned? We need to deal with it, honestly, and be healed of it before we can let it go. You don't need to worry about all this right now," she insisted and took his hand again, squeezed it. "Right now all you need to do is rest so you can get out of here."

"How can I rest when I know you've told our private business to my foreman? How many other people have you told?"

She could tell by the way he winced that every word caused him pain. Despite this, her chin jerked up at his tone. "Pam overheard our argument. Alex knows as much as Steve, though he also knows it goes a lot deeper than what I said. So, only the three people closest to us know anything at all, and Pastor Hebert."

"How can I expect to have his, or anyone's, respect after this?"

"Because he's your friend and because he loves you. We have to learn to trust people besides each other, Trevor. Who better to trust than him? Now, that's not to say we need to spread our business all over the world. Steve's promised to keep our conversation confidential, and I believe he will. Pastor Hebert wants to help us in every way possible, and you know how Pam feels about you. Do you think she'd say anything to hurt or humiliate you or us?"

"What about Alex?"

Taylor considered her words with care. "Alex has been the ultimate gentleman, Trev. He's kind and gentle and . . . I trust him. More than I ever thought I'd trust any man other than you. I trust Steve too," she admitted, and realized how true those words were the moment she spoke them aloud.

She sensed the turmoil their conversation caused him, both physical and emotional, and took his hand in hers once more. "Please Trev," she whispered, "Let's not talk anymore. I don't want to argue, and you need to stay quiet so your throat will heal."

Trevor closed his eyes but not before she saw the pain and fear in them.

"I don't want to argue either and my throat hurts too much to talk," he grumbled, and choked back a sob.

"Maybe I should ask the nurse to give you something for the pain."

Trevor knew the pain was an escape, and a weak one at that, but right now he'd agree to anything to avoid thinking about the mess he was in. The mess he'd gotten them in. He nodded.

Taylor waited with him while the nurse administered a dose of pain reliever and then stayed until he began to feel its effect. "I love you, Trevor," she whispered, and laid her head on his shoulder.

He slid his arm around her, pulled her close. "Love you, too," he murmured, and then succumbed once more to the welcome void of a drug-induced sleep.

"How is he?" Pam asked when Taylor returned to the waiting room.

Taylor smiled. "He seems to be okay, anxious to get out of here or at least into a private room, even argued with the doctor."

"He's not the only one," Pam murmured, "So, what now?"

Taylor brushed a hand down her arm in a gesture of affection. "I think I'll go back to the office for a while, unless you're ready to go home?"

Pam shook her head. "I'd like to stay."

Taylor nodded. "Okay. I'll be back in a while to relieve you," she promised then turned to Alex with a grin. "Back to the office, cabby."

Alex bowed elegantly and offered her his arm. "At your service, ma'am."

Once they arrived at the office, she insisted that he leave her alone and tend to his own business. He protested.

"I have a laptop, I can set up anywhere," Alex said.

Taylor shook her head and poked a finger in his chest. "You can go to your office. I appreciate all you've done, but I have work to do."

"I don't want to leave you alone," Alex insisted. "I'll set up in the kitchen or lobby, and I promise not to disturb you."

Taylor rolled her eyes and stood her ground. "I don't need a babysitter and whether you mean to or not, you distract me."

He took a step closer. "Is that a good thing or bad?"

She smiled. "I'm not sure yet."

He ran his hands down her arms, clasped her hands in his and raised them to his lips. "Okay, I give up. I'll go to my office, but don't you dare get mad at me if I call and check on you."

Taylor tugged their clasped hands away from his mouth, rested her cheek on them. "Deal."

Alex released her hands, cupped her face in his palms, brushed his lips across hers in a tender caress, and then left.

Taylor sat in the ICU waiting room, pads and pencils spread out around her. She sketched and scribbled notes. She'd only seen Trevor once since she returned after lunch to relieve Pam.

Pastor Hebert had come by earlier and they'd spent almost an hour in the hospital chapel for prayer and counseling. It amazed her how comfortable she felt around him and how easy he was to talk with. With his guidance and wisdom, she began to realize that, though far from complete, her emotional healing didn't hinge on Trevor's and that it was okay for her to move forward even if he didn't.

Trevor had a choice. It was not her fault, nor did she have to feel guilty, if he chose not to move forward. She also began to understand that in her attempt to help him, she'd taken on a burden she wasn't supposed to carry, closed herself off to the leadership of the Holy Spirit, and interfered in God's efforts to touch his life.

Pastor Hebert also helped her to realize that only God could truly help and heal Trevor, but she must release him into God's hands and leave him there in order for Him to do so. Taylor closed her eyes, took a deep breath, and whispered the words he taught her.

"I release him to You, Lord. Forgive my interference; heal me in my weakness. Let Your Spirit touch his heart and mind and change his life. In Jesus's name I pray. Amen."

A sense of peace and wholeness enveloped her, and she spent the next several minutes in silent meditation, thanks, and praise. Startled, she looked up when someone spoke her name.

"Can you come with me?" a nurse asked, her voice thick with concern.

"What's wrong?"

"Your brother seems to be in some sort of trouble, but we're not sure exactly what it is or what may be the cause. His heart rate is elevated, erratic, and his breathing shallow. There is no medical reason why this should occur. His skin is hot to the touch, but his temperature is normal. He seems to be caught up in a nightmare of some sort, and we think that you might be able to coax him out of it."

Taylor hurried in the room and took his hand in hers. "Trevor?" she queried in a soft voice and ran her fingers through his hair.

"Hot," he mumbled.

The nurse handed her a cool cloth. Taylor bathed his face and neck with it and continued to speak, her tone gentle.

Trevor hovered in the place between wakefulness and sleep, darkness and light, heaven and hell. He could hear his sister's voice, but he couldn't see her, couldn't find her in the darkness, and couldn't reach her in the red haze of pain and fear. He was hot, so hot. He burned with anger and shame and shook with the fear that kept him bound, unable to get to her. He felt trapped, helpless. She called to him again, but it was the sound of a little girl whimpering. He mumbled her name, assured her he was there, that he'd save and protect her. It wouldn't happen again, he promised and struggled to jerk his hands from their restraints, to break through the darkness and rescue her.

Fear tightened her chest when Taylor realized the nature of his nightmare. This nightmare had been all too real. She took his hand once more, continued to stroke his face and neck with the cool, damp cloth, and injected strength in her voice in an effort to coax him from the place of horror in his mind.

"Can't you administer something to help calm him?" she asked the nurse when he continued to fight her and the battle going on in his soul.

The nurse shook her head. "Not with his heart rate so erratic and breathing so shallow, anything we give him could be danger-ous."

Her words elicited a sense of panic. Taylor doubled her ef-forts to drag him from the past into the present. She climbed up beside him and took his face in her hands.

"Trevor, listen to me," she insisted. "It's alright. I'm here. I'm safe. We're both safe." He struggled and nearly shoved her off the bed.

Taylor asked the nurse to hold down his hands so he couldn't push her away and straddled him. She placed her forehead against his and continued to speak, her voice gentle but urgent. "It's over, Trev. It's over. I love you, and I forgive you. Please come back to me."

She sighed with relief when his struggles stopped and he began to calm. "That's it Trev, I'm right here. It's all right. Come on now, open your eyes," she urged.

She heard the nurse's relieved sigh, glanced at the machines, and watched his heart rate ease into a calm, steady beat and his breathing register closer to normal. When he tugged his hands from beneath hers, the nurse let them go.

Trevor's eyes remained closed, and he listened to the sound of his sister's voice which was calm now, not frightened or hurt. But there were tears in it. So many tears. He felt them well up in his throat and eyes, roll down his cheeks.

"Taylor?" he mumbled and drifted toward the sound when she continued to speak to him.

"That's it, Trev, c'mon, come back to me."

He heard the urgency in her voice, felt the weight of her on him. A sob escaped. He sat up, wrapped his arms around her, and pulled her close.

"I'm sorry, Tay, so very sorry. I couldn't stop it. I couldn't protect you," he muttered, and buried his face in her chest.

Taylor cradled his head against her breast and sighed in relief. She ran her fingers through his hair and then over his back and shoulders.

"It's okay," she whispered. "You did what you could. We both did what we had to, to survive. But it's all over now. I'm safe. You're safe. We're going to be all right. It's all over."

When his sobs subsided, she stretched out on the bed and continued to hold him and talk softly until he drifted off once more, this time into a peaceful sleep.

CHAPTER FIFTEEN

Taylor awoke, stiff and achy from sleeping in one position for so long, surprised that the nurses had left her there. Trevor rested quietly beside her. She took a quick glance at the monitor to gauge his vital signs. Everything looked fine. She placed her hand on his chest and felt his heart beat strong and solid against her palm. Careful not to disturb him, she eased from the bed and left the room. One thought reiterated itself in her mind: *Please, God, let it finally be over. I don't know how much more we can bear.*

Alex was in the waiting area when she got there. He set his laptop aside and rose from his chair. "Hey," he murmured. "I've been here a while. When you didn't come out, I asked the nurses and all they would tell me is he had a 'spell.' What kind of spell? How is he?"

Taylor couldn't stop the tears this time. They welled up in her eyes, rolled down her cheeks. "He had a nightmare. Actually it was more like he was trapped in a nightmare. Like he was reliving our childhood, stuck in the past. They couldn't seem to pull him out of it, so they came and got me."

She began to cry in earnest. Sobs tore through her in painful torrents. Alex pulled her in his arms, cradled her head against his chest, and stroked her hair. "It tears my heart out to see you like this," he murmured against her hair. "But cry all you want, sweetheart. Get it all out of your system."

"I hate to be weak like this when he needs me to be strong,

but I don't know how much more I can take," she wailed.

"You've fought to be strong all along, and it's time for you to let go and let someone else carry the load for a change."

She could do little else in the face of his tenderness and the strength of his embrace. Taylor wrapped her arms around his waist and soaked his shirt with her tears.

"I never realized how much control the subconscious has over the mind and body," she muttered, as the tears slowed, the emotions spent. "If they hadn't come and gotten me, I really think we might have lost him. Then he'd have been stuck in that horrible place forever," she mumbled. Fresh tears streamed down her cheeks.

"Let me take you out of here for a while," he urged.

She shook her head. "I want to call Pam and see if she'll run by the office and bring me a change of clothes."

"Taylor, you need to rest . . ." his words trailed off when she shook her head again and stepped out of his embrace.

"I won't rest until I know he's okay. I won't leave him again either," she insisted, a stubborn jut to her chin.

Alex sighed. "At least let me take you out of here for a little while, an hour or two at the most. We'll grab a bite to eat. Then I'll take you home. You can shower and change, and I'll bring you back up as soon as you're ready. That way Pam won't have to get out alone this time of night."

"I will not leave," she reiterated. "He should be moved into a private room in the morning. I can shower and change then."

Alex ground his teeth in frustration, and the muscle in his jaw throbbed.

"No point in arguing with you is there?" he asked.

She shook her head.

"And there's no sense in Pam getting out when I'm already here. Call her, tell her that you'll stay tonight, and see if she'll go to the office in the morning. I'll go by there now and get you a change of clothes then pick up some food. What are you hungry for?" He hushed her protests with his finger against her mouth. "Don't even try to tell me you're not hungry."

Taylor frowned at his authoritative tone, felt her stomach rumble, and winced when it downright growled.

Alex chuckled, brushed his lips across hers. "I'll pick up Chinese. Where's your office key?"

Taylor hesitated. The thought of his hands on her intimate apparel made her uncomfortable. A flush filled her cheeks, her eyes lowered. She cleared her throat and thought fast. "Pam can bring me a change of clothes in the morning."

Alex grinned, and laughter lit his merry hazel eyes, but he didn't tease. He pulled her close a moment, feathered his lips over her forehead, promised not to be gone too long, and vanished down the hall.

Taylor figured he'd be gone at least thirty minutes, so she called Pam and got things lined up for the next day. She then went into the bathroom, washed her face, then returned to her brother's room and found him awake, sitting up, and drinking water. He took one look at her face and put down the cup. Water couldn't wash away the evidence of her emotional outburst.

"You've been crying. What's wrong?" Trevor probed.

Taylor smiled, sent up a silent, fervent wish that for once in her life she would carry makeup in her purse, and avoided the question. "How are you feeling?"

"Better. Tired, though, like I've wrestled with the devil all afternoon. Now tell me why you've been crying."

She eyed him a moment before she spoke, not sure if she should bring up the incident or not. "You don't remember what happened?"

He shook his head.

"You had some sort of nightmare, like you were stuck in the

past. Your vital signs went haywire and the nurses couldn't pull you out of it, so they came and got me out of the waiting room. The incident upset me, but I'm fine. I don't want to discuss it, and I don't want you to worry about me," she insisted when he opened his mouth to do just that. "Is your throat still sore?"

He nodded.

She placed her hand against it and prayed for a quick recovery. "Now, I don't want you to utter another word until it feels better. Understand?" Again he nodded.

Taylor snuggled her face against his shoulder. "I love you, Trev," she whispered. Since she forbade him to speak, Trevor wrapped his arm around her and hugged her close.

Taylor knew how concerned he must be, so she filled him in on her thoughts for the office for the next few days. "Sound okay to you?"

He nodded, smiled.

"Do you feel up to a male visitor?" His eyebrow arched in interest. "Alex has gone to pick up Chinese food for me to eat. The man has gotten on my last nerve. I thought maybe I could send him in here to bother you a bit."

She knew the tone of her voice belied the severity of her words when Trevor grinned and shook his head no.

"Please, Trev," she pleaded, and then added a very noticeable whine to her voice. "Just long enough for me to eat in peace."

Trevor relented with a tiny smile and nod, but she saw the shame and fear in his eyes.

"It's okay, Trev," she promised. "He's really sweet, and he honestly cares. We have to open up and trust people. It's the only way we'll ever be able to live normal lives. Just a few for now, him, Pam, Steve, and Pastor Hebert. The rest will come in time. But I don't want you to worry over any of that tonight. I want you out of here and in a private room tomorrow. The only way that will happen is if you rest, deal?"

Trevor rolled his eyes at her insistent tone. "Yes, ma'am," he muttered.

"Don't talk," she added and placed her finger on his lips. "Alex's probably back by now, I'll send him in." Trevor grabbed her hand before she could pull away and lifted it to his cheek.

Taylor heard the whispers of his heart. She smiled and stroked his jaw. "I love you too, Trev. Everything will be fine," she promised.

She went to the waiting area and found Alex had indeed returned. He handed her a bag from her favorite Chinese restaurant. She smiled. "Thank you. Trevor's awake if you want to see him. Just don't let him talk too much. His throat's still sore from the episode with the breathing tube."

Alex knew he'd been dismissed. He grinned, brushed his lips over her cheek, turned on his heel, and went to see Trevor. He knocked lightly on the open door then entered. "Hey guy, how's it going?" he asked, and then held up a hand to ward off Trevor's answer.

"I've been ordered not to let you talk so just smile or nod or blink," he said with a smile that broke the icy tension in the air. Trevor grinned.

"Bossy little chit you have for a sister, stubborn too. Don't laugh," he insisted when Trevor chuckled. "That's probably too close to talking, and Taylor will have my hide."

Trevor laughed. "Had I tried to warn you, would you have listened?"

Alex chortled, shrugged. "Probably not, glad to see you're better." Trevor swallowed hard and blinked back the tears that rushed to his eyes.

"I'm so sorry."

Alex wanted to ease Trevor's embarrassment, so he patted his knee. "Don't even go there, Trevor. Don't fret over it. We all lose it from time to time. I'm just glad I was there to help."

Trevor swallowed convulsively and avoided his gaze.

"Can I get you some water?" Alex offered.

Trevor nodded. "Thanks."

Alex filled the cup and handed it to him. They sat in awkward silence for several moments as Trevor concentrated on the water. He smiled when Trevor put the cup back on the bedside table. "I'll let you get some rest now, but I'll see you again soon," he assured.

Trevor nodded. Words couldn't express the depth of emotions in his topaz gaze. A bond of some sort passed between them, connected their hearts and lives. Alex winked, grinned. "I won't tell her you talked, if you don't tell her that I let you," he promised.

Trevor smiled back and held out his hand. Alex shook it and then left Trevor to himself. He arrived in the waiting area moments after Taylor had finished her meal.

"How is he?" she asked and got up to throw her trash away.

"Good."

She walked back to where he stood. "You didn't let him talk too much, did you?"

Alex pulled her into his arms with a soft laugh. "I don't ever want to hear you complain that he worries too much or that he's overprotective. You're just as bad," he teased, then tapped her nose with his finger. "I'm sure the man knows when he's talked enough. But just to ease your mind, no, I didn't let him say too much."

Taylor seemed to welcome the comfort of his embrace. A thrill rushed through him when she rested her head against his heart.

"I'm so afraid," she whispered.

"Of what?"

"That something else will go wrong and I'll lose him. We've been through so much and he's so much a part of me that I

160

don't know if I could survive without him."

"He's doing really well." Alex assured her. "Don't borrow any more trouble than you already have."

"I know, physically he's doing all right. But what if he still won't get any help? What if I can't talk him into it this time either? I can't bear the thought of him so lost in the nightmare of our past forever, and yet, I can't seem to move forward without him. Pastor Hebert says that it is okay for me to move on and that I shouldn't feel guilty about it, but I just can't seem to help myself. Nor can I seem to get anywhere."

Alex pulled her down on the couch beside him and chose his words with care. "Life goes on, Taylor, no matter what happens. It's up to us to go on with it. I believe Trevor knows that he needs help. I don't think Pam will rest until he's gotten it either. Between the two of you, the poor guy doesn't stand a chance," he added with a grin, then cupped her cheeks in his hands. "Whatever the case, you don't have to bear the burden alone anymore."

Taylor gazed into his eyes for a long moment. Alex knew his heart and the emotions in it were reflected there and that she heard what he hadn't said aloud when she placed her hand against his cheek.

"Thank you," she whispered.

A soft groan escaped him. He pulled her closer, rested his forehead against hers. "I want to kiss you so much," he admitted in a husky voice. "But this is not the place for the kind of kiss I want."

He felt her tremble at the intimate admission. She looked at him, her eyes a kaleidoscope of emotions—a hint of wonder, sparkle of fear, glint of shame. He wished they were someplace private where he could show her the tender side of love, especially when she brushed her lips lightly across his and whispered, "I want that too." Heat rushed to her cheeks.

It took every ounce of self-control he possessed for Alex to keep himself from ignoring propriety and ravishing that lovely mouth of hers. Instead, he settled for the taste of her skin. He pressed his lips against her forehead, cheeks and finally, brushed them across hers. He pulled her close, cuddled her to his side and sat with her for a while. When she got up to go check on Trevor, he picked up her sketchpad, surprised to find that his face graced several pages.

She'd deleted his mustache in one, shaded in a beard in another and colored his eyes in each—a surprisingly accurate combination of light brown and green. Whether with a quirk of lips or brow, a full grin, or just laughing eyes, he smiled in each one.

There were prayers, poems, and notes of changes to be made scribbled in the margins of the many sketches of his house and grounds. He continued to flip through the book amazed at the depth of talent she possessed, only to be shaken by the final few sketches. Pictures of violence and abuse filled the pages.

In one a little girl cowered in the corner of a bed clutching a torn and tattered nightgown to her bruised and battered body. Her eyes were wide with terror, face streaked with tears. A monster towered over her. Another contained images of a young boy wrestling with the monster, and in yet another both children clung together, obviously terrorized by the being. But the final two shocked him the most.

The boy, no longer little but a young man, naked and bleeding and obviously bearing the scars of numerous beatings stood over the monster with a gun. The girl, now a young woman, also naked and bleeding clung to his side. More than physical damage was evident in the portrait, the spiritual implication was clear—shame and fear evident in the faces, tears streamed from the eyes, broken hearts dripped blood down the exposed breasts of the children.

The last was a continuation of the other with vivid scenes of a fierce battle going on around them. The air teemed with angelic creatures that warred with demonic ones. Angels surrounded the children and covered their nakedness with wings. In the final scene all of the demonic creatures were gone as was the monster. The children stood clothed in white, surrounded by heavenly beings, healed and whole and full of light. In the margin were the words, *for we war not with flesh and blood but with powers and principalities of darkness.*

Alex put the sketchpad down. His heart ached, his stomach lurched, and his mind was reduced to a jumbled mass of emotions. If the sketches were any indication of what the twins had suffered, he understood completely why Trevor finally snapped. He also understood the hope portrayed in that final scene. Hope that, by the grace of God, they would be healed and made whole.

Alex buried his face in hands that shook and prayed, really prayed for the first time in his life. He asked God to grant her that one wish and that he would be of service to Him in fulfilling her hope. For in that instance he knew he loved Taylor as he'd never loved before and would never love again.

He flipped back to the pictures she'd drawn of him. She'd certainly flattered him, he thought. Hope hammered a tattoo in his heart that she might feel for him as he did her. He stood when she walked back in the waiting room and held out the sketchpad.

"Is this how you see me?" he asked, his voice thick with emotion. Taylor's eyes searched his, and he knew she could tell he'd looked further in the sketchpad than the pages now exposed. Her gaze lowered, cheeks heated, and hands trembled when she reached for the book and clutched it to her chest.

"You do occupy my mind quite a bit," she admitted in a soft, hesitant voice.

Alex lifted her chin with his finger and waited until she raised a wary gaze to his. Shame darkened the beautiful topaz eyes. Fear lurked deep within the shadowy depths. He brushed a thumb over her lips, resisted the urge to take her in his arms, bit back the words *I love you,* afraid it was too soon for such a declaration, that he may frighten or scare her off.

He gazed at her for long, tender moments, and then pulled her gently against his chest. He pressed her face to his heart and stroked her hair.

"And you certainly occupy mine, sweetheart," he whispered, his voice filled with awe and wonder and a host of other feelings he dare not put a name to yet. "You certainly occupy mine."

CHAPTER SIXTEEN

Taylor stood by while the nurses prepared to move Trevor into a private room. After he read about the nightmare episode in Trevor's chart, the doctor reiterated his advice to put Trevor on a mild anti-depressant. Again, Trevor refused. They met with the hospital psychiatrist alone and together, and he agreed with the doctor that Trevor did not need to be in the psychiatric ward but advised him to seek some kind of help to deal with the emotional distress he felt instead of burying the feelings in hopes to forget. He too suggested an anti-depressant, but Trevor resisted the idea.

Taylor didn't argue. Drugs were not what her brother needed to be healed. Faith is what he needed, and the healing balm of Gilead. Oh, how she prayed he would be open to Him now.

She picked up the bag of clothes and personal items Pam brought by for her earlier and followed them out of ICU and into a room. Once they were settled, she called Pam to give her the room number then took a shower.

"I'll be glad when I can get one of those," Trevor muttered when she walked out of the bathroom.

Taylor understood completely how he felt and smiled. "You will. The nurse said someone would be in to help you get one a little later this morning."

"Why don't you go home?" Trevor asked, while she towel-dried her hair.

"I'm not about to leave until I know you're settled and okay," she replied.

"I am settled and okay. You need to rest."

She sat on the chair, which folded out to a cot and began to comb the tangles out of her thick, honey-colored locks. "This is comfortable enough. I'll rest when you do. And don't dare argue with me," she declared when he opened his mouth to do just that. "I'm not leaving until you do."

"What about the office?"

"Pam can handle things over there."

"It's not her place," Trevor snorted and glared at her. "One of us needs to be there. And suppose I want to see Pam and spend some time with her?"

"She'll be by later with some lunch, then again after five. If things are slow and the crew doesn't need anything, she can close the office and come here."

"Then will you go home?"

Taylor bit back a smile when he continued to glare at her. "I might, if she can stay a while."

Trevor ground his teeth.

"You make me crazy, Taylor Marie."

She giggled, placed the comb in her purse, then stood up to snuggle her head against his shoulder. "I love you, too, Trev. You'd be the same way if our roles were reversed, and you know it. So stop fussing at me."

Unable to argue with her point, Trevor surrendered with a grunt, then wrapped his arm around her and pulled her close.

"I love you, Tay," he whispered.

"Sounds like your throat is better," she remarked.

"Doesn't hurt much at all anymore."

"Amazing what a little prayer can do," she commented.

"Don't start on that," he mumbled.

"Why do you doubt so much? Why are you so determined to

stay angry with God? What happened to us is not His fault."

"He didn't stop it though, did He? Tell me why He didn't stop it."

"I can't answer that, Trev. I wish I could. I've prayed and prayed to understand, but that's one question that may never be answered. The only thing I can figure is that He gave man free will and He cannot, or will not, impose His will on ours."

"So how can you trust Him?"

"Because I believe He is the only answer, the only way for us to get over our past and move on with our lives."

"Why couldn't He have done something to make it stop? He could have done something, anything, taken away the lust and perversion."

"He did Trev, physically at least. But look what happened then," Taylor replied. Trevor's cheeks darkened with anger. Shame and wrath sparkled to life in his eyes.

"That's what I hate the most. I should have let him beat me into a pulp before allowing him to force me to hurt you that way."

"You never hurt me," she said, and laid her hand against his cheek. "I don't blame you, Trevor, for any of it. We were just kids."

"Still," he began.

His words trailed off when she placed her finger against his lips. "Still, nothing, it's over, in the past, and it needs to stay there. The shame and guilt are too much to bear, and I want you to stop it. It's over. I don't blame you. I forgive you. Not that you were the one that needed forgiveness for the evilness of another," she added quickly. "But if it'll ease your mind, I forgive you. It's time to let it go. Pastor Hebert will help us, Trev. But you have to be willing to believe that God can and will heal us."

"It's not that easy," he argued. "It can't be that easy."

"I believe it can," she countered. "Look how far we've come already. We're both remarkably intact despite all we've suffered. We have a successful business and what could be wonderful, life-long relationships with people we've come to know and care about. There's a whole world of love and understanding and acceptance out there. We just have to open ourselves up to it."

She took a deep breath and continued before he could interrupt. "The Bible promises that what the devil means for harm, God can, and will, turn around for good and that we'll get a double recompense for our sufferings if we trust Him enough. I know it won't be easy and it won't happen overnight, but I believe we can have normal, healthy lives in spite of our past. I want that, Trevor. I want that more than anything else in the world. You said you wanted it too. I firmly believe this is the only way it's going to happen."

"I'm so afraid to dig up all that trash again," he whispered. "But neither can I seem to get past it. When I think about Pam and how much I care about her, I feel so . . ."

He trailed off and Taylor knew he searched his mind for the right words to describe the shame and guilt he carried in his heart.

"Dirty," he said for lack of a better word.

"I know, Trev, I feel the same way sometimes," she admitted, and took his hand in hers.

"But those feelings lessen the closer I get to God. I believe it's time for both of us to let it go completely. We're never really going to be able to get over it and move on with our lives if we don't deal with it once and for all and get rid of it for good. It's time to dig it up, all of it, empty our hearts and minds of everything evil and let God heal our souls." She hoped the passion in her heart was reflected in her voice and eyes as, perhaps for the first time, he listened in earnest to what she said. What she'd said for years.

"You really believe all that, don't you?"

"Yes, Trevor, I really believe. Almost from the first moment I let Him in my heart," she admitted, her voice filled with wonder and awe. "The Bible says that when we come to Jesus and let Him in our hearts that His blood washes us as clean as snow and that God removes our transgressions as far from us as the east is from the west. Believe me when I tell you that it's a wonderful feeling. It's so liberating, so freeing, so peaceful. It's a refreshing, cleansing feeling . . . like walking in the rain and then standing in the sun with rainbows all around you.

"I don't really know how else to explain it other than saying that there's a blessed relief that's almost overwhelming in its warmth and goodness, a peace and wholeness that comes with continued prayer, praise and thanksgiving."

She hesitated, unable to put any more words to the emotions in her heart.

"Sometimes I wish I could just bottle up what I feel inside and pour it into you so that you could feel it too, so that you could understand and believe for yourself. I want that for you, Trevor. God wants that for you. He loves you, Trev, enough to die for you."

She raised his hand to her cheek. "I love you that much too, but as much as I'd like to, this is the one thing I can't do for you. And I can't seem to get any further without you. Pastor Hebert said that my healing isn't directly linked to yours, but he doesn't understand. No one understands how close we really are. I can't go on unless I know you'll be all right too. Promise me that you'll at least consider talking with Pastor Hebert."

He cupped her cheek in his hand. "Okay, Taylor. I'll consider it. But," he paused. An idea came to him, grew. "I'll consider it if . . ."

His eyes lit with gentle humor. A smile tugged at his lips. Taylor knew she'd been had. She waited, knowing she'd give anything, do anything, if he'd agree to talk with Pastor Hebert. He knew it too and grinned.

"If you promise you'll go home."

She laughed. "I promise I'll go home after we've set an appointment with Pastor Hebert and if, and only if, you let someone else stay with you," she countered. "And that's the only counteroffer you'll get out of me. Otherwise, I'll not leave whether you agree to talk to the Pastor or not."

Trevor rolled his eyes with a grunt. "You are one stubborn female," he complained. "Poor Alex doesn't know what he's up against."

Alex, who happened to walk in at that moment, overheard Trevor's remark and chuckled. "Poor Alex is always up for a challenge," he remarked with a grin when the twins looked at him, obviously surprised at his entrance.

"How long have you been there?" Trevor asked.

"Not long. I knocked but guess you didn't hear." Both shook their head. "You look good, Trev. Sound good too. Guess your throat is better?"

Trevor nodded. "A bit."

"Great. So, how long are you gonna be in here?" he asked, then walked around the bed to stand beside Taylor when Trevor shrugged. Alex stroked a hand down her arm.

"And how are you this morning?" he asked but didn't miss the way Trevor's eyes narrowed when she flushed prettily, smiled up at him, and answered that she was fine.

"Know what, Tay? I sure could use a cup of coffee," Trevor said.

Taylor rolled her eyes at Alex, smiled at the pout in her brother's voice, and inserted just a tad of southern drawl to her tone when she answered, "I'll fetch you one right away."

Trevor grinned. "Thanks."

"Would you like one too?" she asked Alex, after he laughed at the two of them.

"Sure." Though he stepped back so she could pass, the limited space still didn't allow much room. Her body brushed his just lightly enough to send lightning sparks of desire through his entire body. Alex shoved his hands in his pockets to keep from reaching for her. His eyes followed her every move. Trevor cleared his throat and arched an eyebrow at him when Alex's gaze returned to his.

"I like you, Alex, and I'm indebted to you so I won't threaten to beat you within an inch of your life for the way you look at her. But I will warn you to tread with care."

Alex heard the thread of steel in his voice, knew exactly what Trevor meant, and nodded. "Warning heeded, though absolutely unnecessary," he said in quiet assurance.

"She's been hurt in ways you can't even imagine. I won't stand by and let her be hurt again."

Alex acknowledged the words with a slight nod. "Then maybe you should consider the way you're hurting her," he observed, his tone quiet, undertone serious.

Trevor flushed. Anger sparked to life in his brilliant topaz gaze.

"What do you mean?"

Alex kept his voice soft, with no trace of anger or threat. "You've got her on a leash so short she's about to suffocate. I know you worry over her, Trevor and from what I can gather you have every right to do so. But the past is over, done with. You've got to give her room to breathe," he chided, his tone gentle but firm.

He waited a beat then continued. "I promise you this much though, I will never physically hurt her. She's strong-willed and we're bound to butt heads from time to time, but I will never lay a hand on her in anger or in any way meant to hurt. You've got my word on that."

They eyed each other for a long, tense moment. Trevor saw the depth of emotions in Alex's eyes and allowed himself a moment of sadness followed by joy. He wouldn't be the only man in her life anymore, he thought with a touch of bittersweet emotions, and then nodded his approval in silent consent when his sister walked in with their coffee. Alex's smile was quick and rich. His eyes spoke volumes. With a wink he turned his attention to Taylor when she handed out cups.

"So, what's on the agenda for today?" he asked her.

"I'd like for her to go home," Trevor grunted before she could answer.

Alex chuckled. "Good luck with that request."

Before either of them could respond, a knock sounded on the door and Pam walked in with Steve close on her heels.

"Isn't anyone working today?" Trevor asked. Pam giggled and brushed her lips across his cheek.

Steve laughed. "Yep, just took a break to come by and see how you are."

"I'm doing fine," Trevor remarked. "Would be a lot better if I knew my business wasn't left unattended."

Steve chuckled. "Your business is fine. In fact, I thought maybe you'd like a break from these yahoos," his wave encompassed Pam, Alex and Taylor. "And we could discuss a few things."

Trevor heaved a huge sigh of gratitude. "Oh, yes, thank you. These two are about to drive me insane." His gesture indicated his sister and secretary. "And believe me, it's a real short trip," he admitted with a grin.

"You," he pointed to Pam. "Back to the office. You, home," he told his sister then turned an imploring gaze to Alex. "You make 'em go, please."

Alex laughed, nodded, and threw his coffee cup in the trash.

"You heard the man, ladies," he said and took Taylor gently but firmly by the arm.

"Now wait just a minute," they protested in unison.

Before either could argue more, another knock sounded on the door, and Pastor Hebert strolled in. "Well, good morning everybody, how's our patient today?"

Trevor rolled his eyes. "Trying to get these women out of my hair so I can discuss business with my foreman."

Pastor Hebert bit back a chuckle, arched an eyebrow at Trevor, then winked at Alex and Steve. "Man doesn't know how good he's got it," he said with a solemn shake of his head.

"Two beautiful women hang on his arm, attentive to his every word, and cater to his every whim. He complains and tries to run them off. We do need to talk," he said, his voice tinged with mirth.

Laughter erupted throughout the room. Trevor had the grace to grin. He glanced up at his sister, saw the hope in her eyes, felt it spring to life alongside the doubt in his heart.

"See how many people love you," she whispered, and then continued aloud before he could respond. "You win. I'll go for a while."

She glanced over at Steve. "How long will you stay?"

He shrugged, "A while, we have a few things to discuss. I thought I'd hang around till after lunch sometime, then head on out to the jobsite to check on the gang."

Taylor nodded her approval. "Good. Pam?"

Pam shrugged. "Guess I'll go on back to the office for now and come back later."

She looked back at him, and Trevor could see she was still hesitant to leave even though he wouldn't be alone much at all. "Go," he insisted. "I'll be fine."

"Okay," she sighed and squeezed his hand. "I'm going," she said, but hesitated.

Her gaze sought Steve's. "You won't leave him alone, will you? You'll make sure Pam or me or someone is here before you go."

Trevor snorted when Steve nodded and breathed a sigh of relief when Alex chuckled and took her by the arm.

"C'mon, I'll take you home before I head back over to the office."

"Thank you," Trevor mouthed. "Make her rest," he said aloud.

"Make her rest," Alex muttered, a woeful expression on his face, wistful smile on his lips. "Do I look like some kind of magician to you?"

"I'm counting on you," Trevor insisted and grinned when his sister glared and made a face at him. He glanced up at Pam. "You too, go."

Pam mimicked Taylor and made a face at him also. "Yes, sir."

Her voice dripped with sugar-coated sarcasm. She hesitated and laid her hand against his cheek. "I'll see you later," she promised in a soft voice.

Trevor covered her hand with his, moved it around to his mouth, and kissed the palm. "Thanks." She brushed her lips across his then hurried out to catch up with Alex and Taylor.

Trevor closed his eyes and heaved a relieved sigh. "Finally. Those two fuss worse than a mother hen over a brood of chicks."

Steve chortled. "Talk about the pot calling the kettle black."

Pastor Hebert laughed and patted Trevor on the knee. "I won't stay since you two have business to discuss. I'll drop in on you later. Glad to see you're better."

Trevor thanked him then turned his attention to Steve once the pastor left. Steve sat on the chair, propped one foot over his knee and regarded him with laughing eyes.

"It's about time you opened up to that one," he remarked. "She's been in love with you since day one."

Trevor frowned. "I thought we were going to discuss business, not my personal life."

"We could discuss both."

Trevor heard the edge of hurt in his voice, felt a sharp stab of guilt prick his conscious. "You have been a good employee and friend, Steve, and I appreciate you more than words can express," he admitted, his voice soft and sincere. "I'm just not sure how to show it."

Steve shrugged. "You can start by confiding in me. That's what friends do. I don't expect you to tell me all of your deep, dark secrets or childhood woes. But there is no sense in allowing things to build up inside you so much that you snap the way you did."

Trevor nodded. "I'm not used to having anyone to rely on but myself or Taylor," he admitted. "But I'll remember that from now on." Steve nodded and Trevor could tell he, too, was glad they'd gotten that out in the open.

"Good. The gang sends their love and said to tell you that all is under control and to hurry back."

Trevor sighed, grateful he hadn't pried and relieved the conversation finally turned to business.

CHAPTER SEVENTEEN

Taylor pushed away from her desk with a sigh of frustration, unable to concentrate. Her body was tired, heart heavy, eyes gritty, and mind a wreck of emotions. What frustrated her the most was she couldn't pinpoint a reason for the unrest. She walked over to the window, gazed out, and thought of all that had happened.

In the two weeks since the doctor had released Trevor from the hospital, life had pretty much gone back to normal. She'd replaced the hanging lamp, and Steve had repaired the windowsill in Trevor's office. The area where his blood once stained the carpet cleaned up without a trace.

His physical healing seemed remarkable, the damage to the muscles in his back and shoulder miniscule. Though he tired more easily than before, he returned to work with fervor and renewed vision. Other than the fact they argued daily because she wanted him to be more careful and take things slowly and because he wanted to go to his own home but she wanted him to stay with her, things seemed to be fine.

They had talked with Pastor Hebert only a handful of times, twice before Trevor was released from the hospital and three times since. Today he'd agreed to meet with the pastor alone, and it suddenly dawned on Taylor why she was so uneasy. The talks with Pastor Hebert were a wonderful help to her, but Trevor had remained quiet during the sessions. She sensed he wavered between hope and doubt, desperately wanting to believe, just as desperately afraid to. Though she continued to attend morning meditation as well as Sunday and Wednesday services, Trevor hadn't.

Oh, God, please let today be the day.

Before she could cross the office to her prayer closet, a knock sounded on the door and Pam entered.

"How are you?" she asked, a slight quiver in her voice.

Taylor sighed. "Worried, afraid, hopeful, excited, concerned." Pam's smile was tender.

"Me too," Pam said. "We haven't had the time to really talk since the accident. You want to now?"

Taylor shrugged. "I don't know what to say, Pam. I'm sorry you had to find out what you did the way you did, but I don't know what else there is to say."

Pam smiled again, took her by the hand, and sat with her on the loveseat.

"I don't need all the gory details, Tay," she assured her. "I just want you to know that I'm here if you ever need or want to talk."

Taylor nodded. "Thanks, Pam. Has Trevor opened up to you any at all?"

It was Pam's turn to sigh. "Not really. He seems very hesitant, afraid, bitter even. I don't push or pry, thinking that if he knows I'm here for him, he'll open up in time. Like I said, I don't need the details. I just want him to know that he can trust me and that I'll always love him no matter what," she said and blinked away tears that rushed to her eyes.

Taylor hugged her. "Just stay patient, Pammy. He loves you too, but it's all mixed up with pain and shame and guilt. Maybe he'll open up to Pastor Hebert today and the healing can begin."

"I sure hope so," Pam breathed.

"Me too," Taylor agreed.

★ ★ ★ ★ ★

Trevor sat in his truck for a long time. His heart pounded, palms sweated. He took a deep breath, closed his eyes, and wondered why he agreed to this.

His sister was driving him crazy, that's why.

Oh, she was clever about it, not pushy or aggressive. But the quiet joy and silent hope in her eyes made him want to believe that all he'd been told was real. That he could purge himself, or rather God could purge him, of the pain and fear of his past. That he could be healed and whole and someday love without shame or guilt.

Still, he was afraid, afraid to hope, afraid to believe, afraid to dig up the trash of his childhood and lay it all out for a complete stranger.

He climbed out of his truck, thought about the previous meetings with Pastor Hebert and how the man had always been gentle and non-intrusive. He hoped the pastor would be the same today.

Dan had something else in mind altogether. He lit a single candle on the table in the sanctuary and added what he considered the final touch to the environment he wanted to create. In previous sessions with the twins, they'd met in his office. He'd wanted Trevor to feel comfortable, not pressured by atmospheric conditions. Though he acknowledged Dan's extensive education and training, Trevor had remained tense and quiet during the meetings. Dan hoped today would be different, which was why he'd suggested they meet in the sanctuary.

Sunlight streamed in through the skylight as well as the stained-glass windows, creating rainbows throughout the room. Music played softly on the sound system. He'd chosen a variety of quiet worship songs that reflected the awesome power of

God to heal, and he hoped the reverent words would somehow speak to Trevor's spirit even as they talked. He stood before the cross in silent meditation.

The door opened, he turned, and saw Trevor walk through. Dan stepped off the platform and walked to meet him, hand outstretched. "Hi Trevor, how's it going?"

Trevor shook his hand and shrugged. "Okay I guess."

"No sling today?"

Trevor shook his head. "No. Dr. Forrestier said I could go without it," he said, frustration evident in his tone. "My sister is about to drive me nuts."

Dan chuckled.

Trevor blew out a frustrated breath then smiled. "I know, I know, turnabout's fair play."

Dan agreed. "Why don't we have a seat," he suggested and led the way to the front of the church where two chairs were set up, facing each other. He gestured for Trevor to take his pick. Once they were seated, he said a quick prayer and asked for God's guidance and blessing on the meeting.

"How about we do things a little different than before?" he asked.

Trevor shrugged.

Dan nodded. "Ever play twenty questions with your sister?" he asked, hoping this was the right tactic to take.

Trevor shook his head. "No. Never heard of it."

Dan smiled. "Well, it's a game some people like to play when they're getting to know each other. I'll ask you a question. You answer then ask me one and so on. Sound okay?"

Trevor shrugged again. Dan sensed his guard go up and sent a quiet prayer for God to intervene. After a moment of silence, he began. "Is there any question you'd like to ask or comment you'd like to make?"

Trevor shook his head. "Not really," he admitted. "I just

don't see the sense in talking about all this so much."

Not much, but a start, Dan thought. He welcomed the opportunity and nodded in response to Trevor's words. "I've often wondered about that myself. Psychologists believe that when we talk things out it makes them less daunting. But I'm not sure they understand how much power words have."

Trevor frowned. "What do you mean?"

"Well, if you go back as far as Genesis and the Creation, when God spoke, things happened. Proverbs teaches us that the power of life and death are in the tongue. I'm afraid most people don't realize that, or the fact that words can hurt, even kill. We've all been taught the old adage: sticks and stones may break my bones, but words will never hurt me. But that's not the least bit true. Think about it," he urged. "Have you ever seen a child's face when his parent corrects or berates him?"

Dan knew by Trevor's expression and the quick way he winced that he'd struck a chord. He waited a beat, then continued. "Words can devastate a soul and kill a spirit. I imagine that you and Taylor both know the power of words to destroy. But do you realize that, just as they have the power to hurt, words also have the ability to heal?" he asked. He sat in quiet anticipation of Trevor's response.

Trevor hesitated. "You said I could ask questions," he began, then continued when Dan nodded. "No holds barred?"

"No holds barred," Dan promised. Trevor leaned forward in his chair, his jaw tensed, eyes blazed.

"Taylor has this lovely idea that if we surrender all this garbage to God, He will make it go away. Well, I've asked her this and she can't seem to answer so I'll ask you. Where was God when our father abused our mother or us?"

Dan considered his words with care. "Well, the Bible does say that when we're born again, we become a new creature in Christ, so she's right to hope and believe it'll go away. Maybe not completely, but it will lose its power over you. As for the other, from what I know about God, I'd have to say He wept over the fact that He'd entrusted you and Taylor to your father for safekeeping and your father not only abused you, he dishonored God and disgraced the position God placed him in as the head of his house."

"What good did it do for Him to weep? Why didn't He just put a stop to it?"

Again Dan considered his words with care. *Oh, God, what do I say to him, how do I explain that?* he wondered, and heard the reply deep in his heart.

On high I dwell and in holiness . . .

"I'm not sure I have an answer that would appease you, Trevor. I could give you all the theological reasons why He didn't just come down from heaven and stop it, but they wouldn't make any sense, just as what happened to you makes no sense. I will say this much though, God is love, and He loves people more than anything, enough to die for them. But He is also a just and holy God, and as much as He loves sinners, He hates sin. And I can assure you that, unless he repented, your father stood in judgment before God and met His wrath."

"Well, I know he didn't repent," Trevor snarled. "He didn't have time to repent."

"For that I'm sorry," Dan said. "He'll suffer throughout eternity for what he's done."

"Eternity's not long enough," Trevor insisted and pushed out of the chair with such force it nearly toppled. "I can't do this," he stated and turned on his heel.

Dan rose from his chair and started after him. "Trevor, wait."

Trevor held up his hand and shook his head to ward off any words Pastor Hebert might utter. His breath came in ragged pants, his stomach churned.

"I can't," he reiterated and escaped into the safety of his

truck. With no conscious thought or plan of action, he left the church and drove to the jobsite. Steve met him the moment he disembarked from the vehicle.

"Are you all right? You look like you've seen a ghost."

Trevor flushed and avoided his gaze. "Might as well have. You said we could talk."

Fear and confusion filled his soul, so thick, so tense so . . . tangible, he could almost feel it emanate from his very pores. Steve put a hand on his shoulder in a gesture of support.

"Anytime," he assured. "Want to take a walk or a drive?"

"Walk's fine, away from the crew."

Steve keyed his walkie-talkie. "Greg, take over for a bit, will you?"

Greg radioed back affirmative, and the two men started out in the opposite direction from where the crew worked. A tense silence accompanied them.

"Want to tell me what's on your mind?" Steve ventured.

"Do you believe in God?" Trevor asked.

Steve nodded. "Sure do."

"Okay, do you believe in some high, lofty God or a more personable one?"

"Both."

Trevor stopped in his tracks and glared at him. "What kind of answer is 'both'? Care to elaborate?"

Steve grinned. "I'd love to elaborate if I knew what you wanted to know. Care to ask a direct question or give me some clue of what you want me to elaborate on?"

Trevor sighed and raked his fingers through his hair. "I just bolted from a meeting with Pastor Hebert."

Steve's eyebrow arched in curiosity. "And?"

"And if God is so high and mighty, why didn't He just stop the abuse?"

"Did you ask the pastor that?"

Trevor nodded.

"What was his response?"

"Said he couldn't really answer that, but then he gave me some cock-and-bull story about God being a just and holy God. He said that any theological reason probably wouldn't make sense, just like what happened to me and Taylor didn't make sense."

Steve frowned. "So why are you asking me?"

Trevor blew out a frustrated breath. "Because he's a preacher, he's supposed to say those things. You're just a man. I want to know what you think, how you believe. Do you really feel that if I just let go, give up, surrender, or whatever, that God can take away my past?"

Steve remained quiet for long moments, and Trevor knew he considered his answer with care.

"I'm not the most devout or religious person you'll ever meet, Trevor. But I do believe in God, and I do believe He can heal you from the pain of your past. I'm not sure what all that might entail, but I believe that it can be done, if you want it bad enough and choose to believe it too. Can I ask you a question?"

Trevor hesitated, gnawed on his lower lip, then nodded.

"I'm not about to delve into all of your deep, dark secrets, Trev, but don't you think it's worth a shot to give God a try to possibly gain a measure of peace in your life?"

Trevor huffed out a sigh and dragged the heels of his hands over his face. "I guess."

"So, what now?" Steve asked.

Before Trevor could answer, his cell phone vibrated. He looked at the number and groaned, then pushed the button to send the call straight to his voice mail. "Now I guess I'll have to face my sister and explain what happened, then set up another appointment with Pastor Hebert."

"Sounds like a good plan," Steve assured. "Just remember,

buddy, I'm here for you, anytime."

"Thanks, Steve." The two walked back to where he parked his truck. "Do you guys need anything?"

Steve shook his head.

"Okay, I'll see you tomorrow or the next day."

"No problem," Steve assured. "Got it all under control over here, you just take care of yourself and get some rest."

"Will do," Trevor promised. He unlocked his truck, climbed in, and considered what to do next. He picked up his cell phone and felt a surge of irritation at the number of calls he'd missed, even more so when he realized they were all from the office. He lingered at a stop sign. The last thing he wanted was to go there and answer a bunch of questions from Taylor and Pam. He wanted to be alone. He punched in the office phone number, then turned his truck around and headed for his apartment.

"Is Taylor in?" he asked Pam when she answered the phone.

"Yes," Pam said her voice soft. "Are you alright?"

"I'm fine. Put her on, will you?"

Pam put the call through and within moments his sister answered.

"Hey, Trev, how are you?"

"I'm fine. I'm going home for a while," he replied.

"Okay. I'll see you this evening then. Is there anything you need? Anything I can do?"

Trevor inhaled a sharp hiss through clenched teeth. "No, Taylor. I'm a grown man. I can do for myself, and I'm going to my apartment. You've been hounding me ever since we moved to Louisiana to let go and to let you live your life. Now it's time for you to ease up on me. I'm not going to do anything stupid again."

He heard his sister's sudden intake of breath and felt a prick of guilt at his choice of words and his tone of voice. He sighed. "I'm sorry, Tay, the meeting didn't go well."

"What happened?"

"I chickened out."

"Oh."

He heard a wealth of disappointment in that one-syllable word and cringed. "I know you're disappointed in me, Taylor. Believe it or not, I'm just as disappointed in myself. I'll call Pastor Hebert and set up another appointment, but for now I just need to be alone."

"Okay," she whispered. "Will you call me later?"

He heard the quiver of fear in her voice. "Yes. And tell Pam not to worry, I'll call her later too," he said and hung up before she could reconsider or argue.

Once ensconced in his apartment, Trevor allowed his emotions to run their course. Exhausted and in pain, he took a couple of pills, stretched out on the couch, fell into an uneasy slumber, and dreamed.

He stood alone in a meadow. Two lions approached, one scraggly and unkempt, the other stately and regal. He turned as they circled in on him, closer and closer until he could almost feel their breath on his neck. One grunted, growled, and snarled. The other responded likewise. They crouched, prepared to attack, then lunged. He ducked, rolled out from beneath the tangled mass of muscle and fur, and watched them go at each other in a battle of wills. Within moments, the large, regal cat had the other pinned beneath his huge paws, his teeth clasped in the throat of his foe. He snarled, shook his head, and released the lesser animal which then pounced to his feet and ran off with his tail tucked between his legs. The big cat roared in triumph then sat, head high, and eyed Trevor.

Trevor kept a wary eye on the lion and inched backward until a tree stopped his escape. Though his eyes followed his every step, the animal never flinched. Trevor watched and waited for him to pounce, but the lion didn't so much as twitch a muscle. That's when he noticed the crown. Trevor shook his head and rubbed his eyes. Sure enough the crown remained, embedded in the animal's scalp. The crown turned to thorns. The lion's face changed into that of Christ crucified and then back into a lion's face.

Trevor rubbed his eyes again and shook his head. "Who are you? What do you want?" he felt compelled to ask.

"I am the Lion of Judah, the King of Kings, and Lord of Lords. Come, Trevor, follow me," the cat answered and turned to walk away.

Trevor awoke with a start. His heart thundered in his chest, sweat poured from every pore. He lunged from the couch, winced in pain, and paced the floor. The dream played over and over in his mind until he figured he'd gone mad. In a quick, decisive move, he fumbled with his cell phone, scrolled through the numbers, found the one he sought, and hit the call button. Concern and relief resonated in Dan Hebert's voice the minute he answered the phone.

"I hoped and prayed you'd call or come back."

"I'm sorry I ran out like I did. Do you still have time to see me?"

"Sure, come on over."

"I'll be right there," Trevor said and left the apartment before he could change his mind.

CHAPTER EIGHTEEN

Dan watched for Trevor and met him when he drove into the church parking lot and climbed out of his truck. The poor man looked as though he'd wrestled with the devil since he'd left earlier. Dan took pity on him and led the way to his office. They sat in awkward silence for several minutes then Dan spoke. "I'm glad you came back, Trevor, but I can't help you if you don't want to be helped."

Trevor raked his hands over his face. "I don't know what I want," he muttered. "No, that's not true. I want to be free from the past. I just don't know how to get free. And I don't understand why I have to hash it all out over and over. We've seen counselors, talked the situation to death, and not a damn thing got accomplished. We're still haunted. And now, on top of the usual nightmares, I'm having hallucinations in the middle of the day."

"What kind of hallucinations?"

Trevor rose from his seat to pace the floor and recounted the dream with the lions. He left no detail uncovered. "Makes no sense to me. Guess I've finally lost my mind."

Dan chuckled. "You haven't lost your mind, Trev. The Bible says in the book of Joel that in the last days, God will pour out His spirit on all flesh and that women will prophesy, old men will dream, and young men will see visions."

Trevor snorted. "So you think God appeared to me in a dream or vision?" he asked, his tone incredulous.

"He works in mysterious ways," Dan remarked. "The Bible speaks specifically about two lions. Jesus is referred to as the Lion of Judah, and First Peter, chapter five, verse eight warns us to *be sober and vigilant for our adversary, the devil, roams about like a roaring lion seeking whom he may devour.* So, you see, it is very possible that God tried to speak to you through your dream."

"Ridiculous, the whole concept is beyond me."

"Maybe it's beyond you because you're looking at the whole thing logically. Faith is a heart issue, Trevor. You have to turn off your mind and listen to your heart."

"How do I do that?"

Dan rose from his chair and placed a hand on Trevor's shoulder. "You've made a good start by coming here," he assured. "The next thing you have to do is open your heart and mind to the truth of who God is and His love for you. Do you have a Bible?"

Trevor shook his head.

Dan walked back to his desk and retrieved the Bible he planned to give to Trevor earlier. "I've marked numerous Scriptures to help you get started," he said, and handed the book to Trevor.

"Read them, say them aloud. Memorize them if you have to. Just as you believe in your heart and confess with your mouth that Jesus is Lord, begin to see and acknowledge yourself as God does. See yourself as cleansed, healed, made whole. Acknowledge that you are a new creature and the righteousness of God in Christ Jesus. Give yourself a couple of days, immerse yourself in the Word, dwell on the love of God, allow yourself to feel and experience that love, and then come see me again."

Dan saw the skepticism on his face and sighed. "The choice is yours, Trev. You said you wanted to be free of your past and that nothing else has worked. You can take a chance this will be the one thing to work, or you can continue to live as you are now and hope that one day you'll have victory."

Trevor thumbed through the Bible and saw the different colors highlighting various sections, then looked up to meet Dan's eyes. "Okay, I'll give it a shot."

"Good," Dan replied.

"I'll see you in a couple of days." Trevor left the church and, on the way back to his apartment, called his sister and Pam, then stopped for a bite to eat. When he arrived home, he opened the Bible and read the scriptures Dan had highlighted. He fell into an exhausted slumber, the Bible still open on his lap.

Dan paced the sanctuary, fidgeted with candles, picked up prayer and song books and returned them to their proper places. To use the term "worry" for his unrest would be an understatement. He had spent an hour with Taylor after meditation earlier that day, but he'd not heard from Trevor since they'd met three days ago. Other than a couple of phone calls a day, Taylor hadn't heard from him either. Her worry caused doubt to plague his mind. Fear of failure ruled his heart. As usual the foot of the cross drew him in and he found a measure of peace. He'd been on his knees mere moments when the door burst open. No quiet, reverent entrance, but a loud, obnoxious arrival. He rose, turned. Trevor's blazing eyes and tense jaw assured him the battle had begun. A battle he intended to win. Trevor tossed the Bible at his feet.

"I thought God's love was great, infinite, and unconditional."

"It is," Dan assured.

"Bull! It's all conditional. Be angry and sin not. Don't let the sun go down on your wrath. That's impossible."

Dan could tell by the myriad of emotions in Trevor's eyes that he'd probably never realized how much anger he harbored until he read those scriptures, nor had he ever felt convinced that his emotions were wrong or unjust. He met that anger head on, acknowledged it with a slight nod. "Nothing is impossible. May I ask you a question?"

Trevor nodded, his eyes wary. Resentment radiated from him.

Oh, God, give me the words to reach him.

Speak the Truth in love came the answer.

Dan took a deep breath, sent up another silent prayer that this would be the right tactic, and then went straight to the heart of the matter. "I know you're angry . . ."

His words were cut off by Trevor's violent snort.

"Angry? You think what I feel is as simple as anger? Think again."

Dan conceded with a nod. "Oh, I'm sure what you feel is much more than anger. I've no doubt that bitterness, resentment, and rage are uppermost in your heart too, Trevor, and I do understand why. But let me ask you this, who is affected by your emotions, who do they hurt?"

When Trevor didn't answer, he continued. "Is it your father?"

Trevor hesitated then shook his head.

"Then, who?"

Dan sensed the struggle within Trevor's heart and knew in his own that Trevor had to not only face the truth of his actions; he had to get it out in the open. He had to admit it. "Take a guess," he insisted, his voice gentle.

Trevor shook his head and backed away, but Dan saw the light of revelation dawn in the brilliant topaz gaze. Dan remained silent and fought the urge to go after him when the younger man swallowed convulsively, dragged a shaky hand over his face, turned on his heel, and fled.

Sometimes the truth comes with its own share of pain and anger.

He knew the battle would rage in Trevor's heart until he saw the need to repent for his part in keeping the past alive through his emotions.

Trevor fumbled with the key to unlock his truck then climbed in mere seconds before his legs collapsed. His chest was so tight even the slightest breath seemed to stab through his lungs. His eyes stung, his head swirled. He swallowed hard to dislodge the knot of bile in his throat. His mind cried out in denial of what he knew in his heart to be the truth. His anger and bitterness had and would continue to hurt and possibly destroy his sister. The sister he loved more than life. *Oh, God, that can't be!* But it was. Trevor knew from the depths of his soul that his emotions caused his sister a deeper pain than the abuse they had suffered could now that she was saved. The revelation blinded in its brilliance. He put his head down on the steering wheel and let the tears come.

His cell phone rang. Trevor forced a measure of calm into his voice and answered. Steve's voice sounded over the line.

"Hey, Boss, you headed this way today?"

Trevor jumped at the opportunity to focus his mind on other things. "Sure, whatcha need?" He grabbed a pad and pencil when Steve rattled off a list of materials they needed to finish out the day. Glad for the reprieve from his tortured thoughts, he hung up with Steve then called the office.

"Hey, sweetie," he said, inserting a note of cheer into his voice when Pam answered the phone, though it sounded false even to his ears.

"Hi, how are you?" she asked.

He hated that question, despised the way she and Taylor skirted the issue of his meetings with Pastor Hebert. He knew they ached to question him but didn't dare since he told them three days ago the subject was off limits. He wondered for a brief moment what either would say if they knew he was about to lose his ever-loving mind, but he bit back the retort.

"I'm okay. Where's Taylor?" he said.

"She's not in. Called a little while ago and said she would be in later. Didn't say why or where she was headed, but she sounds good, relaxed, even happy."

Trevor felt a twinge of envy that his sister could be happy when he struggled for the slightest bit of peace. Guilt followed. With deliberate intention, he shut off his whirlwind of thoughts. "Well, I'm headed over to the lumber yard to pick up a few things for the guys then out to the jobsite. Holler if you need anything."

"I only need one thing," Pam interjected before he could ring off.

Trevor waited in expectant silence.

Pam continued to the tune of one of her favorite songs, "I need to hear you say that you love me."

Her voice danced over the line and sent a quick shiver of joy through his heart. His voice softened, "I do love you, Pammy, a whole bucketful."

She giggled, and his heart lightened another degree.

"That's fine but I'll take it. Besides, I love you more because I love you a whole barrelful."

He chuckled. "You got me there."

Her laughter rang in his ears, echoed in his mind, and chased away the cobweb of emotions tangled there. Trevor managed to push his troubles away for the remainder of the day, but with evening they returned and brought with them nightmares of the past. Only these nightmares were different because the Lion King sat on the edge of them. Sometimes He watched, sometimes He wrestled with the demons in Trevor's mind, but always He reiterated His command, "Come. Follow Me."

Trevor walked along the beach in Cameron and watched the

sun rise over the horizon in a glorious display of light and color. He took a deep breath and tried to quell the tumultuous thoughts that haunted his mind. He'd been up and down all night. He'd fought demons, entertained angels, swore he heard the still, small voice of God and knew if this didn't end soon, he would truly go insane. Though the Bible he had thrown at Dan Hebert remained in the pastor's care, scriptures floated around in his mind. They brought with them a measure of calm alongside the turmoil in his soul, and he knew the time for another session fast approached.

"Oh, God," he whispered into the silent sky. "I don't know if I'm strong enough to hash this out again or to face any more truth," he muttered, a sob stuck in his chest.

The truth will set you free.

Trevor heard the words deep in his spirit. "I'm so afraid."

Fear not, for I am with you always.

"If that's so, then where were You, God, when all of this took place?" he asked, angry all over again. He shook his fist at the sky and yelled, "Where were You? Why didn't You stop it?"

On high I dwell, and in holiness, to revive the spirits of the dejected, to revive the hearts of the crushed, I will heal them and lead them, I will give full comfort to those who mourn for them. I have always been with you, Trevor. I am with you now. I will never leave or forsake you.

"Then why do I feel so empty, so forsaken?"

Because you've yet to believe.

Trevor felt the truth of those words like a shaft of hot iron straight through his heart and knew he'd reached an impasse, a crossroad between the past and the future. He also knew that very soon he would have to make a conscious, heartfelt decision to let go of one in order to embrace the other. Like steel through his veins, resolve strengthened his heart to do what he knew must be done. He called Pastor Hebert and set an appointment. Forty-five minutes later he drove into the church parking lot to find Dan waiting in the sanctuary as promised.

Dan heard Trevor enter and greeted him with a smile and handshake. He could tell by the haunted look in his eyes that the past few days had not been easy on the man. He also knew the hardest part was yet to come. Though repentance brought freedom, confession was never easy. He gestured for Trevor to take a seat.

"I see you've thought about our last conversation," he ventured. "Have you discovered the answer to my last question, who your anger affects?"

Trevor took a deep breath. "My sister."

Dan nodded. "The one person closest to you," he remarked his tone quiet, gentle. He saw by Trevor's expression that the words struck deep and true. "Who else?"

Trevor closed his eyes, took a deep, ragged breath. "And everyone else around me."

"Including God?" Dan asked.

Trevor nodded again.

"You're right. But you haven't mentioned the one person who hurts the most," he remarked, and then continued when Trevor remained silent.

"Hatred is like poison, only it is we who drink it. It has no effect on the person we hate because if they cared in the first place, they wouldn't have done what they did to hurt us so deeply. And, as in many cases, your father has lost the opportunity to come to that realization and make amends."

Dan knew he'd never forget the brilliant color of his eyes when Trevor looked at him. Truth shone in the topaz gaze. He watched Trevor struggle, then surrender. Every stronghold crumbled under the flood of tears when he buried his face in his hands and wept deep, heaving sobs that shook his entire frame.

"Oh, God, I've never thought about it like that. I've felt this way for so long. I'm not sure if I can feel anything else."

Dan shivered when he realized that he'd been given the words to reach him. The relief was so profound that he could have wept. Instead he placed a gentle hand on Trevor's shoulder and sent up silent prayers of thanks and praise that God had entrusted him with such a glorious mission.

"Of course you can," he assured in a tender voice when Trevor's sobs subsided. "You already have. You've felt this all-consuming love for your sister. Now what you need to do is allow yourself to feel it for yourself, for others, and for God."

"I don't know if I can. I just don't understand why things like that happen. Why does God allow it to go on?"

"I don't understand either, Trevor. I doubt anybody does. The Bible says that we should lean not unto our own understanding, but trust in the Lord with all our heart and He will make straight our paths. It also instructs that in the midst of our suffering we should consider Jesus and whether or not we've suffered to the point of shedding blood."

"But I have. Not mine, but my father's."

"I know," Dan said, his voice soft, not reproachful. "That's what hurts me the most. That a child would feel he has no way out but murder. All I can tell you is that the love of God and the blood of Jesus have the ability to cleanse and renew the hardest of hearts, heal the most wounded of souls, and forgive the ugliest of sinners."

"I don't know where to start," Trevor admitted. "Or how."

"Open your heart to God, Trevor and let Him heal your soul of all the pain, the anger, and the unforgiveness."

"I don't think I can ever forgive my father for what he did," Trevor muttered.

"Forgiveness is a choice, just like believing is a choice. Forgiveness doesn't mean that the past disappears from your mind. What forgiveness does is strip the past of its power to control you and your emotions. Not only do you need to forgive your father," he said, raising Trevor's chin with his finger, "but you need to forgive yourself for things you had no control over. You have to forgive the child."

"I don't know if I can."

Dan heard the fear and confusion in those whispered words. "Again, who does it hurt if you don't?"

It took less than a moment for Trevor to realize the answer to that question and to understand that there were no excuses for him to stay where he was any longer, no more reasons to remain stuck in the past when there was a lifetime of hope and a future ahead of him. Dan saw the comprehension flicker in Trevor's eyes and anticipated the next question.

"How?" he asked, in a voice full of confusion, underscored with hope.

"First you let God into your heart and ask His forgiveness for your sins. Ask Him to wash you in the Blood of His Son and make Jesus your Lord and Savior. Once you've done that, you continue to abide in Him and His Word." He picked up the Bible Trevor had thrown at his feet a week ago and handed it back to him.

"Continue to read, to trust, to believe, and when you're ready, come to church. This whole congregation will stand with you, support you, and love you until there is no room for doubt left in your heart." Dan watched him get up to pace and wondered if he'd bolt again.

"I find it hard to believe it's that simple," Trevor admitted. "None of this can change what happened to us. Even if the memories lessen or fade, I have scars to remind me."

Dan's smile, though tender, slightly mocked. "No one said

that it'll be easy, Trevor, just the opposite in fact. The devil has kept you bound in this prison of anger and shame, of bitterness and hatred for so long, he will no doubt come against you when you start to believe the truth of who you are in Christ."

Trevor ran a hand over his face in agitation. "So it's not simple at all. It won't just go away."

Dan heard the disappointment in his voice and rose to place a hand on his shoulder. "No, Trev, it won't just go away, but this time the battle is in your hands, yours and God's. You'll no longer be under Satan's thumb.

"Jesus said to fear not those who kill the body, but to fear the one who kills the soul. Though God is the only one who can kill a soul by eternal damnation, Satan has attempted to do that here and to destroy the gift that is within you and your sister. However, if you continue to believe and confess what God says about you and your life, you have the power to pursue your enemies until they are dust under your feet.

"The Bible says that too," he continued when Trevor remained silent. "In a letter to the Corinthians, the Apostle Paul spoke of Abraham saying, *'he believed therefore he spoke and as we believe, therefore we speak.'* The Word of God holds the divine energy of God and when we speak His Word over our life, we release that energy to change the situations and circumstances from what they are to what they are supposed to be. By *'calling those things that be not as though they are'*, we have the ability to change things.

"You can't erase the past, Trevor. But what you can do is put the past where it belongs and rob it of its ability to control you and your emotions any longer. You can take away its power to determine your future. As I said, it may not be easy and it may not happen overnight. But if you stick with it, God will deliver you. In fact, He delivers us immediately. It just takes a little longer for our minds to believe what our heart knows is the truth and for our lives to line up with that truth."

Trevor sighed and rubbed his forehead, a frown marring the skin between his eyes.

"It's all so complicated. I mean, it seems simple yet complicated at the same time."

"I know this is a lot to absorb all at once. You're tired and in pain, aren't you?"

Trevor nodded.

"Well let me just say one more thing. I want you to know that I'm here for you, Trev. Anytime, day or night, all you have to do is call and I'll be available to talk with you for as long as you need or want me to."

"So it's all up to me now, isn't it?"

Dan nodded and quoted scripture, " 'I have set before you life and death, therefore, choose life.' " Tears filled his eyes, and Dan knew Trevor finally understood and realized that this is exactly what his sister had talked about and hoped for, for years.

"With faith the size of a mustard seed, right?"

Dan smiled and nodded then led him in the sinner's prayer as Trevor took a chance on hope and a future. He asked Jesus to come into his heart and prepared for the biggest battle of his life, the battle for freedom from a past too horrendous to live with any longer.

CHAPTER NINETEEN

Trevor couldn't say that when he left Pastor Hebert he felt like a new man, only that he felt exhilarated and exhausted at the same time. Mentally, emotionally and physically worn out, and yet, incredibly alive. As though the pastor had drained all of the hatred and resentment from his body and replaced it with something else—with hope. That hope took a life of its own, curled in his heart, renewed his spirit, and reached toward his mind. He picked up his cell phone and called his sister.

"It's over, Taylor," he whispered. "It's finally over."

Taylor hung up the phone, put both hands palm down on the desk to keep them from trembling and resisted the urge to call him back. Fear warred with the hope in her heart and showed in her eyes when she looked at Pam.

"How did he sound?" Pam wanted to know.

"Tired," Taylor admitted.

"Well, what exactly did he say?"

Taylor buried her face in her hands and thought about the call. She wanted to believe what she'd heard, yet was afraid to. *It's finally over.* His words circled in her mind, tumbled with doubt and fear until only hope remained.

"He said it's finally over."

"He did it, Tay! He opened up! I just know he did!"

Pam's excitement reached clear to her soul. Taylor closed her eyes. "Oh, God, I hope so," she whispered and felt His peace fill her entire being with assurance.

"Thank You," she added, then joined Pam in a jig around the office. They danced and laughed and wept with relief.

Back at Way, Truth & Light Christian Church, Dan Hebert did his fair share of rejoicing at Trevor's deliverance, though he wouldn't be found dancing around his office. He was, however, at the foot of the cross on his knees in heartfelt praise and worship, grateful that God saw fit to use him in such a manner. He heard the door to the sanctuary open. He rose and turned to greet the visitor, surprised to see Alex Broussard walk in.

Though formally introduced to Alex at the hospital, he had only chatted with him on occasion. He sensed great depths of goodness in the man, as well as his love for Taylor.

Dan smiled. "Hello, Alex, how are you today?" he asked, hand outstretched.

Alex shook his hand and smiled. "I don't know, you tell me."

Dan eyed him, his eyebrow arched in question.

Alex grinned. "I want to know how Trevor is doing."

Dan smiled back. "Well, I'm afraid I can't breach any confidences, but I can tell you that Trevor is much better. How are you?"

Alex shrugged. "I'm fine, just concerned, mostly about Taylor. But, maybe now that Trevor is better, she can settle down, get some rest, and not worry so much."

Dan couldn't help but smile when he realized the deeper reason Alex wanted Taylor to settle down.

"I imagine it's hard to pursue a relationship with her when she's so obsessed with her brother," he remarked, careful to keep his tone clear of condemnation, judgment, or any other negative connotation. A dark flush crept into Alex's cheeks. They eyed each other for a long moment.

"It is."

Dan chuckled, then sobered. "How have you been since the accident, Alex, really?"

"Honestly?"

Dan nodded.

"Frustrated, angry, confused, worried. I'd like to get my hands on their father and beat the life out of him. It's a good thing he's dead, otherwise I'd tear him apart with my bare hands and leave him for the vultures like the garbage he is."

Dan understood exactly why Alex felt the way he did, but he also knew that anger, even on their behalf, was not what the twins needed. Anger, especially the all-consuming kind of anger he saw in Alex's eyes, would destroy any hopes of a relationship with Taylor if the man didn't deal with it and let it go.

"Well, that's honest, I guess," he remarked, again careful of his tone. "But anger is not what the twins need from us. Nor do they need our pity. What they do need, however, is unconditional love, understanding, and acceptance. That kind of anger is not healthy for you either," he warned and continued when Alex remained silent.

"You are aware that fear of intimacy is probably the biggest obstacle you'll have to overcome with Taylor?"

Alex nodded.

"Meditate on First Corinthians, thirteen. You'll be fine."

"Okay, thanks."

"And go slow," Dan added. "An occasional dinner or movie, maybe double-date with Pam and Trevor. Take it easy, get to know her."

He hesitated and eyed Alex, an elaborate lift to his brow. "Come to church with her."

Alex chuckled. "I knew you'd get around to that one sooner or later."

Dan had the grace to grin.

"I'll definitely consider it," Alex promised, shook Dan's hand again, and then left. He arrived at T&T Enterprises within minutes after he left the pastor. Privy to backdoor liberties, he entered the office via the kitchen. The atmosphere was festive, and music played on the stereo system. The entire building seemed to smile. Taylor's voice came over the intercom.

"May I help you?"

He pushed the button. "Yeah, you can tell me where to find a beautiful woman with honey-colored hair and topaz eyes."

"I'm sorry, sir. We're an interior design firm, not a match-making establishment."

He chuckled, left the kitchen, and made his way into Taylor's office, where she and Pam sat curled up on the loveseat. They laughed like schoolgirls.

"A party going on, ladies, and I wasn't invited?"

"We're celebrating," Pam said, and continued at the curious lift to his brow. "Trevor met with Pastor Hebert this morning. We're celebrating his victory over the past."

Alex eyed Taylor, noted the joy in her eyes, the flush of excitement on her cheeks, and felt a tug of longing clear to his soul. "So, he gave it all up?"

"We think so," she said, her voice tinged with hope. "Or, if he hasn't, he's beginning to. We believe he will and we intend to thank God in advance for his complete healing and restoration. Want to drink and celebrate with us?" she asked and held a bottle of sparkling white grape juice toward him.

Alex shook his head. Taylor didn't have time to protest before he took the bottle from her, put it down and pulled her into his arms.

"I'd rather celebrate this way," he murmured and cupped her face in his hands. His lips covered hers in a tender caress. He urged her closer when Pam slid from her seat and exited through the nearest door.

★ ★ ★ ★ ★

Had Trevor known they rejoiced over his victory, he'd have admonished them not to celebrate too soon. From the moment he arrived at his apartment and opened the Bible Pastor Hebert had given him, fears plagued his heart. Doubt filled his mind and soul. Since the pastor had warned him this would happen, he plodded on through the scriptures. He meditated and read them aloud until his eyes hurt and ears rang from the voices swirling in his head. He put the book down, took a couple of aspirin, and did what he hadn't done in years, he went for a run.

Time passed with explicit swiftness. April slid into May and spring gave way to summer. The days grew longer, warmer, and offered endless hours of time to work. The crew embraced the opportunity with all their hearts. Satisfied with the progress on his home and property, Alex upheld Trevor's rule for adequate time off and provided various outings for the workers and their families. To see everyone gathered around the barbeque pit or crawfish pot, laughing and talking or dancing in the yard was not unusual. Even the children were often seen doing a two-step, waltz, or jitterbug to the French music blaring on a portable stereo.

Alex also took advantage of the longer days to court Taylor. Early afternoon features at the movie theater, dinner, and dancing, and late night strolls along a moonlit beach were just a few of the ways he did so. His kisses remained light, caresses gentle, and though it became more difficult with every breath he took, he tried hard not to rush her too soon into a more intimate relationship.

He adhered to Pastor Hebert's advice and invited Trevor and Pam to join them on many of their dates and often attended church services with them. The way the man preached amazed and surprised him. The pastor taught about relationship in place of ritual and how friendship and fellowship took precedence over rules and regulations. He encouraged his congregation to come to service out of love instead of obligation and urged respect and reverence in lieu of fear. As a result, his spiritual journey took a turn into the intimate, and he found himself seeking, praying, and listening more than he ever had before. He even slipped into church a time or two and joined Taylor for morning meditation, appreciative of the freedom Pastor Hebert offered each individual to worship as they wanted. Some said rosaries, others knelt at the altar or sat in their chair to pray, and still more read or sang in melodious voices along with the soft music that poured from the sound system.

He sometimes took upon himself the task to spirit Taylor away. After quite a bit of work to reassure her brother she would be safe for a whole day in his company, he would take her to visit historic landmarks and plantations. The way she got caught up in the atmosphere of the old places and the ideas that flowed through her and onto paper afterward never ceased to amaze him.

This particular evening, they walked along the beach after having dinner with Trevor and Pam. Alex chuckled at how the two flirted and fussed. Sensual undercurrents accentuated every gesture and nuance of interaction between them.

"What's so funny?" Taylor asked.

"Just thinking about Pam and Trevor. Watching them together is like observing a fireworks display, explosive passions, flashing emotions."

"Yeah, they're pretty well hooked on each other."

Alex frowned at her sulky tone. Trevor's remarkable recovery, both physical and emotional, became more evident with each new day. He laughed and joked in ways previously unimaginable and could often be seen in quiet meditation. But for some reason, the lighter his mood became, the darker Taylor's grew. He stopped, leaned against a table and pulled her in his arms. "Want to tell me what's on your mind?"

"What makes you think I've something on my mind?"

"You've been a bit melancholy lately."

When she didn't answer right away, he cupped her face in his hands. "Don't you trust me enough to talk to me yet, Tay? Haven't I proved to be a friend worthy of your confidence in these last couple of months?"

He felt a flush warm her cheeks and pulled her in his arms once more, resting her head against his heart. "Is it the job, visions?"

She shook her head no.

"I can't help you or be a true friend, if you don't talk to me," Alex said.

Taylor wrapped her arms around his waist and snuggled against him. "My emotions are all jumbled up, and I don't know how to explain what I feel."

"Jumbled how?"

She sighed. "I don't know, just jumbled. I feel so many different things, so many conflicting emotions, and they just seem to tumble all over each other."

"Well, let's see if we can sort them out. How do you feel right now?"

"Happy, safe, secure."

He pulled her closer, rubbed her back, and rested his cheek on her head. "What else?"

"Scared, confused, anxious."

"About what?"

"I'm not sure. I'm just afraid to get my hopes up that all will be well from here on out. It's like I'm waiting for the bottom to drop, expecting the ax to fall, and when it does, my life will be in turmoil again."

"Wasn't it Job who said, 'what I feared came upon me' and doesn't the Bible warn us against borrowing trouble?"

She nodded.

"Well then, why are you?"

She shrugged. "I never thought about it that way."

Alex brushed his lips over her hair. "You need to focus on the blessing here, Taylor, and not the fears. Don't concern yourself with *'what if'* but enjoy each day as it comes."

"You're right. I'll try."

He shifted her in his embrace so he could cup her face in one hand. "Good. Now let's get back to the happy, safe, and secure part. Is that all you feel when you're in my arms?"

Again he felt a flush warm her cheeks. She quivered against him but refrained from comment. He chuckled and lowered his mouth to hers. Within moments she was plastered against him, her hands fisted in his hair. Her mouth clung to his until each breath he took robbed her of oxygen. Desire shuddered through him with such intensity he had to force himself not to pull her down in the soft sand. Alex broke the kiss and buried his face in her hair. His hands roamed over her back and shoulders in a restless caress.

"Okay," he breathed, his voice somewhere between a groan and a chuckle. "Now that we've answered that question, I better take you home before I lose all sense of propriety and ravish you on the spot."

Taylor awoke the next morning to the memory of Alex's kiss and smiled. Her thoughts circled back to their conversation about Pam and Trevor and then honed in on her brother. She had no idea why she felt uneasy with the difference in Trevor as he became stronger in his faith and less dependent on hers. Gone were the late night talks and early morning jogs in which they discussed scripture. And though she was happy, she couldn't help but resent the changes that happened so quickly between them. She couldn't explain it either, and her talks with Pastor Hebert didn't seem to shed any light on the issue. All she knew was, now that she had the brother she'd longed for all of her life, she had to share him with others. She knew it was petty and selfish to feel that way, to feel jealous and threatened, but she couldn't seem to stop the emotions that ruled her. The situation came to a tumultuous head one morning in late May.

Memorial Day weekend was a welcome relief from the hectic pace the crew had set to get as much done as possible while the weather held out. They took Friday and Tuesday off in conjunction with the Monday holiday, prepared to return to work bright and early Wednesday morning. As he had done in the past when a job demanded it, Trevor hired additional workers, one of whom was a carpenter named Colleen.

A pretty woman and a hard worker, she came highly recommended. Her only flaw was in personality. She'd worked alongside men all of her life and as a result was loud and crass and blunt to the point of rudeness. She was an excellent carpenter and made no bones about it. Nor did she make any bones about flaunting the body that reflected her occupation. Long, firm legs, tight abs and buns, sleek, toned muscles, all of which she showed off in skin-tight cut-offs and skimpy shirts.

Steve was head-over-heels with the woman and had no shyness about flaunting that either. They arrived at the annual company picnic arm-in-arm, and Taylor was glad that Alex, who'd left Thursday morning for a week-long business trip, was not around to see the way the woman dressed.

She'd done her best to welcome Colleen into the family of crewmembers that had been with them since the firm had opened, but after she listened to the snide comments and whispered complaints from the regular crew's wives and girlfriends, Taylor knew she had to do something. What made matters worse were the number of phone calls she received Tuesday about the very same subject. By Wednesday, she was fit to be tied.

She arrived at the office late, frustrated, and stressed to the max. A headache brewed behind her eyes. She barely had time to get to her office and collapse at her desk before the phone started to ring. After three calls back to back, she asked Pam to bring her some aspirin and a glass of juice, then unplugged the phone. Pam brought the items to her and waited quietly while she swallowed four pills with a single gulp of juice.

"Alex is on line one," she said, her tone soft.

Taylor plugged her phone back in and answered the call.

"You sound rough," he remarked. "Problems?"

"Just one and her name is Colleen," she said, and glanced up in time to see Pam's expressive green eyes frost over. Taylor arched an eyebrow at her and lifted a hand to signal Pam to wait, then turned her attention back to Alex when he chuckled.

"Ah, the Irish lass," he remarked, the brogue he attempted foiled by his rich, southern accent.

Taylor's attempt at a chuckle sounded more like a groan. "With the maiden name Soileau and current name Fontenot, I doubt very seriously there's a drop of Irish blood in her," she muttered.

Alex laughed. *"Jalou, mon cheré?"*

Taylor rolled her eyes. Even had she not chosen French as a foreign language in school, there'd be no mistaking his question. "No, I'm not jealous. Why is it that every man thinks that a woman is jealous when she's offended by another woman's attitude or appearance?" she mumbled and heard his answering laugh. They talked a few more minutes. Then she hung up.

"Alright, let's have it," she said, and gave Pam her undivided attention after she unplugged the phone once again. Pam hesitated and Taylor knew she was unsure of whether or not she should speak her mind.

"You know I've never gotten involved in that aspect of the business, and I have no desire to now. But I've heard the comments and complaints too. The phone has rung all morning with more of the same and, well, enough is enough. Besides, you know I'm not one to judge or criticize, but I'm not thrilled with the idea of her parading around half-naked in front of Trevor all day either."

Taylor scrubbed her hands over her face with a weary moan. "Seems to be the overall consensus. Get Trevor on the phone and ask him to come in, please. And have him bring Steve with him."

When Pam left and shut the door quietly behind her, Taylor laid her head on the desk and remained that way until she heard the men come in.

Trevor's concern over the coolness in Pam's greeting turned to worry when he walked in his sister's office to find her pale and shaken. Dark circles added color to the bags under her eyes and gave the appearance of bruises on her creamy skin. "What's wrong?"

"I haven't slept in two days, that's what's wrong," she answered and then turned on Steve. "What's this I hear about Colleen, that she showed up for work in a bathing suit top and cut-offs?" Steve's eyebrow arched in automatic reflex at the annoyance in her tone.

"She likes the sun."

"Well she can like the sun in a shirt and shorts, decent ones."

"Her attire in no way hinders her work, and the guys haven't complained."

Taylor rolled her eyes with a grunt. "Well I don't imagine they have or will," she muttered, and then glared at him. "I hate to pull rank on you Steve, but she can't parade around half-dressed anymore. Make her wear decent clothes."

"You can't do that, Taylor. It's called sexual discrimination. The guys wear shorts and take off their shirts. She has the right to dress accordingly as long as it doesn't interfere with her, or anyone else's, work."

"She does not have the right to parade around half-naked in front of a bunch of married or committed men," Taylor exclaimed and slammed her hand down on the desk for emphasis. "I've had nothing but whining and complaints from the wives and girlfriends since you hired the woman!"

Trevor sat there, speechless and shocked at the heated words and violent emotions that poured from his sister as she went head-to-head with his foreman. When he tried to bring a measure of calm to the meeting and stop the argument, she turned on him in an angry whirl.

"As for you!" Taylor exclaimed. "Where's that ridiculously strong sense of business propriety you used to wield like a badge? She's a reflection of this company!"

Steve interrupted before Trevor could form a response to her accusations.

"That's bull! We're working out of the city limits and far enough away from the road that no one can see how we're dressed."

"Or undressed as the case may be," Taylor hissed. "And no one except the wives and girlfriends who drop their men off or stop by to bring you all food or drinks."

"Well, seems to me they're the ones with the problem."

"And it seems to me you're so wrapped up in this . . ."

Taylor's tirade trailed off and she visibly bit back the word that came to mind.

She took a deep breath and continued, ". . . woman that you've forgotten where your loyalties lie. You've worked with these men a heck of a lot longer than you've known her, and I can't believe you're so insensitive to the feelings of their wives and girlfriends." She held up a hand to ward off Steve's retort.

"I'd hate to have to enforce a dress code on you guys, Steve, so it's up to you. You're the foreman. If you don't remedy the situation, I will."

Trevor watched Steve, who trembled with barely controlled fury, lean toward his sister. "Is that a threat?" he asked, his voice deceptively soft. "If so, then you know what you can do with this job."

Trevor had heard all the hollering he could stand. "Enough," he interjected. He stepped between them, placed a hand on Steve's shoulder. "She's not threatening anyone, so just calm down.

"And you, back off," he ordered his sister. "What in the world is your problem? You've been moody and irritable for weeks now, and I've had about all I can stand of your attitude."

Taylor drew in a sharp, painful breath, shocked at her brother's tone of voice. She knew in that moment that their separation was complete. He'd never used that tone with her. At least not in front of anyone. The knowledge that they were no longer one, but individuals, cut to the heart. She began to tremble and blinked furiously at the tears that rushed to her eyes. "Get out," she ordered between clenched teeth. "Both of you just go."

CHAPTER TWENTY

The three stood stock still and glared at each other in tense silence. After a moment's hesitation, Steve turned on his heel and stormed out of the office, slamming the door in his wake. Trevor ignored her order, rounded the desk, and took her in his arms.

"What's the matter?" he asked, perplexed by her moodiness which usually accompanied visions. And he knew she hadn't had one of those in a while.

"Talk to me," he urged when she began to cry.

"I feel like I'm losing my little brother," she sobbed and buried her face in his chest, soaking his shirt with tears.

"You're the other half of my heart and soul, Tay. How can you lose me?"

"I don't know," she cried. "You've just changed so much so fast that I don't know how to keep up. I have no idea what to say or do any more."

"I thought this was what you wanted, Taylor, for me to let go of you and open up to God and to others."

"I did! I do! Oh, I don't know anymore," she wailed.

Trevor held his sister while she cried and thought about how much his life had changed in the last two months. The first few weeks had been the hardest, while he had tried to believe and learned to trust. But he had embraced the challenge as he had every other in his life, and as time passed, he grew stronger. He opened up to the truth of God's word and the joy of new life.

That truth was so much sweeter than the bitterness he'd lived with for so many years and the light so much brighter than the darkness he'd carried around for so long. He embraced it, ran with it, and determined not to look back but to press forward, to the high calling of Jesus Christ and healing power of God's grace.

With a pang of guilt he realized somehow, somewhere along the way, he'd left behind the sister he adored.

He cupped her face in his hands and gazed into her tear-drenched eyes. "I'm sorry, Tay," he whispered and brushed the tears off her cheeks with his thumbs. "I haven't taken the time to thank you. I feel like a new man, and I owe it all to you. If not for you and your faith in God and in me, I wouldn't be where I am today.

"You haven't lost me," he assured her. "You could never lose me. It would be like cutting out half of my heart. The better half." He brushed his lips across her forehead. "I've just grown up. I only wish I'd done it sooner and that I hadn't wasted so many precious years bogged down in bitterness and anger and shame.

"I love you, Taylor. The fact that you don't hate me is a miracle in itself, and I'll be grateful for the rest of my life that you stood by me through thick and thin, through the pain and heartache of our past and the joy and discovery of new life."

He'd always known exactly what to say to ease her fears. Now was no exception. He saw the light come into her eyes, felt the darkness flee and the burden lift from her shoulders as he held her and spoke the words she'd yearned to hear for so long. She stepped out of his embrace, laid her hand against his cheek.

"I could never hate you, Trevor. I love you. You too are the other half to my heart, and I'm sorry." Her eyes searched his.

"It's really over, isn't it?"

Tears filled Trevor's eyes and rolled slowly down his cheeks.

But they were tears of joy. He nodded.

"It's really over Tay, finally and completely. But my love for you is one thing that will never change," he promised and cuddled her to his chest once more.

Steve sat at the kitchen table with his face buried in his hands and waited for Trevor. He regretted the harsh words he'd hurled at Taylor. *She's right about one thing,* he admitted silently. *I'm so wrapped up in Colleen that I've forgotten where my loyalties lie.*

She's right about more than that, he realized. The way Colleen dressed in front of the men left a lot to be desired. His claim that she liked the sun had been an excuse, and a poor one at that. He knew from the intimate moments they'd shared that the woman hated tan lines and frequented tan salons on a regular basis. He'd tried to think of her as just one of the guys and to ignore the insecurity and jealousy aroused in him by her choice of clothes, but it hadn't worked. His heart was too involved. When Taylor had brought it up, it forced his own feelings to the surface. He'd lashed out at Taylor instead of dealing with Colleen as a man should.

To say he'd fallen in love at first sight would be an understatement. Or maybe lust at first sight, he conceded mentally. Whatever it was, it had hit him hard, and he'd been dazzled ever since. He knew it was time to find out where the rubber met the road, and he intended to do so the moment he returned to the jobsite. His mind made up, he went to Pam's office in hopes of borrowing her car to go back out there. He hesitated at the doorway, stunned to see Pam at her desk, her cheeks pale, a frown etched in her forehead, fear in her eyes.

Pam sat glued to her chair. She'd felt the tension brew between the twins for weeks but had no idea that it would escalate to such a degree over something like this. The angry shouts that came from Taylor's office brought memories of another day crashing in on her until she'd covered her ears in an attempt to shut them out. Now she sat immobilized, glad that the shouts had stopped but deathly afraid of what the silence meant. She looked up, startled when Steve spoke her name.

"Are you okay?" he asked.

"What's going on?" she whispered.

"Taylor and I had an argument," Steve said. "I guess Trevor is trying to calm her down."

Her eyes narrowed at the guilt in his voice. "Over Colleen?"

Steve nodded, swallowed hard.

"Are you going to make her wear decent clothes?" she demanded and brushed the coldness out of her cheeks with an angry swipe.

"It bothers you too?" he asked, shock in his tone.

"Of course it bothers me," she snorted. "It would bother any warm-blooded female to have another prance around her man with such a flagrant disregard for modesty."

Steve closed his eyes with a groan. "I never thought of it like that. I'll take care of it right away, Pammy. Can I use your car?"

Pam nodded and handed him the keys. Before he could walk out, the twins strolled down the hall, joy and laughter accompanying them. Taylor walked up to Steve, put her arms around his waist, and rested her head against his chest.

"I'm sorry, Steve. I shouldn't have lost it like that. I should have been a little more tactful."

Relief flickered across his features. He hugged her back.

"And I should have been a lot more sensitive," he admitted. "I'll take care of the situation as soon as we get back."

"As long as you take care of it before Alex gets home from his business trip," Taylor said with a smile.

Steve chuckled.

Trevor stepped through the door into Pam's office. "Are you alright?"

She smiled, relieved to see them happy and at ease. "Guess it's been a rough morning on everyone. I'm fine," she assured.

"How about some lunch?"

"Are you gonna stay in this afternoon, or do you want me to order some food for you to pick up for the gang?" Pam asked.

She could tell by the way he hesitated and the quick flare of emotion in his eyes that he wanted no more than to escape the frustrations of the morning and spend the afternoon with her. She also knew by the way he glanced over at Taylor that he didn't want to leave his sister alone either. He grinned, held a hand out to both of them, and, when they clasped his in return, turned to Steve.

"I thought I'd take my two favorite ladies to lunch and we'd play hooky the rest of the afternoon. Can you handle things at the job?"

Steve arched an eyebrow at him. "What if I want to play hooky with my favorite ladies this afternoon too?"

Trevor grinned. "Then I'd have to pull rank on you." Steve chuckled.

"Here, take my truck," Trevor said and tossed him the keys. "We'll pick it up later, or I'll hitch a ride out there in the morning."

Steve caught Trevor's keys and handed Pam's back to her in one smooth movement. The significant look he shot her said he knew the twins would not be back at the jobsite that afternoon. He shook his head and grinned.

"Yes, sir, boss," he said. "I'll see you tomorrow."

"Why don't you give the gang an extended lunch," Taylor suggested before he could turn away. "Then the guys can go home to their wives and families for a little while. It doesn't get dark until late, so there's plenty of time for y'all to work this evening."

Unspoken intention hung in the air, and they all understood she'd just given him the opportunity he needed to figure out what to say to Colleen and how to say it.

"Sounds like a plan," he remarked and then left.

When Steve arrived at the jobsite, he parked Trevor's truck where it would be safe for the night and pocketed the keys. His sharp whistle got the crew's attention. He made a gesture across his throat to signal them to shut it down and waved for them to gather around him. Once they were all there, he told them to go to lunch or home and report back at three o'clock.

He took the spare shirt he always carried off the hanger in his truck and held it out for Colleen, "Any plans for lunch, want to grab a bite with me?"

She eyed him for a long, luxurious moment. Heat sparked to flame in her eyes. His heart did a slow swirl into his stomach, followed by the swift kick of desire. His body tightened with need when she replied, "Depends on what we're having," in a husky, suggestive tone.

"Whatever you want," he assured, and tugged the shirt closed over her skimpily clad bosom. For the next hour they reveled in each other's company over an intimate lunch, and the next two were spent engaged in a heated discussion about her work attire. They arrived back at the jobsite still in the midst of an argument.

Steve sighed, his stomach in knots, his head aching. "Look, I don't want to argue with you in front of the guys. Just wear the shirt. Please."

"What's there to argue about?" she seethed. "Your boss is a prude, and you're a male chauvinist pig," she accused and jerked the shirt open. She tucked the tail under and tied it just below her breasts with short, angry movements.

"She is not a prude. She's just worried about the continuing marital status of the rest of the guys. And I am not a male chauvinist pig. I just don't like for you to flaunt what's mine."

"Well, they're all a bunch of prudes," she bit out. Her voice trailed off, eyes narrowed when she realized what he'd said.

"What do you mean by 'what's mine'?" Colleen pressed.

At his wits end, Steve could only think of one reply. He jerked her in his arms. His mouth covered hers in a fiery embrace. When he was sure she no longer trembled from anger, but desire, he ended the kiss by slow degrees. "Does that answer your question?" he queried, his voice soft, tender.

She lowered her gaze but not before he saw the heart reflected there. Hope beat a tattoo in his chest.

"All that tells me is you lust after my body."

A throaty chuckle rumbled from deep in his chest as Steve caressed her face, tugged the ponytail holder from her hair, and buried his hands in the luxurious brown mass.

"You're a terrific carpenter and a beautiful woman, and I lust after more than your body, little lady," he assured in a husky, tender tone.

He stepped away from her, loosened the knot out of his shirt, retied it around her waist and buttoned the top buttons. "It's your heart I desire the most," he confided in a whisper, as his lips left a trail of moist fire across her forehead, cheeks and nose before capturing hers once again, this time with devastating tenderness.

When the guys started to drag in after three, it was obvious none had enjoyed a peaceful time with their families as Taylor had apparently hoped when she'd suggested the extended lunch period. Steve took into consideration the sorry shape they were in and his own need to spend time alone with Colleen and made a decision that his status as foreman allowed him to make.

He sent them all home.

When the twins arrived at seven-thirty the next morning they were hard at work to make up for lost time. Steve climbed down off the scaffold to confer with Trevor and give him back the keys to his truck.

"How's it going?" Trevor asked.

"Good," Steve said. "Didn't get much done yesterday so we all got an early start today," he said and then explained when Trevor arched a brow at him in question.

"The guys dragged back in after lunch like a bunch of whipped dogs. I sent them all back home."

Trevor grinned and shook his head. "Women," he muttered.

Steve agreed with a soft laugh.

"What about women?" Taylor asked as she walked up behind them after parking her car.

Trevor grimaced, winked, and then turned to her. His smile charmed, voice placated.

"Lovely creatures, huh Steve?"

Steve chuckled. "Lovely."

Taylor's eyes searched his, then Trevor's. When neither offered further comment she rolled hers then glanced back at the house. He could tell she was pleased at the progress since the last time she'd visited the site.

She spotted Colleen and remarked, "Good to see she has clothes on."

Though she wore shorts, they covered her legs to about mid-thigh. She had on a sleeveless, gray T-shirt and tennis shoes. Her hair was in a ponytail and a paint-splattered sun visor shaded her eyes. "Yes she does," Steve answered. "And I'll thank you to give her another chance," he said and explained when both twins eyed him, unanswered questions in their gaze.

"She's had it rough all of her life. Daddy was disappointed that he didn't get a son and made sure she knew it every moment of her life. Then her husband used and abused her before he left her with a broken heart and a pile of bills. Like her father, he always ridiculed her desire to be a carpenter. But Jesus was a carpenter, and the son of one, and that's what she wanted to be.

"She apprenticed through the local union but found that in order to get any respect at all she had to play up her assets but act like one of the guys at the same time. She hated every minute of it. Underneath that rough and tough facade, she's really a sweet and gracious lady."

"Well, you sure got to know her pretty well in a short amount of time," Taylor remarked.

Steve shrugged, grinned, and winked at her brother. "Couldn't wait around for you forever."

Taylor took his teasing in stride and then frowned when she glanced back at Colleen.

"Isn't that your shirt?" she asked, when she recognized the ragged V cut out of an otherwise round neckline and college logo that had long since seen better years.

Again Steve grinned. "Was. Looks better on her, don't you think?"

"It sure does," Trevor piped up and then laughed at his sister's expression. He poked her in the side with a grin. "You staying or going?"

Taylor made a face at him. "I'm staying," she said, then glanced back at Steve with a smile. "There's a lady I'd like to get to know."

Steve saw Colleen glance up toward them when their coworker Greg, who was next to her, waved and called hello to them. As she'd lain in Steve's arms last night, they'd laughed and talked and watched TV. He told her a little more about the people they worked with and asked her to give Taylor and the guys a chance to show that this crew was like no other she'd ever worked with. This morning she'd talked less and observed more and soon discovered he was right. No one laughed or mocked because she showed up dressed decently and spoke politely. In fact, they seemed relieved and appeared to accept her even more. Shame, pride, and fear flickered across her features as Steve and Taylor approached, but she held her chin high and Steve imagined she waited to see how the boss lady would act toward her after yesterday. He glanced down at Taylor and knew by the tenderness in her eyes that she too, saw the play of emotions across the other woman's face.

Taylor smiled. "Morning, Greg," she said, and then turned to Colleen with a nod. "Love your shirt."

Colleen glanced down at the shirt Steve had given her the night before, then back at Steve as he slid his arm around her waist and sent her an encouraging smile. She ran her hand over the logo. The scent of his cologne clung to the fabric, drifted up from her movements. A flush colored her cheeks. A smile bloomed along her lips. "It was a gift."

Taylor brushed a hand over Colleen's arm then linked hands with her and lowered her voice. "You've got to tell me how you managed to wrangle that shirt away from him. I've told him numerous times it's ready for the rag bag."

"Hey, watch how you talk about my favorite shirt!"

Colleen giggled. "Oh no, it's just now good and broke in."

Steve knew the instant the two women walked off together that life would be a lot sweeter for him and Colleen because if Taylor accepted her, the others would soon follow suit.

Chapter Twenty-One

Alex turned the truck's air conditioner up a notch, slipped in a CD, and settled in for the trip home. His one-week business venture had turned into two. Two weeks of twelve-hour days filled with meetings, followed by evenings where he had wined and dined prospective clients. *Two weeks away from Taylor.* The thought made him frown despite the joy he felt because he had snagged the accounts he had coveted for nearly two years. The commissions he would make off their investments would substantially fill out his current income.

Monetarily the trip was worth it, but emotionally he wasn't so sure. In all of his thirty-eight years, he'd never dreamed he could miss someone as much as he missed Taylor. Talking to her every day hadn't helped but had only added to his loneliness. By God's grace, he'd never have to leave her again.

He coaxed the cruise control up a tad over the speed limit and thought about the future. Not the distant future but the immediate one. The one just a short while away when he'd hold her in his arms again. The thought of her sent an ache to the depths of his soul, and he wondered how long this instantaneous reaction of his body would last.

The feelings were novel, like being drunk only better. His arms ached with the need to hold her, mouth watered at the thought of the taste of her lips and skin, nostrils flared as though he could smell the sweet, feminine scent that was hers alone.

Anticipation beat a slow thud through his veins as the miles flew by.

Taylor slipped into the barn, careful not to be seen. No doubt her brother would have a conniption fit had he even the slightest clue she dared to enter the dilapidated old structure, but she'd put it off long enough. Curiosity got the best of her, and she couldn't wait another day. She had to find out if Jean Lafitte had carved his initials into a board as rumored. The flashlight trembled in her hand when she turned on the beam to inspect the area around the door she'd just entered. Sunlight filtered in through the cracks of decayed wood, and darkness loomed in the shadows. Her heartbeat jumped into overdrive, and her breath hitched when a winged creature dove at her. She ducked, raised an arm over her head, and choked back a scream.

Maybe this wasn't such a good idea after all.

Resolve straightened her spine. She would not let a bat scare her off! Not when the treasure she sought would add authenticity to the stories that surrounded this property, not to mention value to the property itself. Collectors, history buffs, and museums would no doubt pay a fortune to harvest the wood that bore the initials of the famed pirate. Her desire however was not to sell or give the item away but to display it in the house. She pictured it above the mantle in Alex's office and that vision drove her to disobey strict orders to stay away from the building unless someone accompanied her, which no one would. Trevor had seen to that. The thought ticked her off. Who was he to boss her around, anyway?

She nearly jumped out of her skin at the impression that something or someone moved behind her. She twirled around, took a step back, tripped, and landed with a thud on the hard-packed earth. The flashlight bounced out of her hand and went out. Oh, God, what am I doing in here? A pulse at the base of her skull began to throb and familiar vibrations stole over her. She had no choice but to ride out the sensations and buried her face in her knees. What ensued was no vision, but a nightmare. Like the din of bees around a hive, the low drone of voices thrummed in her ears. Evil lurked in every corner and assailed her from all angles. The shadows came alive. She began to whimper and crawl around, desperate to find a way out.

Alex arrived in Lake Charles and headed straight for Taylor's cottage, then cursed to find her gone. Since it was Saturday, he figured she wouldn't be at the office but drove by there just in case. He circled through the parking lot and then steered in the direction of his property.

He arrived and parked among the multitude of vehicles present. His heart pounded, palms sweated, mouth dried as though he had swallowed a cup of dust. He punched the automatic lock button on his key chain and slid the keys into his pocket, then chuckled at the way his hands shook. He took a deep breath and forced a semblance of calm on his intense emotions. He walked toward the house. His eyes searched for Taylor with each step.

He tried to be polite as he made his way forward, only to be interrupted by what seemed like hundreds of handshakes and hellos, and then sighed with relief when he reached Trevor, who was conferring with Steve. The two men turned to greet him.

"Where's Taylor?" he asked, before Trevor could utter a simple hello.

Trevor grinned. "Well, hello to you too."

Alex rolled his eyes with a sigh, politely shook Trevor's, then Steve's, hand, then asked again for Taylor's whereabouts. Trevor shrugged, his eyes scanning the vicinity.

"She's around here somewhere, sketchbook in hand I'm sure."

Alex nodded and walked off in search of her. He approached Trevor a few minutes later. A worried frown creased his forehead.

"I can't find her, Trev."

"What do you mean you can't find her?"

"Just what I said," Alex growled. "I've looked everywhere, and I can't find her. You don't think she left with someone do you?"

Trevor shook his head. "Not that I know of."

They turned at the sound of a crash in the barn and realized where she was. Trevor spit out a curse. "I told her to stay away from there."

They headed toward the decrepit old structure. "We should have torn it down on day one," Alex growled.

But they hadn't. They'd left it in order to concentrate on the house.

The barn stood as it had for years, about as steady as a drunkard's hand. Alex and Trevor halted in their tracks when they heard Taylor's scream and watched in horror as, with an obstinate groan, the building began to collapse. Trevor shouted his sister's name and took off at a run with Alex close on his heels.

Steve and the others heard the commotion and Trevor's bellow and followed suit. Steve got there first and then turned to block their way as Alex and Trevor bolted for the still crumbling debris. "Hang on guys, let it settle."

"My sister's in there," Trevor argued and struggled against the hold Steve had on him. "Let me go, damn it, or you're fired!"

"If you barge in, matters will only get worse!" Steve insisted and held him back with every ounce of strength he possessed.

Once Trevor and the structure settled, Steve let him go and then turned with them to examine the damage. He nodded at the guys and joined in as they lifted the fallen roof and tossed it aside.

Alex was the first to spot her, lying deathly still beneath a pile of debris. "Someone call an ambulance," he said and reached for her hand. He felt a pulse and breathed a prayer of thanks.

"She's alive. Let's get the rest of this crap off her."

They worked to uncover her, careful to be gentle with the rotten wood and other debris.

"Don't move her," Steve cautioned, when Trevor knelt by her limp form and took her hand.

She had a knot on her forehead and scratches on her face and arms. Trevor brushed the hair off her face and repeated her name over and over. Alex took her other hand and forcefully restrained himself from pulling her in his arms.

The paramedics arrived and tried in vain to wake her. They loaded her onto a stretcher and took her to the hospital with Alex and Trevor close behind. The two men paced the ER waiting area, anxious for some word, and turned in unison when a doctor called for her family.

Trevor introduced himself and waited in tense silence for the doctor's report.

"She has a nasty bump on her head, some scratches, and she's bruised badly all over. She hasn't come to, and I'm positive she's suffered a concussion. There don't seem to be any internal injuries besides that, but we're going to run a few tests to be sure. I'll let you know the extent of damages as soon as I can. You'll need to fill in the paperwork to have her admitted."

Trevor nodded and swallowed the hard knot of bile pooling in his throat. *Oh, God don't let her die! Please don't let her die,* his heart cried over and over as he waded through the admission forms. He felt a hand on his shoulder and looked up at Alex.

"I'll call Steve."

"Thanks. Call Pam, too, and Pastor Hebert."

Alex nodded and walked outside the emergency waiting room to make the calls. In a few minutes, the place swarmed with people. Steve and Colleen, Pastor Hebert, and Pam gathered around Trevor and Alex.

Pam enfolded Trevor in her embrace and held on tight while he relayed what the doctor had said. Whether it took an hour or an eternity for the doctor to come back, he was unsure, but he'd about reached the end of his patience when the man finally appeared.

" 'Bout time," he mumbled. Pam shushed him and they stood together to hear the results.

"Well, there are no broken bones or internal injuries and very little swelling around the brain, but she's still unconscious. We'll have to watch her to make sure no other problems develop, but we won't know the total extent of damage until she wakes up."

"When?" Trevor demanded.

The doctor shrugged. "Minutes, hours, days . . . it's entirely up to her."

"How encouraging."

"Wish I could give you more, but the truth is we never know with head trauma. Some people breeze through with little more than a headache. Others stay in a comatose or semi-comatose state for days or weeks, even months. We will watch to make sure there is no additional swelling or bleeding around the brain and do what we have to if there is. The rest is up to her. You might want to have someone with her all or most of the time, bring her some music, read to her, whatever you can think of to coax her back from whatever place she's drifted to inside her mind."

"Jesus," Trevor sighed and raked a hand over his face.

"That'll work too," the doctor assured and put a hand on his shoulder. "The nurse should have a room number for you. You

227

can go on up. She'll be there soon."

Trevor thanked him and turned to check with a nurse. He took a mere two steps when his knees buckled. Alex and Steve caught him before he hit the floor and urged him into a chair. He doubled over with a groan. His breath heaved in and out in jagged pants.

"Did he just say what I think he said? She's in a coma?"

Pam knelt at his feet and cupped his face in her hands. "Yes, but there's no broken bones, no internal injuries, and just a little swelling around the brain. She'll be fine, Trev. I just know it."

In a moment of quick desperation he grabbed her by the arms. "Promise, Pam," he whispered, his voice raw.

Before she could respond, a nurse approached. "Mr. Forrestier?"

He nodded.

"Your sister is in her room if you'd like to go on up now," she said and then told him the number. He thanked her and stood, flanked by Alex and Steve. Pam and Colleen followed with Pastor Hebert in tow as the group made their way to the room where she lay. Trevor took one look and bolted. Pam followed him into the hall. Alex sank into the chair by the bed, took her hand in his, and rested his forehead beside her. Steve and Colleen gathered at the foot of the bed. Dan walked up along the other side, made the sign of the cross on her forehead, whispered something to her, and then left to check on Trevor.

"Are you all right?" he asked.

Trevor took a deep breath and swallowed hard. Fear battered him like a thousand tiny tornadoes, but he nodded.

Dan touched his shoulder in a gesture of support. "Like Pam, I believe she'll be fine, but you've got to hang tough, Trev, until she finds her way back."

"I will. Thanks."

"I'll be in and out. You know how to reach me if you need to. Anytime you need to."

Again Trevor nodded.

"Okay, I'll see you later then," Dan said, and left.

Steve and Colleen stepped out the door. "We're going to head on back to the jobsite and fill the crew in on what's happening," Steve said.

"Thanks, Steve. Looks like you've got control of the reins again," Trevor remarked.

"Not a problem," Steve assured. "I doubt you'll be able to pry Alex away from the chair he's in right away, but you two might want to work out a schedule or take shifts. No need for the both of you to wear yourselves out keeping vigil."

"We'll figure it out later," Pam said before Trevor could answer. "I'll take my turn with her too."

"One thing's for sure, she'll never be alone. Not even for a minute," Trevor asserted.

"Good deal," Steve said and took Colleen's hand. "We'll see you later."

Once they turned away, Trevor and Pam went back into the room where he settled in for what would be the first in a long string of sleepless nights.

Trevor sat beside his sister's bed, her hand in his. They'd been there five days and still no change. The doctors had found no medical reason why she had yet to wake and encouraged them to keep vigil. He and Alex took shifts, one during the day, and the other at night. Oftentimes, their shifts overlapped, one of the men reluctant to leave. Sometimes they talked; other times they sat in silence. Pastor Hebert dropped in on a regular basis and chatted with them. Pam came after she closed the office, and Steve was a regular visitor, not only to give Trevor and Alex a break but to keep them informed of the progress of the job.

The nurse came in and ran him out while she bathed and dressed Taylor. Pam arrived, and they paced the hall outside her room until allowed back in.

Music played on the portable stereo he brought in. Pam brushed Taylor's hair. She chatted the whole time in order to keep Taylor informed of what went on at the office. Trevor stood over her and spoke in a gentle but firm tone.

"Time to wake up Taylor. We need you here. Wake up now," he urged. "Please, Tay, squeeze my hand or something, anything to let me know you're there."

Nothing.

He raked a hand thorough his hair in frustration. "Damn it, I feel so helpless!"

Pam put the brush down and braided Taylor's hair, then walked around to enfold Trevor in her embrace. "I know. We all do. But we've got to hang on, Trev, and not give up hope that she'll find her way back soon."

"I don't know how much more of this I can stand. She's so lifeless, so fragile."

"She's stronger than you think. Why don't you go home for a while? Alex will be up soon. I'll stay until he arrives."

Trevor sighed. "Think I'll run on out to the jobsite for a bit before I go home. Promise you won't leave her, not even for a minute."

Pam promised, walked with him to the door and kissed him, then turned back to Taylor. After a moment's indecision, she picked up a book she'd started a couple of days ago and continued to read aloud in hopes the sound of her voice would draw her friend back to consciousness.

Trevor arrived at the hospital early the next morning while Alex was still there. Pastor Hebert arrived shortly after.

"Glad to find you both here," he commented.

"What's up?" Trevor asked.

"I'd like to talk to you both. As you can imagine I've said a lot of prayers since the accident, and I've also studied numerous cases of coma victims and after or near-death experiences and I think I may have an idea of what we need to do."

Both men perked up and sat a bit straighter. Dan took a deep breath and sent up a silent prayer then plunged right into the heart of the matter.

"I think we need to give her permission to not come back." At the startled gasps from both, he held up a hand to ward off their comments.

"Let me explain," he urged, and took their silence as acquiescence.

"In all of the material I've studied, there are three reasons why a person either gains or does not regain consciousness from a coma. One is medical, the other is emotional, and the third is spiritual. Now, we know there is no medical reason why Taylor hasn't come back to us. I don't think emotional comes into play either, despite the trauma she's suffered, you two have suffered," he said with a nod at Trevor. "We know she's dealt pretty well with all of that. So, the only option left is spiritual. As I said, I've studied numerous cases of after and near-death experiences, and I've uncovered a couple of interesting facts."

Encouraged by their rapt attention and the fact neither interrupted him, he continued. "The spiritual cases narrowed down into two categories, those who did not want to come back but did so because of loved ones and those who wanted to come back or were sent back because they felt their mission here on earth was not complete. I believe Taylor is in the first category. She may not want to come back but is afraid to let go and die because of you two. I think we need to give her permission to go instead of clinging so tightly to her that she is afraid to do what her heart desires." He stood stock still and waited for one or the other to respond.

Trevor sat in stunned silence for a moment then leaned toward him, his face ravaged with shock.

"Are you suggesting that we give her permission to die?"

"To put it bluntly, yes, but more like give her permission to make the choice."

"Never!" Alex interjected. "I'll never let her go, and I'll curse God until the day I die if he takes her from me now." He rose from his chair and bolted from the room.

Trevor sat back with a sigh. "I can't believe you'd even suggest such a thing, or that God would ask this of me."

Dan walked over and put his hand on Trevor's shoulder. "You've heard the old adage, if you love something let it go; if it loves you, it'll return?"

Trevor nodded.

"Well it's something like that. Now, I'm not saying Taylor wants to die, but I do believe she should have the choice to live in eternal glory if she so desires. I know this won't be easy, but think about it. Pray about it and if you can't do this alone, I'll be here if you want. Either way, I'll stand behind you."

The blood drained from Trevor's face but he nodded. "I understand. I'll give it some thought."

"Good. Now, let me see if I can find Alex. He'll probably be ready to bite my head off, but I'll take that chance." He left the room and went to search, surprised to find him in the hospital chapel. A tangible air of desolation surrounded him, reached out and tugged at Dan's heart. He stepped through the doorway and watched Alex stiffen.

"I don't want to talk to you right now."

He sat anyway. "We don't have to talk. I just want you to know I'm here."

Silence stretched between them, tense, wary, uncomfortable.

When Alex turned to face him, wrath sparkled to life in his usually merry hazel eyes.

"I can't do what you've asked. I can't let her go without telling her how much I love her."

Dan reached out and placed a hand on his shoulder. "Tell her now. Medical evidence has proven that the comatose hear when they're spoken to and what goes on around them."

"So she probably heard your speech. You think it's wise she hear something like that?"

"I'm not sure, but I think it's only fair that she know someone understands where she's at and the dilemma she may be in. I'll tell you what I told Trevor, this is not something you have to do right away. Think about it, pray about it, and if you need me to be with you when you make the decision, I'll be there."

When Alex remained silent, Dan got up to leave. The agony in Alex's voice stopped his departure when he asked, "Is it true you can't bargain with God?"

Dan hesitated, chose his words with care. "I'm not sure what you mean by bargain. I know of people who've made a promise to God in return for answered prayer."

"So you can bargain with Him."

"I wouldn't call it a bargain, more like an exchange of favors, but Alex, be careful what you pray for and more careful what you promise."

His only answer came in a curt nod. Dan left.

Alex sat for long moments after the Pastor left, his heart heavy, his mind a mass of jumbled emotions. Anger, pain, frustration, and grief sliced through him with equal clarity until all that remained was profound resignation.

Taylor's recovery was out of his control. He couldn't wish her back, will her back, force her back, or even pray her back. He had to let her go. He had to let go and let God do whatever His will entailed.

Tears pushed through the wall he'd erected around his heart and for the first time since the accident, he wept. Huge sobs wracked his entire frame until only emptiness remained.

Oh, God, I don't know if I can do this!

Trust in the Lord and lean not unto thine own understanding . . . The scripture floated though his mind but didn't bring much comfort.

Despair washed over him in fierce waves. "I know what I said earlier about cursing you was wrong and I'm sorry. I just don't think I can ever love again the way I love her. And I haven't even told her!"

Again the words came, *trust in the Lord and lean not unto thine own understanding,* only this time they brought a measure of peace.

"OK, God, I'll let her go, but not before I tell her how I feel. If You bring her back to me, whole and healthy, I'll serve you with everything I have until the day I die."

He didn't know if God would accept his bargain, or "exchange of favors" as Dan put it, but he was prepared to do whatever it took and to promise all within his power to have her back.

Chapter Twenty-Two

Taylor walked where angels trod. She gloried in the peace of heaven and traipsed through the coals of hell, always strong, always victorious.

On some level, she heard all that transpired around her.

She heard her brother's voice, felt the emotions that clouded his words . . . Anger, *almost lost you to a stupid piece of wood!* Frustration, *I feel so helpless!* Grief, *please come back, Tay, I don't know if I can go on without you.* And finally, resignation, *I love you, Tay, but I'm releasing you to God. I hope you come back, but I'll do my best to understand and accept if you choose to stay in heaven where there's no pain or fear and no more nightmares.*

She felt his kiss and the sense of relief that flowed through the atmosphere.

She also heard the others, Pam, Steve, Pastor Hebert, but Alex's voice drew her the most. Her heart leaped a little when he spoke. Her senses hummed when he stroked her hand or arm. Her stomach fluttered when he pressed his lips to her forehead or mouth.

Today she basked in the glory of the Lord. She knelt at the feet of Jesus, clung to the hem of His robe, and waited for His direction, while Alex's voice assailed her senses.

"Oh, Lord, what should I do?"

The choice is yours, my child.

"But to leave you . . ."

He lifted her chin with nail-scarred hands. *Tell Alex to*

remember his promise. With those words, He disappeared and left her to decide her fate.

Alex's voice shimmered through the haze of indecision and tugged at her heart.

"I love you, Taylor. I wish I'd told you weeks ago then maybe you wouldn't have been so foolish to enter that barn alone."

She felt his face on her shoulder and tears in her hair; she heard the anguish in his voice.

"I'm supposed to release you now, but don't know if I can. You're the woman I've longed for all of my life, and it's hard to let go."

She swam through the darkness toward the sound of his voice. Her hand twitched. He grabbed it.

"Taylor, sweetheart, can you hear me?"

She nodded.

"Oh, God, thank You!"

Taylor turned toward him. "Trevor?"

Trevor, who had just stepped in the door, stopped when he heard her voice. "Did she say my name?"

Alex nodded. "I believe so. Taylor, open your eyes, honey."

She did and squinted at the fluorescent glare of the overhead light. "Help me up," she said and tried to push herself into an upright position.

"Hang on, let's get the doctor or a nurse in here," Trevor urged.

"I don't need a doctor or a nurse. I need to sit up."

Alex put a firm hand on her shoulder. "You've been flat on your back for nearly six days now, you can wait another minute or two," he insisted while Trevor rang for the nurse.

Taylor sat back with a heavy sigh. The doctor and a nurse arrived within a few minutes and examined her, then helped her to sit up.

"How do you feel?" the doctor asked.

"Fine, a bit weak but fine."

"I'd like to run an MRI and a few other tests to make sure you haven't suffered any brain damage."

Taylor nodded her consent, and the nurse went out to prepare the way and get the test set up.

The doctor informed them that she'd be gone an hour or more. When they left with her, Trevor called Pam and then Steve. Alex went to Frank's florist shop. He returned after they had brought her back into the room and knocked softly on the door. He entered when he heard her voice. Her eyes widened at the multicolored spray of roses he carried.

"A dozen roses," she murmured, "how sweet."

"Two dozen," he corrected. "One for every year of life you scared out of me."

She buried her face in the flowers in an attempt to hide her smile in the soft petals. "I'm sorry."

"Yeah, right, so what's the smile for?" He did his best to sound disgruntled despite the relief that soared through his veins. Taylor lifted her face, her eyes dancing with humor.

"Because you're so sweet," she said, her voice little more than a purr.

He resisted the urge to take her in his arms and glanced around the room. "Where's Trevor?"

"I made him leave. We figured you'd be back soon, so he went out to the jobsite for a while. Reluctantly I might add. I'm sure he'll be up here later, with Pam, and the two will fuss enough to drive me nuts."

"Serves you right."

"Are you going to stand there and chide me or come over here and kiss me hello?" she asked, her eyebrow arched.

Alex gave up his pretense of being angry. He sank down on the bed and pulled her gently against his chest.

"You've no idea how much you scared me," he mumbled and

buried his face in her hair. She snuggled against him for a moment, then lifted her face to receive his kiss.

His arms remained gentle, lips tender, until his fingers brushed the skin revealed through the opened back of her hospital gown. The response of her body pressed intimately against his chest nearly drove him over the edge.

A moan of pure, primitive pleasure escaped her and spilled into his mouth like fine wine, as his hands traveled over the smooth skin of her back to bury themselves in her thick, honey-colored hair. His lips clung, molded and shaped hers to his until each ragged breath he took robbed them both of oxygen. *Just one more moment,* he thought, dazed, and jerked his mouth from hers. His hands ran over her back and shoulders in a restless caress. He'd hold her one more moment then let her go. Though he had no idea how on earth he'd do so.

Taylor remained locked in his arms, held firm against his chest. Her breath came in sharp, almost painful pants. Her limbs felt flushed, heavy. Blood pulsed and throbbed through her veins, settled into tingly pools of pleasure, and ached in places she'd never imagined. Shocked and surprised at her body's response, a blush stung her cheeks. Shame washed over her in angry waves, fear nipping at its heels. Alex must have felt her stiffen because he laid her gently back against the pillows.

"Are you alright?" he whispered. His lips brushed across her forehead tenderly.

She could feel the intensity of his gaze when she tugged the blanket up and nodded.

"I didn't hurt you?"

Taylor kept her eyes closed for fear he'd see the emotions warring in her soul reflected there, and shook her head no.

"Look at me," he urged, his voice gentle.

When she opened her eyes, she noticed the smashed flowers

on her lap. "Oh, look," she gasped and blinked back the tears that rushed to fill them. "They're crushed."

Alex lifted her chin with a gentle hand and waited for her to look at him. Wary, afraid, Taylor lifted her gaze to his, certain that her eyes, aching with unshed tears, reflected the emotions in her soul.

"Something so fragile and lovely should never be handled roughly. It won't happen again."

Taylor knew by the tenderness in his gaze and the tone of his voice that he did not refer to the flowers. Her hand trembled when she raised it to his cheek.

"You have never handled me roughly," she assured, her voice soft, full of emotion.

Alex covered her hand with his, closed his fingers over hers, and placed her palm over his heart. "And I never will," he promised. "I love you."

Hope sang to life in her heart at the whispered admission and tears rolled slowly down her cheeks. A smile trembled on her lips.

"I love you too," she admitted, her voice tremulous.

Joy glittered in his expressive hazel eyes. Alex brushed his lips over hers, then took the pitcher on the bedside table and filled it with water for the roses. Not two minutes later a nurse's aide came in. She shook her head and put her hands on her hips.

"That's supposed to be for drinking water," she scolded, with a wink at Taylor.

Alex did his best to look contrite despite the smile tugging at his lips. "Sorry, it's all I could find."

With another shake of her head, she rolled her eyes, filled one of the extra pitchers she carried on her cart and placed it beside the one with the roses. She made sure Taylor didn't need any books or magazines. Then she left them alone once more.

Trevor and Pam arrived after Pam closed the office. Each

carried a bag of goodies. Pam's contained a pair of pajamas, a robe, and toothbrush as well as a sketchpad, pencils, and pencil-colors. Taylor rummaged through the items and murmured her thanks while Pam shooed the guys out of the room so she could change. When they returned, Trevor handed her the bag he carried.

"I think this is what you've been looking for."

Taylor opened it and gasped with pleasure. The board had splintered in a uniquely symmetrical manner. In the center were the initials JLF carved within a circle by the pirate's knife over a century ago.

"Wow," she breathed. "Look how neatly it broke. It'll make a beautiful mantel piece or wall plaque after we preserve it."

"Or a great whipping stick for hard-headed women," Trevor remarked, and grinned at Alex who quickly chimed in his agreement.

Taylor made a face at them. "You were going to tear the structure down anyway. I just saved you the trouble," she teased. Though her brother grumbled about her audacity and foolishness, she saw the relief and the love in his eyes when he leaned down to brush his lips across her cheek.

A knock at the door caught their attention. They turned as Steve, Colleen, and Pastor Hebert strolled in, followed by her doctor. Everyone made room so the doctor could approach her bedside.

"How do you feel?" he asked while he checked her pupils.

"I doubt I could run a marathon right now, but I actually feel quite well, very . . . rested for lack of a better word. I would love to get out of this bed and walk a bit, though."

He chuckled. "Well, I suggest you do just that. All of your tests are normal, so recovery is imminent. You may be weak for a bit, but that too shall pass. If all goes well tonight, we'll release you tomorrow."

"Wonderful," she breathed. "How soon can I go back to work?"

"As soon as you feel well enough, within reason of course. Take it easy and don't try too much too soon."

"Oh, don't worry, she'll take it easy," her brother interjected. The doctor nodded his approval.

Taylor frowned over at her twin. "I should have run you out of here when he arrived," she muttered, then turned back to the doctor. "He'll try to control my every movement now."

This time Alex's voice interrupted any reply the doctor may have made. "If he doesn't, I will," he asserted. Everyone in the room added their assurance that they, too, would make sure she took it easy.

The doctor laughed. "Well, looks like I don't have to worry. I'd like to see you again in a couple of weeks, just to make sure all's well, but there's no doubt you'll be right as rain in no time."

After the doctor left, others trailed out. Steve and Colleen were the first to leave, then Pastor Hebert.

Before he walked out, Pastor Hebert turned to Alex. "I'm sure Pam will come back up in a couple of hours to relieve you."

"No need. I'm not leaving."

The pastor's eyebrow arched. "I don't think it's proper for you to spend the night here with her awake. I'm sure Pam won't mind. Will you?" Pam smiled and shook her head.

"Oh for heaven sakes, she's in a hospital bed," Alex protested.

Pastor Hebert shook his head. "In a private room with a door that locks."

Alex snorted and glared at Trevor. "A little support here would be nice, buddy."

Trevor grinned. "I happen to agree, but hey, she's a grown woman so the choice is hers."

He turned to Taylor. "Are you really going to let them run me off?"

Taylor couldn't help but smile at the argument between them. "Well, the Bible does say we should avoid the appearance of sin."

Alex rolled his eyes and relented.

Pam and Trevor left not long after, and she and Alex were alone once more.

"Can I get you anything?" he asked.

Taylor nodded. "I'm hungry, and I'd like to take a walk."

"Let's see what the nurses say you can eat first. Then we'll walk," he replied and rang the nurses' station. The nurse responded that she shouldn't overload her system with heavy foods yet, but she could eat things like yogurt, juice, Jell-O, crackers, soup, and ice cream, all of which he could buy in the cafeteria. Alex thanked her and turned back to Taylor.

"Would you like to walk now or wait?"

"We'll wait."

"Okay, I'll be right back."

When he returned, he sat next to the bed while she ate. When she indicated she was ready, he helped her into the robe Pam had brought, slipped his arm around her waist, and walked with her down the hall. The moment she appeared weak, he picked her up, carried her back to her room, and settled her in the bed.

He urged her over, sat beside her, and wrapped his arm around her. "I can't believe you let them run me off. I've spent the night with you before."

She flushed. "If I recall correctly, I didn't have much choice in the matter that time."

He chuckled. "I ought to not give you a choice in the matter this time either, but out of respect, I'll go once Pam is here and I know you're okay."

She turned where she could snuggle her face in his shoulder

and put her arm around his waist. "I appreciate that."

He stroked her hair, pressed his lips against her forehead, and whispered his love.

Taylor kissed his cheek. "I love you, too. I have a message for you, from the Lord."

He cocked his head, his eyes curious.

"He said for you to remember your promise."

Amazement shone in his eyes. He hugged her close.

"That's one thing I'll never forget," he whispered.

CHAPTER TWENTY-THREE

June slid by with summer in full swing, its old dog days interrupted by an occasional shower or thunderstorm. In answer to their prayers, God, in His wisdom and mercy, saw to it they were nighttime showers and thunderstorms or weekend rain spells which enabled the crew to work steadily on Alex's house and still have adequate time off.

Though the groundwork would continue well into the early part of next year, Alex was more than pleased with the progress on the house and amazed on a daily basis at how quickly things came together. The whole place began to look and feel more like a home than the original showpiece he'd wanted.

The house was no longer just a frame or shell, but actual rooms, floors, and ceilings. The kitchen, breakfast nook, formal dining room, den, master bedroom suite, and Alex's office were all downstairs. The upstairs housed three guest rooms with private baths, a library, and a ballroom for when Alex held parties or entertained clients.

Just as her brother had warned early on, Taylor insisted they maintain the original style and structure of the house as much as possible, especially downstairs. There were exposed beams in the ceiling, bare cypress walls, and hardwood floors. Antique doorknobs and plumbing fixtures graced the rooms. Except for the chandelier in the ballroom, most of the light fixtures resembled coal-oil lanterns, candlestick lamps, and other early American lights. She allowed very little carpet in the house, all of it restricted to the upstairs rooms.

Alex gave her free rein with the design and décor with one exception, the master bedroom and bath. There he insisted on carpet in the bedroom and a full-sized Jacuzzi garden tub in the bath. Taylor protested. Vehemently.

"It throws off the whole scheme of things."

"It's one area of the house, two rooms. No one will see them except me anyway."

"That's not the point! All of the upstairs baths have antique, claw-footed tubs with shower stalls tucked discreetly in closets. Why can't this one be the same?"

"Because this is my private domain and I want it to be comfortable. You can tuck the shower stall discreetly into a closet too, if that's what you want, but the carpet and tub are not an option."

Taylor sighed. "All right, I'll compromise and allow the carpet. Make sure it's light with a natural look and feel. But the tub is out of the question. It's too big, too modern."

Alex fought the urge to take her in his arms and shake, or kiss, some sense into her. "Modern is exactly what I want. And it has to be big enough for two."

She flushed at the images his words conjured up. He chuckled. "I see you get my drift."

She rolled her eyes and allowed him to pull her against his chest. Awareness shimmered between them. Alex lowered his mouth to hers, nibbled on the tender skin around her mouth and lips.

"Now all I need is someone to share it with," he murmured and felt her tremble.

"I'm sure you'll find someone," she hummed while her arms crept around his neck and her lips reached up to receive his kiss, the argument forgotten for the moment.

They had another clash of wills a few days later.

While he shopped for office furniture and kept in mind what Taylor said about all wood, oak or walnut, maybe cherry, preferably dark, and the antique look, Alex found the perfect carpet for his bedroom. He decided the unique blend of natural and synthetic fibers with rich earth tones and a subtle pattern that reminded him of a forest floor would look good in his office too.

He arrived back at the house with samples of the carpet and pictures of the furniture he had ordered. He asked for Steve's assistance and made his way through the house to the room designated for his office only to find Taylor on her knees, sander in hand, as she prepared the floor to be lacquered to perfection and waxed to a high gloss finish.

Jeans, worn in very interesting places, clung to her shapely hips and legs. A T-shirt, splotched with patches of sweat, revealed nearly as much as it covered, the smooth shape of shoulder, enticing curve of breast. Tiny wisps of hair escaped her French braid to curl around her face and clung damply to her neck.

He made a manful attempt to swallow a groan and resisted the urge to send Steve away, tiptoe in there, brush the hair off her neck, and taste the salty sweetness of her skin. Steve's throaty little chuckle indicated he understood Alex's sentiments.

Taylor looked up when they walked through the door, and her eyes narrowed at the tape measure in Steve's hand. She glared at him then Alex.

"What do you think you're doing?"

"Measuring for carpet," Alex replied.

She turned on Steve. "If you touch this floor with that tape, you're fired."

Steve hesitated, glanced back at him with a grin, and waited while Taylor scrambled to her feet, ready to go head-to-head with Alex. Before she could snarl the first word, Alex handed her the carpet sample. She gasped and ran her fingers over it, a look of pure sensual pleasure on her face at its texture and softness.

"It's beautiful," she breathed. "Wherever did you find it?"

Alex told her.

"It's perfect," she admitted. "For the bedroom," she added before he could comment and shoved the sample back in his hands.

"I want it in here too," he said and nodded for Steve to proceed.

Steve hesitated again when she glared at him and threatened to break both of his hands if he so much as thought about touching the floor with the tape. He shrugged and tossed the steel rule to Alex with a grin.

"Man, I hate to deny your request, especially since you own the place and all, but I'm not about to measure this floor until you two get this ironed out. Give me a holler when, if, you do," he added with a chuckle and made a beeline for the door.

"Traitor," Alex grumbled.

Steve laughed. "Hey, I know who wears the pants in this company and who signs my pay checks," he teased and made his escape.

Alex turned back to her, eyes narrowed, prepared to do battle for what he wanted, until he saw the dark circles beneath hers and the tears that shimmered in them.

"What am I supposed to do with all these wood floors?" he asked.

"Buff and wax them, regularly."

"Not a chance," he mumbled.

"Then hire someone to do it," she insisted. "You've got more money than sense anyway," she muttered.

She sounded every bit as tired and petulant as she looked. Alex arched an eyebrow, ground his teeth and let that one pass.

"When was the last time you slept?"

"You mean, the last time I had a full night's sleep?"

He nodded.

She shrugged, ran a hand over her hair. "I don't know. A few days ago I guess."

"Visions?"

She nodded.

"Taylor, you can't keep going like this without adequate rest. Have you thought about taking an over-the-counter sleep aid to help you relax?"

Taylor sighed and only half-listened to the admonishment. Her brother and Pam had harped on the same thing for days now. No one understood. She had no choice. The visions came when they wanted, no warning, no reason. Sleeping pills wouldn't help. They'd only hinder her ability to successfully draw and thereby make matters worse. She'd learned to live with the situation and knew the visions would lessen as the project moved closer to completion. She'd rest then. Besides, not only dreams and visions interrupted her sleep. Nightmares plagued her also, though she would never admit that to Alex or her brother.

Funny how when she had lain in a coma she had trampled the devil under her feet, but in the flesh he still had the power to render her helpless with fear.

She heard Alex's exasperated sigh and flinched in automatic reflex when he threw up his hands in defeat and muttered, "Forget the carpet." He turned on his heel but spun back around to face her as her reaction dawned on him.

"Whoa, wait a minute," he said, his voice whisper soft. He took a step closer. "I didn't mean to frighten you, sweetheart. I'll never raise a hand to you," he promised, then groaned when a lone tear escaped to leave a moist trail down her cheek. He took her in his arms, and pulled her against his chest. She buried her face in his shirt and wept soft sobs that shook her entire frame.

"I'm sorry. It's your house. Do what you want," she mumbled when the sobs subsided.

"It's not my house; it's our house."

Taylor dared not dwell on what he meant by the declaration.

"We'll discuss the carpet later," he said, and cupped her cheeks in his hands. "Right now, I'm taking you home, and you're going to rest, whether you like it or not."

She fought the smile tugging at her lips and the hysterical little giggle that bubbled in her throat. "Yes, sir," she complied as meekly as possible.

Before he could lead her out the door, Steve returned. "What's wrong?" he demanded, and gave Alex a hard, steely look, exactly the kind Trevor would give him if he were to notice the tear streaks on his sister's cheeks.

"She's exhausted," Alex answered. "I'm going to take her home and put her to bed."

"Good idea," Steve murmured and brushed a hand down her arm when they passed by.

"Are you hungry?" Alex asked once they were on their way.

"Let me rephrase that," he insisted when she shook her head. "When was the last time you ate?"

Taylor rubbed her forehead where a headache brewed between her eyes and sighed, "Yesterday, I think," she added under her breath.

Alex rolled his eyes and turned as though he would take the bypass to her favorite restaurant.

"I really can't eat a whole lot, especially if I'm going to go to bed."

"Fine, I'll prepare a light meal at your place," he said as he turned the SUV around and headed to her cottage. Once there, he commanded her to sit with her feet propped up and wait while he whipped up some scrambled eggs and toast.

While she ate, he brewed a cup of herbal tea and carried it into the bedroom. She heard the water run in the bath and smelled the scent of her favorite bath crystals and the candles placed throughout the bathroom as he lit them. He closed the door behind him then rejoined her in the kitchen.

"You have exactly thirty minutes, forty-five max, and if you're not out by then, I'm coming after you," he warned. "Then you're going straight to bed."

Taylor made a face at him but bit back her comments at his tone of voice. Though exhausted, she had the presence of mind to retrieve her pajamas from the bedroom and noticed that he'd turned down the covers on her bed. She disappeared into the bath and sank gratefully into the warm, frothy water. Its scent combined with the candles and warm chamomile tea did wonders to relieve her frazzled nerves and weary soul.

Back in the kitchen, Alex paced and forcefully restrained himself from going near the bathroom, determined to leave her in peace.

"Lord, help me here," he muttered, though the prayer did little to stop his imagination from going wild. Images crowded his mind . . . her chin deep in bubbles . . . the way he'd greet her with a warm towel when she emerged from the tub and rub scented oil into her skin. No doubt she'd rest well after a full body massage and the lovemaking that would follow.

He groaned in agony, shook his head, scrubbed the heel of his hands over his face and prayed again. Time enough for all of that after they were married, but, oh how he longed to hold her in his arms. He almost wept in frustration when she emerged from the bathroom with a hairbrush in hand and tugged at her French braid. Her clothes had picked up scent from the candles, and fragrance from the frothy water clung to her skin.

"I thought I told you to go straight to bed," he growled, his eyes narrowed, fists clenched in an effort not to reach for her.

"I can't sleep with this braid," she explained, and curled up cross-legged on the couch.

The need to touch her, to hold her in his arms and feel her body against his, was too hard to resist. He succumbed. "Let me," he whispered and picked the brush up from where she laid it on the arm of the couch.

Though she trembled at the look in his eyes and tone of his voice, no fear marred her lovely eyes. A thrill of joy dashed through him when she turned to where he could reach her and flipped the braid over her shoulder so that it hung almost to the center of her back. His hands shook while he undid the plait. He ran trembling fingers through the thick, honey-colored locks and began to brush out her hair. She all but purred with pleasure at the long, soothing strokes of brush against scalp.

When Taylor's hair cascaded around her shoulders in a silken mass, he tossed the brush aside, slid his arms around her waist, buried his face in her hair, and pulled her firmly against his chest. "I love you," he whispered, his voice husky.

Taylor snuggled against him. "I love you, too. I'm sorry I've been so grouchy."

"I'm sure I'll get used to it," he murmured and tightened his grip in a valiant attempt to force his hands not to stray, lips not to roam.

"Thank you for taking such good care of me."

"I'm not through yet," he mumbled, then slid off the couch and swung her up in his arms.

Fear snuck in, darkening her eyes. She stiffened and opened her mouth to protest. He brushed his lips over hers and silenced her objections.

"I just want to hold you," he whispered and laid his forehead against hers. "That's all. I promise," he added, unable to camouflage the need in his voice.

He'd offered her another step to relinquish her fear and trust him. Triumph lit his expressive eyes when she wrapped her arm around his neck, smiled, and whispered, "Okay," then snuggled her face against his shoulder and let him carry her to the bedroom.

With exquisite tenderness, he laid her on the bed, crawled up beside her, and took her in his arms. Taylor felt the strength of his need in the heat and tensed against the hardness of his body. He eased his grip and propped up on one elbow beside her. His eyes pleaded for grace when he stroked the hair off her face and said in a soft, husky voice, "Please don't be afraid of me; please trust me. I will never force or even persuade you to give more than you're ready to."

They gazed at each other for a long, tender moment. She cupped his cheek in her hand, brushed her thumb over his mouth, then curled her fingers in his hair and urged his head down to fasten her lips to his. A low moan escaped his throat, yet he held himself taut.

Taylor ran her hand over his shoulder and back in a soft caress then wrapped her arms around his waist. "Hold me, Alex, I trust you."

The emotions reflected in his tone caressed her heart when he thanked her in that beautiful velvety-rough voice. He rolled onto his back, pulled the covers over her, and held her while she slept.

Alex awoke with a start when Taylor began to moan and toss in her sleep. He brushed the hair off her face and whispered her name. She jerked away and opened glazed eyes to stare into space. Trancelike, she sat up and fumbled with the bedside table.

"Draw," she mumbled, the word barely intelligible.

Careful not to startle her, Alex reached across and grabbed the sketchbook and pencil from the table drawer and placed them in her hands and then sat in amazement as with frenzied movements she filled the book with pictures and notes of changes to be implemented before completion of his home. When she pushed the items off her lap and buried her face in hands that trembled, he arose and went into the kitchen to pour her a glass of water. He brought it back to her and helped steady her hand while she drank. When she gazed at him, her vision clear, he gathered her in his arms once more and held her while she slept.

June marched into July, hot and humid. The highlight of the season was when the twins decided to be baptized.

They chose the last Sunday in July, which happened to be their birthday, as the perfect day to do it. Just as they'd come into the world minutes apart, they went into the baptismal font minutes apart. Trevor emerged from the water with a shout of victory, swept his sister up in his arms, and twirled her around. They laughed and wept all at once. Alex and Pam watched with tears in their eyes as the whole congregation converged to welcome them more fully into the family of God in which they now belonged.

One month later, Trevor and Pam married. They left the next day for a week-long honeymoon trip to Las Vegas and the Grand Canyon, scheduled to return the Tuesday after Labor Day.

Alex and Pam watched Trevor pull his sister aside for a private moment before he boarded the plane with his wife.

"They've never really been apart," Pam whispered.

Alex acknowledged her words with a slight nod. "I know."

"Watch over her while we're gone."

Alex heard the tremor in her voice and hugged Pam to his

side. "You two worry too much," he admonished with a tiny laugh. "But don't let those thoughts cause you a moment of unease. I promise to watch over her. She'll be fine."

Trevor cupped his sister's face in his hands. "I've done it, Tay. I've gone and gotten myself married," he whispered, joy evident in his tone. "We had a beautiful night, Taylor. Yours will be beautiful too, when the time comes."

His eyes shone with happiness and joy. Taylor smiled, hugged her brother, and bravely fought back tears at the thought of him gone, away from her for a whole week.

"I'm glad, Trev," she whispered. "I know it's your honeymoon, but please call me. Just once or twice so that I'll know y'all are okay."

"I will," he promised. Their flight number came over the intercom with the order for passengers to check in. They rejoined Alex and Pam. Trevor shook Alex's hand then hugged Taylor again. He hesitated a moment, lingered another. Both knew once he passed through to the secured area, they wouldn't see each other again until he and Pam returned next week.

"Take care of her," he admonished Alex.

"I will," Alex promised.

"Don't let her work too hard."

"I won't. Will you two please go before you miss your flight?"

They all laughed. Trevor pulled Taylor close and brushed his lips across her cheek then stepped through the security check. He turned once more and blew her a kiss, then slipped his arm around his wife and left his sister behind for the first time in twenty-eight years.

Chapter Twenty-Four

Rain washed over his windshield like a tidal wave. The wind buffeted the SUV like a toy in the paws of a playful kitten. Alex squinted through the darkened sky, cursed the weather, and envied Trevor and Pam their time in the sunny Nevada desert. They'd made it through the first half of hurricane season without much threat so far. The gale which currently kicked up a fuss just might prove to be the biggest one yet. He adjusted the dial on the radio and listened in concern as Gustav, which had wreaked havoc across the Atlantic for days, traversed the Gulf of Mexico as a category three storm.

Traffic backed up for miles at the intersection, as people began to evacuate the lower parishes to find shelter. Alex waited through two red lights before he could continue on to the house to check on things. Then he'd head to his apartment to bunker down and wait out the storm. His eyes widened in disbelief when he saw Taylor's car parked up close to the house. He slammed out of the truck, made a mad dash for the porch, and still managed to get soaked in the process.

He stomped through the house and cornered her in his office. "What on earth do you think you're doing out here all by yourself in this weather?" he said. "For crying out loud, there's a hurricane out in the Gulf!" Taylor looked up and frowned.

"I'm about to put another coat of varnish on this floor, and you're dripping water all over it," she accused. "Besides, it's not predicted to hit directly. There's even time for it to fizzle out and die before it causes any more damage."

"No matter how close they may come, no one can accurately predict what a hurricane will do or where it'll hit," he muttered through clenched teeth and pushed the stop button on the portable AM/FM radio-CD player which had been playing Taylor's favorite working music. "You should be home where it's safe, not out here all alone, or you should at least be listening to the radio to keep track of things."

She sat back on her haunches with a sigh, shook her head and glared at him. "Other than Rita three years ago, there hasn't been a direct hit from a hurricane to this area in fifty years. This one's liable to do like all the others and fizzle out, turn inward somewhere east of us, or head over to Texas. Besides, it's nice and cool right now and a lot easier to work when there are no people to track in and out or drip water on my floor."

Alex rolled his eyes and resisted the urge to shake her. "Yes, Miss Meteorologist. Only this one has already torn up everything in its path throughout the Atlantic. Though crossing land has weakened it, there's time for it to grow larger, stronger and meaner and regardless where it *may* land, at this moment it's headed straight for Louisiana." Before he could utter another word, thunder roared and lightening flashed across the sky, struck a transformer nearby, and caused the electricity to falter. He muttered a curse and felt his way along the wall to where she was.

"Do you have a flashlight handy? That much sense at least," he growled when she handed it to him. He turned it on and shone the beam right in her face. "Looks like we'll have to wait it out here. C'mon," he took her by the arm and led her down the hall.

"Where are we going?"

"I picked up a few things at the store before I came out here. Essentials you know, like batteries, candles, water, snacks, and such. If you'll hold the flashlight where I can see, I'll run out to the truck and carry them in."

She did her best to hold the light steady despite the strong wind and slashing rain. "Why don't we just leave?" she hollered over the howl of the storm.

"Because we don't know how bad the roads are and whether or not there are power lines down between here and either of our places," he yelled back. "On top of that, the traffic is a nightmare. Cameron is on mandatory evacuation. We'll probably be ordered to leave soon, too."

He grabbed the plastic bags loaded with supplies with both hands and rushed up on the porch. Taylor took some from him, and they went back into the house.

He dropped the bags on the floor of the entryway, brushed the rain off his clothes, ran a hand through his hair, and considered the best place for them to ride out the storm. A pot-bellied stove in the kitchen and a fireplace in the den would provide warmth in either room, he thought, but neither had carpet. The library upstairs, however, had both.

He led the way up there, settled her in with the groceries, and then went back to the kitchen where he found a roll of brown paper that was used to clean paint brushes and hands as well as a stack of wooden paint stirrers. He grabbed a piece of board to put the candles on, then rejoined Taylor in the library and proceeded to light a fire in the fireplace. He fed it paper and wood until it roared to life, warm and cozy. He glanced over at Taylor and noted how beautiful she was, bathed in firelight. *She's beautiful bathed in any light,* he thought with a smile, then asked, "Are you okay?"

She nodded.

"Hungry or thirsty?"

She shook her head.

"Cold?" he asked when a shiver passed through her with a

visible shudder.

Again she shook her head.

"Come here," he whispered and held a hand toward her.

Taylor gave up the pretense of bravery. She scrambled over to where he sat and welcomed his strong embrace. Alex pulled her against his chest then, with a groan, removed her from his embrace. He picked up the flashlight and rolled to his feet.

"I'll be right back."

"Where are you going?"

"Down to the office and get the radio so we can listen to the weather." He touched the bag that contained a bottle of wine and plastic cups with his foot. "Why don't you pour us a cup, and I'll be right back."

Taylor waited until he was out of the room before she attempted the task so that he wouldn't see how bad her hands shook. She wasn't fond of wine but figured she'd need this cup. She hated storms, which was why she'd chosen to work through this one. She guessed she underestimated it. He returned with the radio, a stack of newspapers, and an old, ragged blanket under his arm.

"Where'd you get those things?"

He chuckled. "I saw Steve and Colleen stretched out on it the other day underneath that big oak tree in the yard, where they snoozed instead of leaving for lunch, and I remembered he said they kept it stashed in the den. The newspapers were there also. Guess the guys like to read on break and lunch time." He dropped all but the radio on the hearth. "The newspapers will help keep the fire fed, and the blanket will keep us warm if we run out of fuel for the flames."

He tuned the radio to the oldies station, then put it down. "Might as well get comfortable," he suggested, and kicked off his shoes, placing them close to the fire.

She handed him a cup of wine, then removed her shoes and

placed them next to his. He held a hand out to her and helped her to her feet. He brushed his lips over hers, whispered his love, and then held her close as they swayed to the tune of a classic love song.

Within moments the National Weather Center reported that Hurricane Gustav, a category three hurricane, had slowed to 115 mph and would either continue to die down before it hit land or strengthen and change directions before it headed inward. From the tip of Florida to the toe of Texas, the entire Gulf coast was on alert. Lightning flashed, thunder rolled.

"Don't be afraid," Alex whispered when she shuddered in his arms. "I believe we're safe here."

"I hate storms," she admitted, her voice hardly above a whisper. He eyed her, a curious lift to his brow.

"Then why were you out in this one?"

The memories were too close to the surface for comfort, too vivid to ignore. Taylor sipped her wine and chose her words with care. "Trevor and I have always weathered the storms in our life together. But he's not here, so I decided to stay busy. Although the rain shut the crew down, I knew there were things I could do."

His gaze searched her face a moment. Taylor knew by the concern in his face that every emotion she felt showed in her eyes: the panic, the sheer terror. She could tell the moment he realized her hatred of storms was linked to their childhood. His eyes narrowed and breath caught in an audible hiss. He swallowed his last bit of wine with a gulp, poured himself another glass, and refreshed hers.

"Let's sit," he urged, and pulled her down on the rug with him.

She knew the time had come to tell all, every sordid detail of her childhood. This would be the definitive test of their love, the ultimate step of trust. She had to know that he'd understand

and not turn away after he knew how truly defiled she'd been.

She had to know he wouldn't blame the child.

Her hand trembled when she took a huge gulp of wine then held the glass out for him to refill. Once he did so, she began. "The first memory I have of my father is fear. As I said before, he ruled his house with an iron fist. He never really hit me, but being a little more rebellious, Trevor felt the sting of his hand often. While Mama was alive, she took the brunt of his anger and did all within her power to shield us from it. We were ten when she died. I'll never forget that day as long as I live. That was the first time he came into my room. And it was storming."

She heard Alex gasp and hesitated, watched as he emptied his wine. She drained her own and let him refill both glasses before she spoke again. "When Trevor found out, he started to sleep in my room thinking he'd be able to protect me. When he tried, my father beat him, tied him up, and made him watch." Her voice wavered.

She swallowed the shame and tears, took another sip of wine and continued. "That went on for a while. We talked often about telling someone or running away, but were too frightened to do either. Our father always said that no one would believe us, warned that they'd take us away for lying and put us in foster homes. They'd separate us, and we'd never see each other again. Then he'd go into these long speeches of the horrible things that happened to children in foster homes. The things he told us made us believe we were much better off with him. At least we were together.

"When we were about fourteen, he came into my room, our room actually because Trevor refused to sleep elsewhere. When my father realized he could no longer do the deed, he held a gun to Trevor's head and made him do it. We were both too shocked and scared to do anything but comply." Tears streamed down her cheeks now. Her voice was thick with them. Alex refilled their glasses once again and waited in complete silence for the horror to end.

Both hands trembled when she raised the glass of wine to her mouth. She dared not look at him for fear of what she'd see on his face or in his eyes. "When it was over, we just held each other and cried. The next time, Trevor refused and fought back. My father threatened to kill him, very nearly did. All I could think was that I'd be all alone, with him. So I convinced Trevor to just do it. Don't think about it, I said. Just do it. Who would take care of me if he wasn't there? So he did.

"It didn't take long for the fear to turn to hate. One night when it was over and my father passed out, the gun lay on the floor next to the chair. Trevor climbed out of the bed, picked it up, and shot him in the head."

"Oh, my God," Alex whispered.

Taylor continued, unmindful to the fact that he'd spoken. "It took a moment to register in my mind what had really happened. I started to scream. Trevor just sat down on the floor, covered in blood. I called nine one one. The cops got there and the ambulances. When they pieced together what had happened, had psychologists as well as medical doctors verify our story, Trevor got off on self-defense. They called our uncle in St. Louis to come get us."

"Why hadn't y'all called him before?" Alex asked, and she could tell by the tone of his voice that the question burned in his mind. She took a deep breath and locked her gaze with his.

"We barely knew the man. My father hated him, was jealous of him and his success, always talked bad about him. We didn't think we had an ally in him. Or in anyone for that matter," she admitted. "He'd convinced us that we only had each other and if we made any waves at all, we'd be separated and not be able to see each other for the rest of our lives." Alex picked up the bottle of wine, realized it was empty, and threw it against the fireplace in a surge of fury.

"That was one sick . . ."

Her eyes widened in shock and surprise at the foul name that escaped his lips, the vehemence with which he uttered it, and the steady stream of language, equally foul, that followed. He lunged to his feet and began to pace, ranted and raged, powerless to change what had happened. When he stopped and slumped against the doorframe, his anger spent, she continued in a soft voice.

"My uncle took us in, saw to it that we went to school, saw counselors, and had as normal a life as possible from then on. He wasn't abusive, but neither was he loving and affectionate. He simply did what had to be done. It took a lot of years for me to realize that jealousy and greed over my visions were what drove my father crazy. That only added to the shame and guilt I carried." Her voice trailed off when Alex turned on her in an angry whirl, his face taut, eyes fierce.

"You have no reason to feel guilt or shame. That sorry . . ." He bit off the word this time and visibly struggled with his emotions. "He had no right, no business to treat you two that way," he spit out through teeth clenched as tightly as the fists by his side.

"I know that," she interjected without heat. "Now," her soft voice effectively cut off the remainder of his wrath.

"Anyway, when the visions first began, he encouraged me, took me with him," Taylor continued, determined to finish the whole story.

"Trevor and I were only twelve at the time and both surprised when he started being nice to me. He'd take me with him on projects and encourage me to draw. He saw my gift as the means by which he could be better and richer than his brother. But when he was unable to successfully duplicate what I'd drawn, he took it out on me. He'd take away my sketchbooks and pencil colors to punish me. Soon I quit drawing altogether."

She put down the empty cup, drew her knees up to her chest, and wrapped her arms around them.

"Though a welcome reprieve, the remainder of our teenage years were extremely difficult despite the counseling we received. I mean, we were like a couple of wounded animals in foreign territory, wary, afraid, and unable to trust.

"Trevor adamantly refused to sleep in his own room. He feared that since my uncle and father were of the same blood, he couldn't be trusted either. He'd killed once and wouldn't hesitate to do so again to keep me safe. They went round-and-round over that until at the advice of the counselors, my uncle gave in and put another bed in there.

"Not until we went away to college did we finally begin to feel that we were free. Though still not easy for either of us to trust anyone but each other, we were finally able to start to develop separate identities. And Trevor finally felt free enough to sleep in a room of his own."

She remembered the many nights they ended up in the same room or on the couch together because of the ghosts that haunted their dreams. She smiled slightly. Her breath came easier now that the worst part was over. She took a deep one and finished the story.

"Anyway, that's when I turned to God. Trevor was still too angry and bitter to listen to anything I said, much less believe in Him. We knew we'd have to go back to St. Louis after we obtained our degrees. It was expected, and we felt as though that was the only way to pay our uncle back for what he did for us. When he died, we sold the firm and moved here to start over. And the rest, as they say, is history."

Alex walked over to where she sat and squatted down on one knee in front of her. Taylor saw the anguish in his eyes and the tears on his cheeks. Anger and pain were etched in every plane of his face. After a moment's hesitation, he cupped her cheek in his hand. The deep breath he took shuddered through his entire body. He opened his mouth to speak, stuttered, blinked fast, and swallowed hard. He rested his forehead against hers for a moment then brushed his lips across her skin.

"Words can't describe how sorry I am for what you and Trevor suffered as children. Nor can they express how proud I am for how well you've survived and what you've become. But I can tell you this much Taylor, I love you. I will love you until the day I die, and I'll fight to the death to protect you from ever being hurt again."

He pulled her in his arms, cradled her against his chest, buried his hands in her hair, and feathered his lips over her face, his voice soft, husky, and full of promise when he continued. "I will love, honor, and cherish you for the rest of my natural life, and after that, into eternity. I will never mistreat or abuse you or any children we may have."

Taylor knew she would never love him more than she did in that moment. She struggled to her knees, cupped his face in her hands. "And I will love, honor, and respect you forever," she murmured. "I will not be afraid or ashamed to give you my heart or my body. And I will treasure any and every child you give me," she vowed and wrapped her arms around him. Her lips reached up to receive his kiss.

As the hurricane trekked across the Gulf of Mexico, another of a more intimate, more passionate nature raged between them. Alex crushed her to him. His mouth covered hers in a fiery embrace. He lowered her gently onto the carpet, whispered incoherently soft, sweet words of love and desire.

Swept up in the whirlwind of emotions, all she could do was cling weakly to him as their love rose and crested as high and fierce as the turbulent waves which crashed against the Gulf shore. It wasn't until she felt cool air followed by his warm mouth on her bare flesh that she was shocked into the reality of how deep they'd wandered into the ocean of desire.

"Alex, wait," she moaned. She struggled slightly and placed a firm hand against his chest. "This can't happen. Not now, not like this. It's not right." His hands clenched into fists, and she felt the strength in which he reeled himself in and got a tight rein on his emotions.

"Jesus Christ, help me," he groaned and buried his face in her hair, "Why not?" he rasped. "You said you weren't afraid of me."

"I'm not afraid. But it's not right. We're not married. I know that sounds crazy right now, but . . ." her voice trailed off, not sure how to explain what she'd meant when she'd said what she did. She wouldn't be ashamed or afraid to give her heart or her body to him if he were her husband. She felt him tremble as he fought back another shudder of need. He rose up on his elbows. His eyes danced into hers. He swallowed hard, tried not to smile. She could almost see the gears turn in his mind and anticipated his argument.

"Adam and Eve weren't married. They were just meant to be. Marriage came later. Besides, we've already vowed to one another. We're married in our heart."

Taylor couldn't help but giggle at the conviction in his voice despite the weakness of his words. "Well, we are not Adam and Eve, and this is not the Garden of Eden."

"Can't blame a guy for trying," he muttered, his voice somewhere between a groan and a chuckle. "Give me a minute. Then I'll move," he said and rocked against her gently, pleased at her intimate response and the quick flush of passion that rushed to her cheeks. His voice lowered a notch when he asked, "You sure you want me to?"

She hesitated, trembled, then nodded. With a groan, he forced himself to move away and sat back on his heels.

"Wait," he urged, and stopped her movements with a gentle hand when she attempted to close her blouse. "Let me look at you," he breathed.

Her cheeks heated at his request, but she left the blouse open and waited, eyes lowered.

Alex felt the breath back up in his lungs as he gazed at her. She lay before him like a feast. Her breath shuddered in and out, flesh trembled, skin flushed to a rosy hue. His hands clenched into fists again, and he fought back another wave of need.

"You are so beautiful," he breathed, barely able to get the words past his raw throat. He leaned over her once more, brushed his lips across the tender skin exposed to his gaze, and then forced himself to roll away and lie beside her. He propped himself up on one elbow and tugged her blouse closed to conceal that luscious view from his sight.

"I have a friend who's a Justice of the Peace. Let's get him to marry us tomorrow," he whispered.

"I can't get married without my brother here," she protested and refastened the buttons on her blouse as quickly as possible with fingers that shook like leaves in a hurricane wind.

"Well, let's hop a plane tomorrow, meet up with them in Vegas, and get married there."

She shook her head. "I don't want to get married in a fake church with a fake minister. I want to get married here. I want my pastor to perform the ceremony and my brother to give me away."

Alex rolled his eyes. "I knew you were going to say that," he muttered. "They won't be back until Tuesday so that means we can't get married until next Sunday," he complained, still reeling from the force of the need curling through his system. Her smile was as tender as the light in her eyes.

"I think you can wait that long," she answered, her voice

tinged with laughter.

He tried not to smile and adopted a look of complete solemnity. "I can wait that long, but put me off even another day and I'll seduce you before the ceremony."

Her laughter rang out, music to his ears.

EPILOGUE

The ceremony was perfect, the wedding night, and every night since, glorious. Three and a half months later, Alex found his wife up on a ladder while she put the final touches to the hand-carved molding in the den. Their home was finished and would be completely furnished by the time he and Taylor returned from the honeymoon cruise to the Bahamas, on which they would embark the day after Christmas. Though parishes to the east suffered through Hurricane Gustav and those south and west were damaged by Ike, their home withstood both without losing so much as a shingle. He had no doubt it would hold up through anything Mother Nature tossed their way.

His eyes narrowed when Taylor stretched a little too far and the ladder wobbled. "What in heaven's name are you doing up there with no one here to hold this ladder?" he demanded, and stomped over to do it himself. She turned to smile down at him.

"I'm finishing up. Isn't it beautiful?"

"It's perfect. But you shouldn't be doing this at all, much less alone."

She rolled her eyes. "Oh, please, I'm pregnant, not an invalid."

He shook his head with a sigh and mumbled, "I hope my son isn't as stubborn as his mother."

She giggled. "At least my son won't wear sissy pants," she teased, with a meaningful glance down at his crisply pressed dress slacks.

Eyes narrowed, Alex swallowed a chuckle and forced the smile that tugged at his lips into a frown, albeit a tiny one.

"Sissy pants? I'll show you sissy pants," he muttered, and pulled her off the ladder and into his arms to carry her down the hall to the one room in the house that was completely furnished.

Trevor lay propped up against the pillows, one arm behind his head, and the other wrapped around his wife. *There was nothing sweeter on a dreary winter day than to snuggle up with the one you love,* he thought, then wondered if his sister enjoyed as good a morning.

Although he and Taylor were married only weeks apart, Taylor and Alex had put off their honeymoon until the crew finished the house. Once they returned from the cruise, it would be to begin their new life in their new home in a new year.

Trevor smiled when Pam mumbled in her sleep and curled up more firmly against him. He'd never dreamed life could be this sweet or that he could feel so complete. Love had done that to him, the love of his sister, his wife, his Savior. He thanked God daily for those gifts and the healing power of His grace and mercy. And though he still had his share of doubts, fears, and nightmares, he knew God was in control and, with continued prayer, praise, and thanksgiving, those too would continue to lose power over him.

His mind wandered back over the last nine months and how much they'd accomplished since Alex had walked into T&T Enterprises that fateful morning in early March. Not just emotionally and spiritually or even personally, but professionally.

Though the grounds work would still take a few months to complete, the house was magnificent. An architecture design and review magazine had already done a major piece on it.

They had not only hailed his sister as "brilliant and gifted" but had also praised Trevor and his crew for their ability to successfully create what she had designed. The project was definitely a feather in their cap, and the interest it generated was enough to keep the phone ringing and the crew busy for the next two years.

But the crew's next project was to build his and Pam's dream house on the six acres of land he'd purchased just down the highway from his sister and Alex. And though it wouldn't be as magnificent as theirs, the log home Taylor had designed for him and Pam would be every bit as comfortable.

His attention shifted to the foot of the bed when Bugsby hopped up on it. Trevor smiled, patted his thigh, and called softly to the bunny. When he wasn't with them, the rabbit had a permanent home at Alex's estate. But since they were out of the country, he and Pam had been called upon to baby-sit. *Bunnysit,* Trevor amended with a smile and scratched Bugsby under the chin.

No longer a "bunny," the rabbit weighed in at a hefty six pounds. His fur was thick and luxurious from the constant brushing Taylor provided. She'd also trained him to use a litter box when inside. Trevor still couldn't get over that fact. His sister was amazing, he thought with a pang of loneliness. He missed her, and he'd be glad when they returned safely to the country and settled in where he could see or at least talk to her every day.

A knock on the door startled him out of his reverie. His sudden jerk to awareness caused Bugsby to glare up at him then hop over to cuddle up next to Pam. Had he been a cat, Trevor was sure the animal would be purring right now. The knock sounded again.

Who on earth would get out in this weather to go visiting? He rolled out of bed, careful not to disturb his wife or her new bed partner any more than necessary, slid into a pair of pajama pants, and went to answer the door. A package lay on the front porch of their tiny two-bedroom apartment. He picked up the box and smiled when he realized that his sister had sent a gift. He closed and locked the door behind him, then carried the package into the bedroom.

Pam stirred. "Who was it?" she mumbled.

"It's a package from Taylor."

"What's in it?"

Trevor chuckled. "Can I open it first?"

She turned over, frowned, and opened one eye to glare at him. "Don't be so slow about it."

Trevor hesitated in opening the package long enough to brush his lips over hers. He turned back to the task at hand, unwrapped the box, and lifted the lid. A baby rattle lay nestled in a bed of tissue. He frowned then lifted the note out from beneath it.

Trev, we've always done things together until you decided to get married first. But, I'm still one step ahead of you, little brother.

She'd signed it *Love, Tay* and drawn a smiley face.

Understanding dawned. He chuckled, then threw his head back with a laugh. "I'm going to be an uncle!"

Pam scrambled into an upright position. "What?"

He laughed again and handed her the note. "I'm going to be an uncle." He shook the rattle. "And you're going to be an aunt!"

Pam laughed and threw her arms around his neck. "A baby, oh wow! Lucky cow," she muttered, and he could tell she tried hard not to be too jealous.

"Maybe we should give her a little competition," she suggested and nuzzled his neck. "And give her child someone to play with." Her lips covered his in a tender caress.

Trevor chuckled against her mouth. "You mean someone

other than Bugsby?" he teased and shooed the rabbit off the bed.

Pam nodded and brushed her lips across his again. Her hand ran down his chest.

"My sentiments exactly," he murmured and surrendered to the sweet ecstasy that always awaited him in her arms.

A NOTE FROM THE AUTHOR

Dear Readers,

Abuse of any kind is a shame; abuse of a child is the lowest of lows. If you are an abuser, please seek help. If you are or were abused as a child, don't give up! Don't keep looking back but press on to the high call of Christ Jesus in your life.

For both the abuser and the abused, there is always hope. Not the kind you find in drugs or alcohol or any other form of escapism but true hope. Hope and healing that can only be found in the shed blood of Jesus Christ.

"Though a mother forgets her nursing child, I will never leave or forsake you," says the Lord.

Only God has the power to heal the most wounded of souls.

It is my prayer that if you don't already know Him, you'll seek Jesus as your Lord and Savior and if you do know Him, you'll pursue a closer walk with Him.

Until later, may God bless and keep you—and yours—in the palm of His loving hand!

Pamela S. Thibodeaux
"Inspirational with an Edge!"™

ABOUT THE AUTHOR

Pamela S. Thibodeaux grew up in the town of Iowa, Louisiana, and currently lives there. She is the mother of four (two by blood and two by marriage) and a grandmother. A deeply committed Christian, Pamela firmly believes in God and His promises.

"God is very real to me, and I feel that people today need and want to hear more of His truths wherever they can glean them. People are hungry for practical (and real) Christian values, not some 'holier-than-thou' beliefs that are impossible to believe and impossible to live up to," Pamela says. "I do my best to encourage readers to develop a personal relationship with God. The deepest desire of my heart is to glorify God and to get His message of faith, trust, and forgiveness to a hurting world."

Email Pamela at pthib07@gmail.com
Visit her website: http://www.pamelathibodeaux.com
Or blog: http://pamswildroseblog.blogspot.com